I0638490

ISBN: 979-8-9893244-0-8

Any references to historical events, real people, or real places are used fictitiously. Names, characters, and places are products of the author's imagination.

Front cover image by Kollette Stone
Book design by Kollette Stone

kollettestoneauthor@gmail.com
Instagram: @kollettestone

JUST ONE WOMAN

For my strong-willed girls
Kalyn and Klarke

PROLOGUE

It's funny how humans want to curl up into the fetal position when they're hurt, sick, or emotionally drained. Like the last place they felt safe and warm was in the womb and they're trying to get back there. Kenna was lying on the bathroom floor, hugging her pillow against her chest, wishing she could escape.

"Kenny honey, we've got to get going," Kenna's mother, Victoria, knocked softly on the bathroom door.

"Can't we just cancel it for today? I don't feel good," Kenna called back to her mother.

"You know we can't cancel. Let's just get it over with," her mother replied.

Kenna dragged herself up off the floor and looked in the mirror at her pale reflection. The worry that she felt on the inside was even making her look sick on the outside. She had dark circles under her eyes and her hair looked dull and lifeless. After splashing some cold water on her clammy face, she brushed her teeth and ran a brush through her long, blond hair.

It was a few days after her thirteenth birthday and Kenna's mother was taking her to get her heranon placed. The tires of her mother's car hummed on the pavement as they drove to the surgery center. The closer they got, the more Kenna could feel her heart pounding in her chest. So hard she thought it might just break through her ribs and flop into her lap like a fish flopping on the sand.

The sickening feeling she had fought all morning formed deep in her stomach. It was unrelenting, like something was gnawing on her insides trying to get out. It didn't help that her stomach was empty. They said she couldn't eat today, but that didn't really matter because she was too nervous to eat, anyway.

"Just try to relax Kenna," Victoria said, sensing her daughter's anxiety rising. "Your sister had her heranon placed when she was thirteen too, do you remember? She was perfectly fine. After it's all done, you can lie in bed watching movies all day and eat as much ice cream as you want." She gave a reassuring closed-mouth smile.

"Okay mom, I'll try." She gave her mother a weak attempt at a smile back. She slid her hands under her legs so that she wouldn't fidget with her fingers. Her mother hated fidgeting. The drive seemed to go by faster than expected and they arrived at the surgery center in no time at all.

"Are you ready?" Kenna's mother asked one last time.

"I guess," Kenna shrugged her shoulders in response.

Kenna and her mother got out of the car and went inside. Everything was white and bright. A faint smell of bleach filled the building and it felt sterile. The receptionist was a plump, kind looking woman sitting behind a tall white desk with clear glass separating her from them. She smiled at Kenna and her mother as they approached her. Kenna didn't know why, but this helped calm her.

"Hello dear, what is your first and last name?"

"Kenna Carson," she replied.

The woman stared at her computer screen, which gave her face a white glow and reflected off her glasses. Her mouse made quick clicking noises as she worked.

"You haven't had anything to eat or drink this morning, correct?" the woman asked without tearing her gaze away from her computer.

Kenna shook her head in response.

"You can have a seat over there with the others." The receptionist pointed to the waiting room where there were five other girls who all appeared to be about Kenna's age.

"Honey, you go have a seat I just have to make a quick call," her mother said with her phone already up to her ear as she went to the other side of the lobby.

Kenna took her seat amongst the other girls. They all had their mothers sitting with them. There she sat alone, staring at her feet. This did not come as a surprise to her, her mother worked all the time and was not comforting in nature. Victoria had high expectations for her daughters and Kenna was always on edge, worried about letting her down.

The drone of the television broke the silence in the waiting room, and Kenna was thankful for it. The first girl was called back and rose from her chair, anxiously gripping her mother's hand. Her long black hair hung like a curtain hiding half of her face, but it could not completely conceal her fearful expression. Kenna looked around, sharing brief nervous glances with the others before she returned her gaze back to her high-top sneakers on her feet.

She felt a strange feeling of relief knowing that she was not the only one going through this today. Seeing all the others made this entire process feel more normal, and not like a strange imposition that was forced on her alone. The rest of the girls got called back one by one until finally she was the only one left waiting. Her sneakers tapped the floor as she bounced her legs up and down without even realizing she was doing it. It was like her legs had a mind of their own and acted independently of her control.

"Kenna Carson," a woman in white scrubs and

a white surgical cap called from the door leading to the back area where Kenna was assuming she would have her procedure.

As she stood up, she motioned to her mother that it was time to go. Her mother quickly got off the phone and rushed over to accompany her behind the door, pocketing her phone on the way. Once she was in the surgical area, they had her change into a gown and cap and lay on a gurney. The surgeon came in and explained the procedure to her and her mother.

"We go in vaginally... very minimal dilation of cervix... we use very small instruments...The heranon is about one centimeter long and will be placed in the uterine wall at the very top of the uterus... she can expect some cramping and light bleeding for the next couple days. I will prescribe some mild pain medications to help with the discomfort."

Kenna was trying to pay attention to what he was saying, but she just could not focus. Her mind was hazy, as if she were wandering through a fog, lost and confused. She had never had surgery before and she was frightened.

What if she never woke up? The more she thought about it, the more worked up she became. Suddenly the room felt warm, suffocating her and making it difficult for her to breathe. She thought she might faint or throw up.

Her mother's hand felt soft against hers

as she gave her hand one last squeeze before they wheeled her back to the operating room. Kenna found her mothers touch more odd than comforting. She couldn't remember the last time her mother had held her hand. Before she could really process what was going on, they placed a cold, hard mask on her face. The gas inside tasted funny. She heard a nurse tell her to count backwards from ten.

"Ten, nine, eight, seven..." She felt light as a feather as if she were floating above her body. Then everything went black and there was nothing.

To Kenna, it seemed like mere seconds had passed and she was waking up to her mother's voice. Her head felt thick as she looked around, trying to assess her surroundings. Every one of her muscles moaned with fatigue and her abdomen ached. She was just relieved that it was finished and she had made it through alive.

The sweet juice that the nurse gave her felt good in her dry mouth and she choked down some graham crackers with it. After about a half hour, they could leave.

"How are you feeling?" her mother asked when they got back out to the car.

"Tired and my stomach feels achy, but I'll be okay," she replied, and they started home. They had given her some pain medication before she left and it was doing its job well. Her eyelids felt heavy, and she leaned back in the seat, letting the warm sun spread across her face.

Kenna knew what the purpose of the heranon was. They taught her about it during one of her science classes on reproduction. It was to ensure she wouldn't get pregnant until she was ready. All girls had to get one when they reached thirteen. Once she was old enough and ready to have children, she would have to apply for a child and get approved before she would be allowed to have her heranon removed.

In history class, they had learned about all the terrible things that had happened because of overpopulation in the past. They were killing the planet with their waste, stripping it of non-renewable resources. Water quality was declining every year, and they struggled to maintain enough drinkable water. Power grids couldn't keep up with the amount of people in the country and there were frequent outages that lasted days and sometimes even weeks.

Disease pandemics would arise periodically, rapidly spreading through the population and claiming the lives of hundreds of thousands of the most vulnerable. It became obvious that they could not keep up with a growing population, and it would eventually lead to the destruction of their country.

The government began a reproductive restriction program for population control over sixty years ago. This program evolved over the decades and eventually became the standard.

As the country's population declined, they restructured it into four regions. With Region One being in the North West, Region Two in the South West, Region Three in the South East, and Region Four, which was in the North East. Each region had its own leader, called a region chair. The four region chairs worked together to govern over the country.

They were no longer the United States of America but were instead the United Regions of America or the URA.

As part of the restructuring, they merged people into larger towns and cities. And the small towns slowly died out and disappeared. They then returned unoccupied neighborhoods and entire small towns "back to nature." That's what they called it when they took the previously developed areas and put it back to the way nature intended it to be, creating more green-space.

The government instructed them that reproductive restrictions were crucial for both the planet's survival and their own. They were necessary, and no one questioned it.

CHAPTER 1
The Committee

Conversation buzzed as eleven individuals dressed in suits sat around a long conference room table in the center of a large room. Huge floor to ceiling windows covered one wall, and the view looked out onto the city on the river's edge.

"Next on the agenda, we'll assess the application of Kenna and Emmett Foster." The committee leader walked around the room and handed the others folders. "I know we are all aware that this applicant is the Mayor's daughter, but we are to review the application like we would any other," he stated as he finished handing out the last of the folders.

The committee was comprised of individuals with political backgrounds within the region. They elected many to the committee after holding political office. Some had been judges for many years prior to obtaining their seat on the committee.

The committee leader aimed his remote at the large screen at one end of the room and an image of a man and woman appeared with their names below the photo. The man had dark wavy hair that was kept longer and dark brown eyes under thick but well-kept eyebrows. His face portrayed his confidence. The woman had darker blonde hair that fell below her shoulders and green eyes with just the slightest hint of gold. A kind smile lit up her face.

The sound of shuffling papers filled the room as everyone opened their folders to start the review.

"He is a doctor and is currently going through surgical residency to become a cardiothoracic surgeon. She just started her own psychology practice a few months ago, but it is already looking promising," a woman on the committee pointed out as she scanned their paperwork. "So they will be able to support a child."

Another man on the committee chimed in, "They live in a brownstone townhouse in a pleasant area, with plenty of room for a child. There is even a small backyard, which is unheard of on the North Side near downtown."

"They have been married for three years. Neither one has any medical issues, and their family medical history is not worrisome," another man stated as he peered over the documents.

They continued to discuss the long and

detailed application for another half hour, and could find no fault in the information they reviewed.

"Does anyone have any concerns that this couple would not make suitable parents?" the committee leader asked. There was silence as he looked around the boardroom table at the other members.

Suddenly, there was a buzz coming from one end of the table, the sound of a cellphone vibrating. Everyone turned in their chairs to look down the table and see where the noise was coming from.

"Sorry, everyone," Tom Adkins apologized as he reached for his phone. He was one of the longest running committee members and had made a name for himself as a judge in Region Four. After he glanced at his phone, a puzzled look came across his face. Then he cleared his throat and looked up at the others. "I think we should deny this application."

The other board members darted glances at Tom in confusion as they waited for his reasoning.

"On what grounds?" a woman asked haughtily.

"Well, her practice has only been up and running a few months. That hardly qualifies as a stable career. Plus, we rarely accept applications on the first try, and I don't think this one should be any different." Tom looked around the table.

He met the gaze of certain board members and an understanding passed between them.

"Let's put it to a vote," the committee leader said.

❦

"Kenna, I'm going to go pull the car up out front," Emmett yelled up the stairs to his wife.

"Okay, I'm almost ready!" she called back down.

His keys jingled as he grabbed them from the entryway table and headed out the door. They lived near downtown and parking was scarce. Last time he drove their vehicle, he had to park almost two blocks away. Whistling a cheery tune, he casually walked the distance to their car.

An array of clothes lined the floor as Kenna rummaged through her closet. She was having a hard time deciding what to wear to their application review meeting.

"Too serious," she said, looking at her navy pants suit.

"Too casual," she said to herself as she threw a maxi dress onto her bed.

She settled on some ankle pants, a black blouse and pumps with the tiniest hint of a heel. The lid creaked as she opened her antique jewelry box that had once belonged to her grandmother. She selected her simple, but elegant, diamond studs and single diamond pendant necklace.

Analyzing her outfit in the full-length mirror,

she turned side to side and smoothed her hair back behind her ears. Satisfied with her ensemble, she started down the stairs. After she grabbed her purse off the table in the entryway, she went out the front door, locking it as she went.

Emmett was waiting for her just outside their front steps in the small SUV they shared. She joined him inside the vehicle. She was as ready as she was ever going to be for what lay ahead of them that day.

"I hope I haven't made us late," she said, looking at him worriedly as she fastened her seat belt.

"You know we are still early," he replied, smiling at her. She'd never been late to anything in her entire life.

They started their drive to the Sector Building, which was close to their home on the North Side of town. Blurred images of buildings passed by her window until suddenly they became clearer. They were stopped in traffic. Inching their way forward, they finally got through the morning rush. Kenna was relieved to see they still had plenty of time.

"Let's swing through that drive through for coffee." Kenna pointed out a coffee shop ahead. She figured the Sector Building would have shitty coffee, and she needed a caffeine boost.

Once they made it, they parked in the multistory parking garage next to the tall office building. Grabbing their hot coffees, they then trekked to the front doors.

The Sector Building, a government facility, required identification and scanning your belongings in bins prior to gaining access. They proceeded to the elevator on their left after being cleared. A sign in gold next to the elevator glinted in the light and told them that the application review meetings took place on the fourth floor. Inside the elevator, Emmett placed his hand at the small of her back. His touch felt comforting, grounding.

Ding. The elevator doors opened, revealing a large wooden desk with gold lettering spelling out *Application Review Office*. Several receptionists were chatting behind the desk. They approached the closest one.

"Here for your application review?" She was middle-aged with shorter blonde hair and her name tag read *Karen*.

"Yes, we are. We have an appointment scheduled for nine o'clock under the Fosters, Emmett and Kenna," Emmett answered.

"Here you are," she said, while staring at her computer. "I will just need you each to verify your date of birth."

"September 22nd of 2089 is my birthdate and Kenna's is June 10th of 2091," Emmett replied. She secretly hated when he answered for her but never stopped him.

"Happy birthday," the woman said, looking at

Kenna, surprised.

"Thank you. Just another day," she replied with half a smile.

"You may have a seat until they call you back." The receptionist nodded to some open chairs in a waiting area.

Kenna's shoes clacked on the gray tile floor of the waiting room. Through a window, they could see boats on the nearby river, and the hustle and bustle of cars and people in the city center down below.

Two other couples sat in the waiting area. A man and woman who appeared to be in their thirties, and two women that were holding hands over the armrest of the chairs. In one corner near the ceiling, a TV was playing a morning talk show that Kenna didn't recognize. They sat down and continued to drink their coffee. The talk show was political and they were discussing the upcoming Region Four Chair election that was to take place in the next year. Kenna pretended to be interested in it but couldn't care less. Her mind was racing as she wondered what questions they would ask her and how soon she could get her heranon removed so they could try for a baby.

There was a metal door near the waiting area that looked heavy, and a badge reader was on the wall next to it. It swung open and a short woman wearing a black skirt suit emerged. She called back the two women; they let go of each other's hands and followed the woman behind the door, looking hopeful.

"Are you finished with your coffee, love?" Emmett asked her, snapping her away from her racing thoughts. "I'll throw our cups away over there." He got up and crossed the room to the black metal trash can near the elevators.

Kenna, no longer having something in her hands, fidgeted with her fingers, cracking her knuckles and wringing her hands. She realized what she was doing and instinctively put her hands beneath her thighs to stop herself.

Emmett returned. As he was sitting back down in his chair, the metal door opened again. A petite woman with long, curly auburn hair walked through the opening. Her eyes were red and there were streaks down her face where her tears had run through her makeup. Following her was a tall, muscular man with dark skin and hair shaved very short.

He was leading her by her elbow towards the elevators. The woman appeared devastated as she choked back her sobs. Kenna worried that if the man let go of her arm, the woman would fall to the ground in a puddle of her own tears.

Everyone realized what had happened. The couple's application for a child must have been denied. Kenna's stomach cramped into knots and she regretted drinking her coffee on an empty stomach. Getting denied was her worst fear, and she was realizing it was a real possibility. It was very common, she knew, especially for couples who were applying for the first time. Having never failed at anything in her entire life, she did not want to start now, today, on her twenty-eighth birthday.

The elevator doors opened, and the couple stepped inside. The woman's muffled sobs were no longer heard once the door closed behind them. Emmett reached for Kenna's hand and gave it a squeeze, giving her a look of reassurance. He knew what she was thinking and wanted to put her mind at ease.

"That will not be us," he said.

Kenna nodded in response, but she wasn't so sure. She was all too familiar with the pain that application denials caused, in her psychology practice she had counseled dozens of women through the grief they felt after being denied and helped them find meaning in life again. Then, she was able to remain empathetic and could provide a voice of reason. Now that she was about to be in the hot seat the possibility of getting denied was becoming more real to her personally.

They waited for what seemed like an eternity, but in reality, it had only been another ten minutes before the short woman appeared at the door again to call them back. Silently, they followed her down a dimly lit hallway until they reached another metal door. The woman used her badge to unlock it and let them through before she went to sit at her small desk nearby.

The large room they entered had no windows and the lighting was very poor. There were two chairs next to each other near the center of the room, and there was a large semicircle wooden desk with twelve people sitting behind it. The desk and committee members were on a platform, so they seemed to tower over Kenna and Emmett as they sat in their chairs at the center. In front of each member was a manilla folder and a name plate displaying each member's name.

"Just breathe. No matter what happens here today, we will be okay," Emmett leaned over and whispered in her ear.

"Mr. and Mrs. Foster, are you ready to begin your review?" the committee leader asked, looking over his reading glasses.

"Yes," they answered in unison.

For the next hour, they were drilled with questions from the committee in an interview like fashion.

"Where are you from?" a man on the committee asked.

"I am from Brenzing originally," Kenna answered, "we moved here to Thayes after my father died when I was nine, so that we could be closer to my grandmother."

Emmett answered next,"And I am actually from Region Two originally, a small city called Saxton on the West coast. I came to Region Four for university, and that's where I met Kenna. We stayed here to be close to her family."

"Tell us about your hobbies," one woman asked.

"Well, I work a lot right now, but whenever I get spare time, I usually go for a run or work out in other ways. Kenna also runs and she paints as a hobby," Emmett answered for them both. Although slightly annoyed, Kenna didn't let it affect her game.

"What kind of paintings?" the woman addressed Kenna this time.

"Mostly oil paintings, but I also dabble in acrylics, watercolors, and drawing as well," she answered confidently, looking the woman in eyes as she spoke.

This interrogation carried on and on. The pair had answers to all of their inquiries and it seemed to be going very well. Their confidence was building more and more after each response. Kenna remained composed and rose to the challenge, answering all questions with ease. Emmett always worked well under pressure. He had this never wavering composure and intelligence that left most people in awe.

"I think that covers all of our questions for today," the committee leader spoke. "Your application was impressive for your first time applying and it did not go unnoticed."

Kenna was holding her breath, and her heart was beating hard and fast. She was trying hard to keep her outward expression as neutral as possible, but on the inside, she was all over the place.

"The committee has made its final decision regarding this application. We are denying your request," he paused, "I understand if you find this verdict disappointing. We would like to see Kenna's career stabilize a bit more before approving your application. Other than that, we have no advice or constructive criticism for your next time applying."

After letting out the breath she had been holding, she felt a little lightheaded. Her heart felt as though it had sunk down to the deepest part of her chest, and her shoulders drooped with disappointment. She was able to keep her facial expressions stoic as she and Emmett thanked the committee for their consideration and got up to leave the room, but she felt unsteady on her feet. As they walked out, it took everything she had to fight back the tears that were threatening to spill from her eyes. A knot formed in her throat and she tried to swallow it down unsuccessfully.

The same woman escorted them back to the lobby. Kenna felt like she was on autopilot as they made their way to the elevator and eventually back to the parking garage to fetch the car.

As soon as they were safely inside the vehicle and there was no one in sight, she let it all go.

She slumped forward with her head in her hands and was crying loudly, her voice cracking as she tried to speak. Emmett just rubbed her back in gentle circular motions and handed her some tissues he had shoved in his pocket this morning, just in case. Rarely did Kenna cry and lose her composure, but he had seen it happen a couple of times in grad school when she nearly cracked under the pressure, so her reaction did not alarm him. Although he was disappointed with the verdict, it didn't compare to the heartache she felt.

After giving her a few minutes to cry it out, he asked if she was ready to leave.

"Oh shit! I forgot we are supposed to go to my mom's house for lunch," she said as she pulled down the visor mirror and attempted to fix her makeup. Grabbing her compact from her purse, she salvaged most of it. "It's already ten thirty and by the time we get to mom's on the South Side of town it'll be after eleven."

"Maybe we should call your mom and cancel lunch." Emmett looked at her questioningly.

"I wish we could, but you know Victoria wouldn't approve of us standing her up," Kenna said rolling her eyes as she reapplied her lip gloss.

"Well, we better get going then," he said as he backed out of the parking space to head down the ramp.

Kenna sat back and crossed her arms over her chest. She had to keep reminding herself to breathe and it felt like she couldn't catch her breath. Like the wind had physically been knocked out of her. Her mind was running with questions about why they were denied. What had they done wrong? They were the perfect candidates for a first time approval.

Out of the corner of her eye she stole a glance at Emmett. He was sitting behind the wheel with his face void of any emotion. How could he be so calm? Was he even upset that they got denied. Another tiny tear escaped from the corner of her eye and she carefully wiped it away without disturbing her newly fixed makeup. She felt alone in her misery.

Since their wedding, her thoughts were consumed with having a baby. She had lists of baby names and nursery ideas. She had even made sure the school in their district was reputable before they could purchase their house. They had gotten everything ready for a baby, just as they were expected to do. And now all she could do was wait. A year felt like an eternity to Kenna. A year stood between her and the chance to have what she desired most in this world, a child.

CHAPTER 2
Life Goes On

Driving away from downtown, they briefly went by part of the East Side, which is where all the housing projects in the city were located. Kenna tuned her head away from the window unconsciously, avoiding the view of the slums as they passed.

There were several apartment buildings and run-down houses that had been unoccupied for years. The city had plans to tear most of it down and return it to nature. They had done this more and more as additional areas of the city became scantily populated. But they were not alone in this. It was a common theme across the country. Just as it was meant to happen.

They finally reached the South Side. This part of town was known for its "old money" occupants and had a reputation for being snobbish. After going past several green, luscious golf courses and gated communities, they eventually arrived at her mother's house.

This was the house Kenna had spent half of

her childhood in with her mother, sister, and grandmother. Her grandmother still lived there with her mother, although they had recently considered moving her to an assisted living facility. After considering it, the whole family vehemently decided that Eleanor should remain at home for the rest of her days. How ever many days that would be.

The tires rumbled on the cobblestone driveway as they pulled in and parked next to her sister's vehicle. She was dreading telling her family that their application got denied and this "celebratory lunch" was a lost cause. Emmett parked the car, and she stepped out of the vehicle and started walking toward the house. In front of them was a large Victorian house that was a gray blue and had a white porch, complete with a hanging swing. She had always admired the gardens here, and right now the hydrangeas and peonies were in full bloom, painting an exquisite picture of summer.

Entering the house without knocking, she called out to let her family know they had arrived.

"We're here!"

"We're out back!" her mother yelled from the back patio.

They stepped outside and were greeted with a brief embrace from Victoria. "Happy Birthday kiddo." Kenna stiffened at the embrace that had always felt forced with her mother.

Kenna then went over to her grandmother and gave her a hug as well. "You look wonderful Grandma," she said as she gave her a squeeze.

Her grandmother, Eleanor, was an elegant woman with a thin frame, icy blue eyes, and white hair falling to her shoulders.

"Thank you, my dear. You are beautiful, as always," Eleanor returned with a smile. Kenna reminded her of herself when she was young and seeing her was like looking into a mirror to the past.

"Hey Kass," Kenna said to her sister as she took a seat beside her. Kassi's husband Clayton was on the grill cooking the kabobs for lunch while their two young children played in the sandbox in the yard.

"Well, spill the details! How did it go?" Kassi squealed excitedly.

Kenna's face fell as she answered her sister while everyone was listening, "They denied us." A lone tear almost slipped from the corner of her eye, but she held it back.

"Oh Kenny, I am so sorry." Her sister was the only one that still called her by her childhood nickname. "Almost everyone gets denied their first time applying, and I'm sure you'll get accepted next year," she tried to sound encouraging.

"Easy for you to say. You and Clayton got accepted on your first try. And now you have two beautiful children," she replied, almost pouting.

"We just got lucky, and you will have a child of your own someday." Kassi gave her a reassuring look.

To avoid conversation about their application, Kenna went over to see her niece and nephew in the sandbox. Liam was four and Penny was two, and she adored them. They were trying to build sandcastles but weren't able to figure it out, so she was showing them how it was done. They clapped and cheered as she lifted her pail to reveal a perfect sandcastle. She then found a small leaf to stick on top as its flag. Her sister seemed to have the perfect family and she couldn't wait until she had one too. It was all she could think about since she and Emmett got married and she wanted it so bad that it hurt.

Family had always been important to Kenna. When her father was alive he showered both girls in love and affection while her mother was more subdued and did not put her emotions on display. Ever since her father died Kenna had craved that love. Kassi tried to step in and had always been endearing towards Kenna, but it wasn't the same. Kenna longed to have a baby of her own that she could love and be loved in return.

They sat down for lunch at the large outdoor dining table under the pergola. Kenna sat near her mother at the end of the table.

"Kenna, I know you are probably disappointed with the outcome today, and that is understandable. It's okay to feel sad, but it isn't good to dwell on something you have no control over. Prepare to be better next time," Victoria told her daughter in her sympathetic yet condescending manner.

Kenna knew her mother was right, as always, much to her annoyance. So she just gave her mother a nod of understanding while she continued to eat her salad. Looking around the table, she saw everyone was visiting and smiling like it was any other day. Her world went on spinning, even though she felt like she was being torn apart. She had to wait an entire year before they could apply again, and it seemed like an eternity.

Weeks later, Kenna and Emmett were lounging on their deck in the backyard after work. It wasn't a large space, but it was functional and cozy. They had an outdoor sectional and a gas fire pit they would turn on at night when the air became more crisp. There were a few scattered planters around the deck that she had attempted to plant a variety of succulents in, but these were not taking off as she had hoped. They had a small backyard with nice green grass and hedges around the perimeter. There was one lone tree, an autumn blaze maple that turned a fiery red during fall. A tall privacy fence separated them from their neighbors on all sides. It was like their own little oasis.

When they had gotten home from work, they opened a bottle of her favorite chardonnay and make a cheese and olive plate for supper instead of cooking. Something they did often as they both worked full time and some weeks even more. They were both working on their second glass of wine and they had devoured the cheese and olives, leaving only crumbs on the platter.

She had changed into a pair of comfy gray joggers and her favorite college t-shirt. Sitting back against some throw pillows on the sectional, she plopped her feet in his lap in an attempt to get a foot massage. He chuckled at her not-so-subtle hint and began rubbing her feet with his free hand. Glancing down at her feet, she realized her toenails looked awful. Her pink polish was chipping and had grown out.

"I cannot remember the last time I got a pedicure," she said, thinking aloud.

"Maybe this weekend you and Kassi should have a spa day. You know, massages, pedicures, and whatever else you girls do," Emmett teased.

"You know what? That is the best idea you have had in a while." She winked as she teased him back.

He turned to her more seriously now. "I'm glad to see you have come around. I hated seeing you so down after they denied our application." Watching her become depressed and closed off from the world after their denial was beginning to worry him. He didn't think she would take it as hard as she did.

With how busy he had been lately with residency he was almost thankful they got denied, trying for a baby would just add an extra layer of stress to his already full schedule. He didn't tell Kenna that though, he knew she was devastated and wouldn't understand his relief.

"My heart felt like it broke into a million pieces. But the sting is getting a little better every day." She paused to take a sip of her wine. "I think I have just been focusing on work, you know? Trying to build up my practice so that when we can apply again in a year, I satisfy them with my career." There was nothing she could do to change the outcome of their application, so she tried to pull herself out of her melancholic state by throwing herself into her work.

"I think that's a great plan. We have a year to focus on us, our relationship and how we can balance it with our busy jobs. With me working long hours at the hospital and you working so hard to build your practice, we have spent little time together. This is the first time we have really gotten to sit together and talk for more than a few minutes," he said.

"You're right. We need to make more time for each other. I'm sorry that I've been distant since our application review. I just needed to be sad and process through it on my own," she said.

"But you don't have to do it alone. I am here

for you. We can process through it together." He looked at her with a pleading look in his eyes.

She nodded at him in understanding.

He started to get up from his seat, so she swung her feet off of his lap. "I have something for you. Well, something for us, actually," he said, smiling. "Be right back." He darted back into the house.

Wondering what he had gotten her this time, she sat smiling to herself. He was always surprising her with the most random gifts. Sometimes they were so thoughtful and she adored them, other times he completely missed the mark, but she loved him for trying anyway.

He emerged excitedly from the house. She had her back to him, but she could hear him coming up behind her. Walking around the couch to sit back down, he turned towards her and she could see he was holding a fluff of red fur. She enthusiastically sat up from her perch and reached out for the soft little creature. He handed her a puppy, so cute it melted her heart instantly.

"Oh my gosh!" she exclaimed, "and who is this adorable little guy?"

"Well, this little guy is actually a girl and she doesn't have a name yet," he replied. "She's a Cavalier King Charles spaniel."

The puppy immediately snuggled into Kenna's chest and fell asleep. She had red fur all over, except for the tiniest bit of white on her chest and forehead. Her ears had silky, wavy curls and Kenna stroked them as she slept. She was making the sweetest little grunting sounds as she snoozed, and Kenna could smell her puppy breath as she snuggled her cheek into the puppy.

"Can we call her Ruby?" she asked Emmett.

"Ruby it is," he said, and he leaned in and gave Kenna a kiss on her forehead.

"I love her already! How is that even possible?" she asked, beaming from ear to ear.

"She is ours, and we will take care of her together." He was hoping this would close the gap that had lingered between them these past few weeks since their review.

They sat on the deck a little while longer before heading inside with their fresh addition.

"She's going to need a collar, a bed, and lots of toys," she said as they entered the house.

"Go nuts, buy her everything she needs." He encouraged smiling.

She leaned in to kiss him and stared into his brown eyes. "Thank you for Ruby."

"You're very welcome, love."

CHAPTER 3
Sisters

The following weekend, Kenna drove to the South Side to pick up Kassi for their girls 'day. Her sister and her family had recently moved to that area to be closer to their mother and grandmother. She pulled up to her sister's house, a charming Tudor style home with a large yard and many trees. She was about to get out of the car when she saw her sister already walking out the front door to greet her.

"Let's go! I haven't been out of the house in days," Kassi said as she got in the car. Being a stay-at-home mom left little time and opportunity for getting out, but when she got invited somewhere, she tried to take advantage. Her neighbor's daughter was seventeen and in high school, but was off for summer break, so she could babysit for her.

"So what's on the agenda?" Kassi asked.

"First, coffee," Kenna answered with a smile.

"Yay!" she replied clapping her hands

childishly.

They drove through their favorite coffee shop and both got a caramel macchiato and a chocolate chip scone, treating themselves for girls'day.

"Mmmm, so good," Kassi cooed as she took a sip.

"I made us reservations at The Healing Spa," Kenna said excitedly. "I booked us for massages, facials, and pedicures. Then, I figured we could do lunch at Bianca's before heading home." She knew that was one of her sister's favorite restaurants.

"That sounds amazing. I am so glad we planned a sister's day. We haven't hung out, just the two of us in so long," Kassi said between bites of her scone. They had always been close, but as they got older and their lives got busier, the less time they had to spend together.

They arrived at the spa just before their appointment time. Tranquil music played quietly in the lobby. Marble covered the floors and pillars, and a waterfall flowed along one wall, pouring into a pond that had orange and white coy fish occupying it.

Shortly after they arrived, a woman in a white linen uniform escorted them to a massage room down one hallway. They undressed and laid on the two tables in the room. It was warm and comfortable. The massage therapists arrived and began their work. Gentle scents of lavender and eucalyptus filled the room as a calming melody played softly in the background. Soon, the sisters were drifting off into a trance of relaxation.

"O.M.G. this feels so good," Kassi said.

"I needed this," Kenna replied to her sister as the message therapist rubbed all the stress from her shoulders.

"How have you been doing since your application review?" Kassi asked sensitively.

"It's been really tough, honestly. But I finally feel like I'm getting out of my funk and returning to normal life," Kenna answered as she propped her chin up on her folded arms.

"I know it sucks waiting another year to apply again, but it will happen for you eventually," Kassi said sensibly.

"I know. But you're right, it really does suck." Kenna closed her eyes and tried not to focus on the denial. She was getting sick of everyone telling her it would happen eventually, like that would help her feel better.

After an hour, the massage was over and they were taken to another room for their facials. Again, they laid down on two tables in the room, this time laying on their backs. The esthetician got to work with an exfoliating massage, followed by a clay mask that covered their faces, necks, and chests. She left the room to let the mask sit.

Kenna pulled a cucumber off her eye and looked at her sister. "We look ridiculous."

"I don't care. It's nice just to lie here without little people crawling on me," Kassi replied.

"Be thankful for your little people," Kenna replied with a tinge of jealousy in your voice.

"I am thankful. But I still need a break every now and then. Someday you'll understand."

"I hope so."

Lastly, they went across the hall and picked out nail colors for their pedicures. Kenna chose a candy red and Kassi went with a more neutral taupe polish. Another staff member brought them both cucumber water with fresh mint. The combination tasted fresh and they sipped as they had their toenails painted.

The sisters left the spa feeling refreshed and restored after hours of being pampered.

"We should do that every weekend," Kassi joked.

"Yeah, I wish," Kenna replied

Bianca's was just a few blocks away and they arrived there in minutes. It was still before noon and people were slowly filtering into the restaurant. A bubbly waitress with a pixie cut arrived at their table shortly after they were seated and asked for their order. They both ordered the soup of the day and salad for lunch.

"Oh, and some breadsticks, please," Kassi added to their order.

"Kass, should we get some wine, or mimosas? It is girls 'day, after all," Kenna asked.

"It's not even noon yet!" Kassi teased. "You go

ahead, but I don't want any alcohol."

Gleefully, the girls chatted about what was new in their lives. They gossiped about people they used to know from prep school and where they were now. Joking and laughing in a way that only sisters do, with snorts and even some knee slapping, they had a great time. Finishing their meals, they asked the waitress for the check.

Kassi turned to her sister and she was no longer laughing, but instead had a serious look on her face. "Kenny, I have to talk to you about something. Something that I really want to share with my sister."

"What's on your mind?" she replied, feeling a little concerned by the look her sister was giving her.

"I'm pregnant," Kassi said bluntly. Her hopeful eyes analyzed her sister's face to gauge her reaction.

"What the fuck, Kassi? How?" Kenna asked, taken aback by her sister's news. "I didn't even know you were applying for another child." Shocked and confused, she was immediately angry at her sister.

"We didn't tell anyone we were applying because we didn't think we would get approved again. I mean, it's almost unheard for anyone to get approved for three children. When we got accepted, we started trying right away and I just didn't expect it to happen so fast. I was planning on telling you after your application got accepted so we could go through it together. But then you got denied and I've been struggling with how to tell you ever since."

"I see." Was all Kenna could muster in response, her face stone cold.

"That's all you're going to say? I'm sorry if my being pregnant bothers you, but can't you just be excited and supportive of your sister?" She felt hurt and hoping for some understanding from her best friend.

"No, I can't. Not right now," Kenna said uncaringly, not fully aware of how hurtful her words were.

Arriving with the check, the waitress appeared to sense the tension between them. She seemed relieved when they paid the tab and quickly left.

They sat in awkward silence for the entire duration of the drive back to Kassi's house. Kenna was raging on the inside as she gripped the steering wheel tightly and refused to look at her sister. Kassi sat disheartened looking out the window, occasionally stealing glances at Kenna, hoping to see her come around.

As she was getting out of the car, Kassi looked back at her sister. "I didn't do this to hurt you. It's just the way it worked out." She looked deflated.

"I know," Kenna replied without looking at her sister and then she drove away, crying all the way home.

A week later, Kenna decided to pay her grandmother, Eleanor, a visit with Ruby. When she arrived at her mother's house, she let herself in the wooden front door and called out to let her grandmother know she had arrived. Eleanor, moving gracefully but slowly, met her in the sitting room.

"How are you, dear?" She gave Kenna a side hug before sitting down in the large overstuffed armchair.

"I'm fine grandma, and how are you?" Kenna replied, taking a seat nearby.

"Good, I am good. I was thinking I would work out in the gardens today. It's so beautiful outside." It was late in July now and everyone was trying to soak up the summer weather before fall slowly crept in on them.

"Well, I can stay and help you. I am free all day." Kenna smiled.

"That would be lovely," Eleanor replied.

Kenna introduced her grandmother to Ruby and told her the story of how Emmett had surprised her. They talked about how Kenna's work was going and Eleanor asked after Emmett. Deciding that they should have some tea and cookies, they moved their conversation into the kitchen.

Eleanor looked at her granddaughter the way grandparents do when they know there is something weighing on their conscious. "Why don't you tell me what's on your mind, dear?"

"What makes you think I have something on my mind?" Kenna questioned as she nibbled on a cookie.

"Well, because I am your grandmother, so I know everything" she said with a smile. "That, and your mother told me about you and Kassi."

"Ah, that," Kenna said. "I was just taken a little off guard with Kassi's news and I reacted badly. I haven't talked to her since." She felt guilty about her childish reaction, but she could not come to terms with Kassi's pregnancy yet.

"It's understandable that you would be upset, with your application so recently getting denied. But she is your sister and your friend. She probably believed that your application would be accepted, and you both could experience the joys of pregnancy together," her grandmother said.

"Yeah, but we aren't going through it together. I got denied and now Kassi is pregnant with her third child. I am not even allowed to have one child and she is going to have three. It just seems so unfair," Kenna said, getting upset.

"You will get approved next time you apply, and someday you will look back at this experience and it will seem like a minor problem in the overall picture of your life. And you don't want to jeopardize the beautiful relationship you have with your sister over something that will not matter in five years," Eleanor said wisely.

"I know you're probably right, but right now I'm still sad and maybe a little jealous. I just need a little time to get over it. Then, I promise I will call Kassi and support her like a sister should. But it isn't going to happen today, and tomorrow isn't looking good either." Kenna sipped her tea.

Her grandmother just shook her head and let out a sigh. "Just don't wait too long."

Finishing their tea, they headed outside to enjoy the sunshine. And maybe pull a few weeds while they were there. Walking around the house, they looked at all the different flower beds. They were very well kept and there were only a few weeds scattered about for them to pick.

Eleanor used to manage the gardens herself, but now that she was in her nineties, it was too much for her to handle. So Kenna's mother had hired a gardener to take care of the landscaping needs and he came once a week. Kenna suspected the gardener left a few weeds on purpose so that her grandmother felt like she had something to do.

Summer was half way over but there were still many flowers blooming in the gardens. The walkway around the house was lined with bright orange chrysanthemums, and cheerful pink coneflowers were scattered throughout. Most of the lilies were done blooming but there were still a few in yellow in white that looked like bright stars in comparison to the green foliage surrounding them.

"Grandma, what were the reproductive

restrictions like when you were having children?"Kenna asked.

"Well, they were much different from the way they are now. The restrictions started when I was a young girl, but they were not very strict when they started out. I believe it started with offering free IUDs and arm implants to those who wanted it in hopes that it would prevent unwanted pregnancies," Eleanor said.

"I can't even imagine an unwanted pregnancy," Kenna said, bewildered.

"Oh yes, there were many. There were homes called foster homes and orphanages where unwanted children went. Or sometimes even if the children were wanted, their parents simply were not fit to care for them and the children got taken away," Eleanor said.

"How horrible that must have been! My heart breaks for those poor children," Kenna said as she placed her hand on her chest.

"It was unfortunate, and some children suffered. Then there were those that never had to suffer but also did not get to come to be," Eleanor stated.

"What do you mean, grandma?" Kenna furrowed her brow in confusion.

"Sometimes when a woman would find herself with child but the pregnancy was not wanted, for whatever reason, she could choose to end the pregnancy and not have the baby," her grandmother answered.

"I thought they only did terminations if it was absolutely medically necessary. I don't understand how a mother could do that to a healthy baby," Kenna declared, shocked.

"That is how it is done now, and there is far less need for terminations because all pregnancies are wanted. These women faced hard choices. Sometimes they chose to terminate because of financial reasons, or they simply were not ready to take care of a child. I wouldn't be too quick to judge if I were you. Times were different. Healthcare coverage was very lacking and even when people had access, they couldn't afford it. My older sister found herself pregnant when she was 16 years old, far too young to care for another human being. She needed to finish high school and wanted to go to college, and she certainly did not have the financial means to support herself, let alone a baby. So she decided to terminate the pregnancy, and she went on living her life."

She paused to reach down and pull a weed from its garden bed. "I asked her once if she regretted her decision. She told me that although it was difficult, it was the best choice for her at the time. Others may have judged her, up on their high horses, but I never did." And there she ended her story.

"When did they start requiring pregnancy prevention?" Kenna questioned.

"Oh, not for a number of years. Close to

twenty years, I suppose. After they offered them for free for many years, they then offered to pay women to get implants placed. This did help increase the number of women that were willing to get it. Then, eventually, they made the implants a requirement and over the years, it developed into the system we have in place today," she responded.

"Do you think we are better off now?" Kenna asked with wide eyes.

"There are undeniable benefits to the restrictions and as a whole, I do think our society benefits from them. However, I cannot say that we are better off," her grandmother uttered.

Kenna thought about what her grandmother said for the rest of the afternoon. The restrictions had been in practice her whole life and she didn't know any different. Now she wondered what their world would be like without the restrictions. She pictured a world where people could have children when they wanted and didn't have to ask for permission. The population grew rapidly and there were unwanted babies everywhere.

Now, with the restrictions in place, people had a lot of sexual freedom without the concern for unplanned pregnancy. If they didn't have the restrictions in place there would be many children born to young, unready individuals. It would be chaos, but in this chaos they would have freedom.

CHAPTER 4
Familiar Faces

Kenna was busy working in her psychology office downtown. She had rented space in a charming, old brick building close to their house. It was small and there was only room for her secretary, Glenda, a small waiting area with two chairs, and her office. Trying to make the space comfortable for her clients, she had decorated in calming neutrals with elements of wood and texture in the furniture and decor. Small pops of color were present in the few pieces of her artwork on the walls.

She had just returned from lunch, and following her normal routine, she walked home to let Ruby out during her break. After being outside in the sun and getting some steps in, she felt refreshed. As she reviewed her client list for the afternoon, she looked at her past notes in order to pick up where they left off. There was a new name on her client list, a Rebecca Wilkins. She enjoyed seeing new clients and was looking forward to the appointment. It was her last one of the day.

Later on that day, Rebecca arrived right on time for her appointment and Kenna invited her to sit down in her office. Her curly auburn hair was tied back, but a few strands were loose around her face framing her light brown eyes. They sat by the window, Rebecca on the sofa and Kenna in a chair next to her. Kenna reached for her leather notebook off of her desk so she could take notes throughout their visit.

As she turned to address Rebecca, she realized she recognized her. Although she couldn't quite remember when they had previously met. She thought about it during their session, but she was still drawing a blank.

"So, Rebecca, why don't you tell me a little about yourself?" Kenna started out.

"First off, you can call me Becca. Everyone does. And I guess there's not much to tell. I'm a teacher and I am married." She shrugged, seeming to be uncomfortable or unwilling to divulge much information.

"Why don't you tell me about your job?" Kenna tried to ease her into conversation.

"I teach first grade at Liberty Elementary. I have been there almost ten years now," Becca said as she picked at a loose string on the hem of her shirt.

"Do you enjoy it?" Kenna continued.

"Oh, yes. My kids mean the world to me, and I

couldn't imagine doing anything else. Some days are trying, of course, as with any job I'm sure. But I love it. And my coworkers are great for the most part. There's a few that are harder to get along with...like our principal," Becca shared, rolling her eyes.

"It sounds like you are really passionate about your work." Kenna was skilled in motivational interviewing. It's what made her such a good psychologist. "Tell me about your husband."

Becca's golden eyes lit up and her entire face seemed to smile when she thought about him. "He's amazing, the best man I have ever met. I know this is cheesy, but he really is my rock," she answered with sincerity.

"He sounds like a great guy. And it seems you get along well," Kenna said the statement more like a question.

"Usually, yes. Lately, not so much." Becca's face fell and looked down at her hands folded in her lap.

"What has changed more recently?" Kenna pried gently.

"Well, he is the one who made me come here and I really didn't want to, if I'm being honest. We went through a big disappointment earlier this summer and I have been kind of depressed ever since. He's worried about me and has been encouraging me to talk to someone for a while now, and we have argued about it quite a bit." Becca looked down as she spoke.

"It's very common for people to shy away from talking to a stranger about their issues. Would you like to discuss the big disappointment that you went through a couple of months ago?" Kenna asked.

"Not really. But I suppose that's why I am here, so we might as well get it over with." Becca kept her eyes focused on her hands. "They denied our application for a child."

Immediately, Kenna realized where she had seen Becca before. She was the woman that was hysterical in the Application Review Office when they were there for their review with the committee.

"Getting denied from something so important is understandably very upsetting." Kenna said, welcoming her client to open up about the experience without letting her own feelings on the matter show on her face. She did not mention to Becca that she was there that day. She felt that would be inappropriate and an invasion of her private life.

Tears filled Becca's eyes as she looked up at Kenna. She was trying to blink them back, but it was no use. Kenna handed her a box of tissues and gave her some time to get it out.

"It felt like someone was thrusting their hand into my chest, grabbing my heart and ripping it out of my ribcage. The whole experience is actually kind of a blur. I was so upset it was almost as if I was in a trance. Afterwards, for an entire week I did nothing but lay in bed in cry. I couldn't eat or shower. I was pitiful." She went on to discuss her sadness and how her husband was very supportive, but worried. And how their fighting eventually pushed her to make an appointment with a professional.

Their time was nearing the end of their session. Kenna hated to leave it at such a vulnerable point, but they would have to pick it up at their next visit.

"Becca, I appreciate that you have shared your experience with me and I would like to talk more about it at your next session. Say, next week?"

"That would be fine." Becca looked relieved to be done for the day.

Kenna walked her to the door and advised Glenda to schedule Becca for the same time next week. When she got back to her desk, she reviewed her notes to see if there was anything important she missed and needed to add.

Thinking about Becca and her experience brought up her own feelings of despair after they denied her application. When she thought about it, she still felt the sharp sting of the denial in her chest. She felt a kinship with Becca being denied on the same exact day. It made her feel a little less lonely knowing Becca was going through the same heartache she was going through.

These past couple months had been the loneliest months of her life. Emmett dove into his residency, giving it his full attention and she hadn't spoke to Kassi since girls' day. She missed her best friend and her loneliness was greater than the anger she felt toward her sister. She decided it was time to call her sister. Stubbornly, she had been avoiding it and knew that she was at fault and needed to make it right.

Kassi answered her call right after the first ring. "Hey," she said, a tone of understanding came through the other side.

"Hey," Kenna replied back, feeling sheepish that they had even fought.

"I'm sorry about my reaction to your pregnancy news. I'm a horrible person." Kenna apologized.

"You are not a horrible person. You were just upset. I get it. But you did make me cry, FYI," Kassi replied.

"Well, congratulations on your pregnancy. I am happy for you, jealous, but happy. How have you been feeling?" Kenna asked.

"We found out yesterday that the baby is a boy, so that's exciting. I'm pretty much over the morning sickness part, so I am feeling pretty good." Kassi was relieved to talk to her sister again.

"A boy? That's great," Kenna said, trying to portray more excitement in her voice than she actually felt.

"You should come over soon to see the kids, and you can help me design the nursery," Kassi said invitingly.

"Yeah, sure," Kenna said, ready to be off of the phone.

"I'm so glad you called," Kassi voiced honestly.

"Me too," Kenna stated before ending the call.

Kenna set her phone down and stared at it for a second. She was glad that they were now on speaking terms but after talking to Kassi about her baby, Kenna realized that she was still wildly jealous. Having Kassi around, flaunting her third pregnancy was going to drive her crazy.

The following week, Becca showed up for her appointment right on time. Taking their same seats, they started off talking about the weather and how fast summer was going by. Kenna offered her some water, and briefly went across her office to get them each a glass from the dispenser just outside her door.

"When does school start back up after summer break?" Kenna asked as she set down the glasses on the end table and took her seat again.

"Next week, and boy, I am ready to get back into some sort of routine," Becca replied.

"Routine and getting back to work are usually very good for mental health," Kenna commented before diving into their conversation they had left hanging last week. "At our last session, we were discussing the denial of your application and how that made you feel. I would like to continue with that today." She looked at Becca, inviting her to talk.

"After the sadness and unimaginable heartache softened, it left me just hopeless. Like, I actually have no hope left in me. I just feel defeated," Becca replied with truth in her voice.

"But there is still hope. You can always apply again next year."

Becca rolled her eyes and let out a heavy sigh. "Considering this was our fourth time applying and getting denied, I would say there is no hope for the future," she shared sadly.

Kenna was shocked by this. She had never known of anyone that had gotten denied four times. Usually, you are accepted on the second application or at the very least, the third. "I agree that getting denied four times is quite disheartening. Do you know why you keep getting denied?" she asked curiously.

"When I was a teenager I made some bad choices, and they are still haunting me to this day." Becca elaborated.

"Would you be comfortable telling me about these bad choices?" Kenna asked.

"When I was sixteen, I was dating this boy for all of one month and thought I was in love. He pressured me into having sex with him even though I insisted I was not ready, then afterward he stopped talking to me. He also had apparently recorded some of it and showed it to all his friends. I was mortified and I felt very lost and alone. Thinking that I couldn't show my face at school again, I tried to commit suicide by taking a bunch of pills." Becca looked out the window as she talked, not meeting Kenna's gaze. Even though many years had passed since it happened, it was still difficult for her to talk about.

"Luckily, my mother found me soon after and took me to the hospital to have my stomach pumped," Becca paused and took a deep breath, "after that, I had to spend part of my junior year in a rehab facility that dealt with mental health. Once I completed the program, I went back to school and the boy had graduated and I didn't have to see him anymore."

"And that is why you have gotten denied four times?" Kenna questioned.

"That and when I returned to school, I made friends with some kids that were bad news. We were out partying one night and they talked me into trying cocaine. Then on the drive home I got pulled over and one of my so-called friends had forgotten some of her coke in my car, so I got a possessions charge," Becca shared, finally looking Kenna in the eyes.

"But all of this happened fifteen years ago," Kenna said, bewildered."Surely enough time has passed that the committee could see you are no longer a teenager making irresponsible decisions." Kenna leaned forward in her chair.

"You would think that to be the case, but for some reason they won't let it go." Becca took a sip of water.

They were both silent for some time. Kenna was surprised at what Becca had told her, and she sympathized with her client. Even though they had only had two sessions together, she felt like she was really getting to know Becca and she couldn't help but like her. Kenna found her to be a kind, caring and honest person. In fact, she was almost angry at the thought of such a woman being denied the opportunity of motherhood.

Their session was once again nearing an end. "Would you like to come back next week?" Kenna asked her.

"Let's make it two weeks. I am sure I will have my hands full with the start of school next week."

"Sounds good, I will let Glenda know to schedule you."

Becca grabbed her purse and crossed the room to the door. When she reached the door, she turned back towards Kenna. "You know, Fletcher is working late tonight, so I was just going to go out for a quick bite to eat instead of cooking. Any chance you want to join me?"

Kenna was taken off guard by the unanticipated invitation, and she usually never got involved with clients outside of work because it's unprofessional. However, she liked Becca and felt like they had something in common. And even though she wouldn't admit it, she was feeling a little lonely with Emmett working so much lately.

So she went against her better judgement and said, "Sure."

The two of them left the office together, and Glenda said that she would lock up. They walked around the corner to a small bar and restaurant called Corks and Forks. Taking a seat at a high top table near the front windows, they started looking through the menu. The bar was narrow and long.

They visited in the dimly lit place as a playlist of jazz and R&B played in the background. The air was filled with the buttery scent coming from the popcorn machine behind the bar. When the waiter arrived, Becca ordered a glass of red wine and again Kenna's little voice of reason inside her head told her she shouldn't be drinking with one of her clients.

"I'll have the house cab," Kenna answered the waiter. He then continued to take their food order and grabbed their menus before leaving.

For the next hour, they ate and drank wine and talked as friends, not as a psychologist and her client.

"I saw you that day, at the Application Review Office," Kenna said loosening up after two glasses of wine.

"The day I got denied? What were you doing there?" Becca asked before shoving a handful of popcorn in her mouth.

"We were denied that day too," Kenna replied

with hurt in her eyes.

"I'm so sorry, Kenna. Then you know exactly what I am feeling," Becca said reaching across the table and taking Kenna's hand.

"I do."

At the end of their date, Kenna told Becca that she felt it would be more appropriate for them just to see each other as friends and not in her office as mental health professional and client.

"I agree with you," Becca said. "But here's the thing, I was hoping that in the off chance we apply for a fifth time it would look good if I had some visits for my mental health. You know, to show that I am trying to improve."

"Ah, I see. Well, I'll tell you what, we can do another session or two and if you feel you would like more visits, I can refer you to a different psychologist," Kenna replied.

"Deal," Becca said, smiling.

They parted ways outside the restaurant and walked in different directions home. Just as Kenna had noticed the sky was rather gray and the air had a chill, it started to down pour. She jogged the rest of the way home, thankful that she had worn comfortable flats to work instead of heels that day.

When she arrived home, she grabbed the mail off of the floor in front of the mail slot, put her purse on the entryway table and went to let Ruby outside. After letting Ruby back in, she ran upstairs to shower and change. Emmett was not yet home from work, but that was becoming his new normal.

The bathroom upstairs was one of her favorite rooms in the house. It had black and white octagon tiles on the floor, a walk-in tiled shower, and a beautiful claw-foot tub. She enjoyed going there at the end of the long day for a hot shower and to unwind.

While showering, her thoughts turned to Becca's situation and how unfair it seemed that a mistake made in adolescence would have such a lasting impact on her life. Her brain was not even fully developed when she made those wrong choices and yet, she was being held accountable now as an adult. It did not sit well with her.

She was also troubled by the idea that her friendship with Becca was not professional and wished she had suggested that Becca see a different psychologist. Just one or two more visits and then she would be done and they could just continue on as friends. What's the worst that could happen?

CHAPTER 5
Mayor

Victoria was walking into her office at the Capitol building downtown with her coffee and briefcase in tow. Her secretary informed her that Tom Adkins was waiting for her inside her office. He was early for their scheduled appointment. Her office was large and sophisticated. Bookshelves lined one entire wall and behind her giant mahogany desk there was a wall of windows looking out into the early morning sun. A man in his sixties with graying hair and a mustache was walking around the room looking at the unique works of art she had displayed on the walls and bookshelves.

"Tom, good to see you," she said warmly as she made her way to her desk, setting down her coffee and briefcase.

She invited him to have a seat across from her desk and he obliged. They had both worked in politics in this city for a long time and their paths crossed frequently. Sitting behind her desk wearing a charcoal gray pants suit, she had a powerful presence about her. Her strawberry blonde hair was fashioned in a neat bob, and she peered at Tom through her big, round rimmed glasses. While discussing the new happenings in Thayes and upcoming events, they also shared how their careers were going. Briefly, they talked about how their families were doing as their children were all around the same age.

"Speaking of family," Tom started, "do I want to know why you asked me to have your daughter's application denied? No judgement from me, I am just curious what would drive a mother to do such a thing," he said, bringing up the topic that was the cause of their meeting today.

"Thank you for carrying out that favor for me. I cannot divulge why it had to happen, but it is part of a larger plan. I am sure I do not have to stress the importance that this remains just between me and you?" Her face was stern.

"As always, Mayor, your secrets are safe with me," Tom smirked. "Just remember that you owe me one. I would like to advance to committee lead in the near future and I would appreciate your help to get there." Nothing in politics was done for free or without some sort of debt owed.

"I will see what I can do," she replied. And with that, Tom stood to take his leave. She also stood and shook his hand across the desk, all while looking him intently in the eyes to show that she was not one to be messed with. Over the years, she had made several similar transactions and she had learned along the way who she could trust and who she could not.

After Tom left, she turned in her large, high-backed chair to look out the window at the cityscape while she drank her black coffee. As a mother, she felt guilty for betraying her youngest daughter. She kept telling herself that it was only one year. Kenna would get over being denied, she would get her second application accepted and have the child she always wanted. A year, after all, was such a short period of time in the larger scheme of things. She did not foresee the situation with Kassi, as they had kept it to themselves until they were already expecting. Having done what she did for personal gain, she hoped it would be worth it in the end. She let out a heavy sigh and turned back to her desk to get started on her never ending work.

Victoria had called everyone over for a family dinner the following weekend and her cleaning lady, Marie, who occasionally cooked for her as well, had prepared quite the feast. There was filet mignon topped with an herb butter, parmesan asparagus, a light salad, and turtle cheesecake for dessert. The pleasant aroma of her home cooking wafted from the kitchen to the dining room, leaving everyone's mouths watering. Victoria ventured down the narrow stairs to the basement to get some wine from her wine cellar there. She chose an expensive merlot that she had been saving for a special occasion. She grabbed a couple of bottles and went back upstairs to her guests. Kassi and Clayton sat on one side of the table opposite of Emmett and Kenna while Victoria and Eleanor sat at the ends.

Everyone sat around the table except Liam and Penny, who were eating in the kitchen with their babysitter. Victoria opened the wine and went around the table pouring for everyone, except Kassi, of course.

"I am so glad everyone could make it to family dinner," Victoria said, "even Emmett was able to tear himself away from work for the evening," she joked, knowing that he had been putting in many hours and Kenna found herself at home alone much of the time.

Praising Marie's cooking, they ate their flavorful meal all the while chatting and catching up on each other's daily lives. Victoria was soon running downstairs to grab another bottle of wine as everyone was drinking and conversing merrily.

"I have asked you all over tonight for this special dinner because, well for one, I love seeing all of you and we do not get together enough, and also because I have an important announcement to make," Victoria said.

Everyone was looking at her with curiosity, wondering what she had to share. They had finished their meal and the heavenly cheesecake had just been passed around the table. Waiting for her news before they dug in, they watched her intently.

"I have decided I will not be running for re-election when my term as mayor comes to an end this year," she divulged.

"Wow mom, you're retiring!" Kenna exclaimed. "That's great, and you deserve it after working so hard for so many years."

"No dear, I am not retiring," she replied gently. "I am going to run for our region's chair in the upcoming election," she finished, beaming with excitement.

There were looks of surprise around the table, and then everyone smiled and congratulated her on her newest venture. Eleanor, however, did not seem surprised. Victoria had confided the news to her weeks ago. She was proud that her daughter was reaching for the stars and taking it as far as she could. Running for region chair was going to be a big undertaking, even for Victoria, and she needed all the support she could get.

"I would like to offer Clayton the position of my campaign manager and my personal lawyer. There is no one I would trust more with this significant task, and I hope you will accept my offer," she voiced to her son-in-law.

"Victoria, of course I will accept. I am honored that you are giving me this opportunity to work with you at such a level," he responded. Kassi looked at him adoringly as he beamed with pride.

After dessert, they stayed around the table and were discussing campaign plans with Victoria for her upcoming election. The election was less than twelve months away, which meant that she was a little late to the game already. She would have to come in fast and strong to get the votes she needed to win such a competitive appointment. Clayton was over-the-moon excited and had already come up with several ideas that he wanted to share with her. They decided to meet later in the week to get started on a plan, and he and Kassi gathered the kids and left for home before it was past their bedtime.

"Congratulations mother," Kenna said, approaching her mother in the sitting room. "I'm sorry I thought you were retiring. I don't know why that popped into my head first. But I do think you would make an excellent region chair. You've done so much for our city as mayor, and I know you will do just as much or more for Region Four."

"Thank you Kenna, no need to apologize. After all, I am sixty-five. However, I think I have a few good working years left and I plan to use them," Victoria replied.

Kenna had always admired her mother's work and how she advocated for those who needed it the most. It was the reason she became a psychologist, she wanted to help where she could. Just like Victoria helped where she could.

Kenna and Emmett said their goodbyes to Victoria and Eleanor and headed for home across town. On the drive they talked about the dinner and how fantastic the food and wine was, and the excitement that Kenna's own mother might actually be Region Four chair in about a year's time.

"It was good to get out and have a nice dinner together with family. Lately, we have hardly seen each other, let alone sat down to have a nice dinner together," she commented, pouting slightly.

"I know babe, I am sorry I have been so busy with work. But in my defense, you knew I had a demanding career when you married me," he replied nonchalantly.

"What's that supposed to mean? Like I signed up for this, to be home alone every night for the past month?" she was getting a little worked up, and the wine she had earlier was not helping matters.

"No, that's not what I said. I just mean that in my career I am going to be busy, and sometimes I will be absent and that is just the way it is in my field," he replied.

She did not reply to him and instead turned to stare out of her window for the rest of the drive home.

CHAPTER 6
The Deal

Victoria was sitting in her office when her secretary advised her that Region Three Chairman, Amos Christopherson, was on the line for her. Victoria was not expecting such a call, being mayor she had on several occasions met and spoken with the chair of her own region, but she had scarcely interacted with the other region's chairs.

"Put him though," she replied over the receiver.

There was a click of the call coming through, "Hello Amos, this is Victoria Carson speaking."

"Hello Mayor Carson," he began, "I am calling to extend to you an invitation to dinner with the other chairmen and I tomorrow evening in Thayes."

She was surprised by the invite."Yes, I would love to join you. Thank you," she stated. This call was completely out of the blue and she wondered why he wanted to meet with her.

"Seven o'clock at Waterside downtown. See you then." He hung up the line.

Waterside was an uppity restaurant on the river's edge downtown that was usually impossible to get into without a reservation. She assumed she would meet with the chairmen from regions one, two, and three. The Region Four Chairmen was on hospice care due to lung cancer and he did not have long left, she knew. That is why his seat is up for election this year, even though it was not a typical election year.

Still wondering why they wanted to meet with her, she was hopeful that this meant she was definitely in the running for the position. There were two others running against her and they would be narrowed down to just two candidates by the final election. The other two candidates had already been campaigning for a few months and they were very capable, even likable individuals.

Victoria knew she had her work cut out for her. If she didn't win chair and she didn't run for her mayor position again, she wasn't sure what she would do with herself. This was a sobering thought, and she decided then and there that failure was not an option for her. After all, it never had been and never would be.

The next evening she went to Waterside, arriving just before seven. Her colleagues had already arrived, and the hostess escorted her to their table. The dining room was grand, with high ceilings and multiple large, ornate chandeliers hanging from above. Their table was in a secluded corner of the room, away from wandering eyes and open ears.

When she arrived at their table, Amos introduced her to the other two chairs: Felicity and Jeffrey. Making small talk, she discovered they were in Thayes specifically just to see her. She was honored that they had traveled all this way to meet with her, but also confused as to why. They ordered food and drinks and continued to chat about politics and the Region Four Chairmen opening.

"We wanted to meet with you because we believe you will be favored in the upcoming election and we wanted to make sure you would make an excellent addition to our team. Because that's what we are, a team. And we want to make sure you are on the same page as far as some major elements are concerned," Amos said as the other two nodded in agreement.

Peppering her with questions, they took turns around the table, asking what her stance was on several political issues. How she felt about free healthcare, free college, and returning unoccupied neighborhoods back to nature. What changes would she like to see and her ideas on how to make these changes happen. Victoria answered all their questions honestly. She had nothing to hide and her political beliefs were no secret.

"All of your answers have been right on the mark," Region One Chairman Felicity Porter stated. "But there's one last thing we would like to discuss with you, something that is very important to our team and we are hoping it will become important to you as well."

"It's regarding the reproductive restrictions and the application process," Amos said tentatively.

As mayor, Victoria had little to do with the reproductive restrictions, as they controlled it at a national level. If she was ever involved, it was only to recommend new committee members in their area. As Region Four Chairman, she knew she would be involved in the regulatory process and decision making involved with the application process. The reproductive restrictions and current application process didn't concern her as she considered them reasonable and essential for population control.

"You see, our team has been working many years to make the reproductive restrictions and application process what they are today, and we want to make sure no one tries to undo our work," he said.

"I assure you, I feel the current process is just fine," she replied.

"We have continued to tighten the requirements to be approved during the application process. Raising the income required, the housing standards, and we have been cracking down on those who have past criminal history," he continued.

Felicity chimed in, "We have changed laws and guidelines in order to restrict certain groups of people from reproduction."

Victoria looked at them with confusion on her face. She wasn't understanding what they were getting at. "What group of people?"

"The increased restrictions and hurdles in the application process are there specifically to restrict the lower class from reproducing," Felicity answered with a straight face.

There was silence for several seconds while she processed what was just said to her. "Let me make sure I am understanding what you are telling me," Victoria started, "you are setting it up so that poor people never have their applications approved?"

"That is correct," Amos replied, "and by doing so, we have been decreasing their population at a steady rate. As their numbers decrease and there are more and more unused homes or apartments in the housing projects or slums, we can return those areas back to nature."

"I see," Victoria remarked. She wasn't quite sure how else to respond to the information she had just received. "If you all would excuse me for one minute while I visit the restroom." She got up from the table in search of the bathroom.

The others at the table exchanged glances of speculation and worry. "We need to make sure she will be on board with this before we do anything to help her campaign," Felicity asserted.

Region Two Chairman, Jeffrey Sampson, nodded his head in agreement.

Victoria entered the empty, enormous bathroom. It smelled of fresh soap and was immaculately clean. She approached the mirror framed in gold and placed her hands on the marble counter, it felt cool beneath her hands. Removing her glasses, she stared at her reflection and silently asked herself how far she would be willing to go for power.

Sighing heavily, she hung her head while she tried to organize her thoughts. She knew she was no angel. She was a politician, after all, but in her opinion, this was a new level of wrong and she wasn't exactly comfortable going there. Did she want the region chair position bad enough to compromise her morals, or at least what was left of them? Looking back up at the mirror, being honest with her own reflection she knew she wanted it bad enough. All the work she had put in during her lifetime had led her here, and she knew she would do whatever it took to gain that spot, even this. The reproductive restrictions were essential to the Earth's survival and although she didn't like the thought of wiping out a whole class, she would uphold what was in place. With that, she replaced her glasses, smoothed her hair and reapplied her lip color before returning to the table.

"Sorry about that. I just needed to freshen up," she said to the others with a smile.

They all stared at her questioningly. "So, are you on board with our plan?" Felicity asked.

"Yes. I am on board, and I want nothing more than to be part of your team," she announced enthusiastically.

There were nods of approval around the table, and the three chairmen told Victoria that they would endorse her in the election and do whatever they could to help her succeed. She was elated because she knew that with their backing, she was more likely to win the election and gain the power that came along with it. She sipped her wine and thanked them for their gracious encouragement. But she could not get rid of this nagging feeling, like she had just crossed a line to which there was no return. They exchanged their contact information with Victoria and said their goodbyes before leaving the restaurant.

Victoria spent her commute home thinking about the evening and how peculiar it had been. How could she not have realized their plan to eliminate the poor when it was happening right under her nose in her own city? She supposed they justified it with excuses, such as a higher income is needed to support a child and if someone has a criminal history, they could re-offend. Excuses that it would be for the greater good to decrease the population and return more developed areas back to nature. She was thinking of excuses now herself trying to justify what they were doing, thinking maybe if she could justify it to herself, it wouldn't feel so wrong.

In her past political career, she had always used her platform to help those less fortunate. She did this by advocating for free healthcare, housing assistance, and food programs so that they could have better, healthier lives and be taken care of. On holidays she would drag the girls and her mother to work at the soup kitchens and she did it because she wanted to, not just for the exposure. Now she would work to ensure that the opportunity to have children, to become parents, was denied to these individuals and she needed to make herself accept that.

When she arrived home, she did her nighttime facial routine and changed into silk pajamas. She crawled into her large fourposter bed with a book, but she could not focus on what she was reading. So she gave up and decided just to go to bed, but she couldn't sleep, for her mind was racing with the very thoughts that she was trying to bury.

CHAPTER 7
Emmett

Emmett woke up at five in the morning, his usual wake up time. He threw on some athletic shorts, a t-shirt, and his tennis shoes as he headed out for his morning run. The sun wasn't up yet; the air was cool and felt good against his skin. As he ran through the residential neighborhoods near theirs, there was no one to be seen. Most of the houses were still dark as people slept in their beds. He reached the park that was about a mile from their house and ran along the river, stopping on a bridge that crossed it. It was an old arched stone bridge, and he leaned on the edge as he gazed down into the water, taking a break. The sun was just starting to rise and the sky was getting brighter. He allowed himself a few minutes to appreciate the peace and quiet of nature before continuing on.

He ran the perimeter of the park before starting back home, listening to music as he went. Not thinking about anything except his feet hitting the pavement. When he got back home, he tossed his sweaty clothes into the hamper and jumped into the shower. Steam filled the bathroom as he washed his hair and his body. He stretched his neck from side to side in the shower as the hot water flowed over him and heard a satisfying crack.

As he got dressed for the day, he saw Kenna was no longer in bed. She must have been letting Ruby outside. He grabbed his bag and went downstairs to grab some coffee. Kenna was sitting at the kitchen island sipping from her steaming cup, still in her pajamas. Pouring some black coffee into his travel mug, he wished Kenna good morning before going out the door.

Taking his usual route to the hospital, he walked there in fifteen minutes drinking his coffee as he went. When he arrived, he went past the elevators to take the stairs two flights up to the surgical floor. He grabbed some blue scrubs from the dispenser before going into the locker room to change for the day. After donning his scrubs and surgical cap, he went to look at the surgery board to see the schedule for the day.

The date on the board read August twenty-eighth. He had to think for a moment why that date seemed so familiar to him. Then it hit him and a small feeling of panic came over him. It was their anniversary, and he had forgotten. He immediately started brainstorming to come up with a plan so that the day would not be a total failure. He then went to the office shared by the surgeons to go over his cases and any relevant past medical history that could be useful in surgery. His case load was on the lighter side that day and he was thinking he could leave at a decent time and pick up Kenna's favorite sushi on the way home. Maybe light some candles, have some wine.

After his first two cases, he ran downstairs to the hospital gift shop and found a card and some chocolates. He even managed to find a dozen red roses there. He thought the day was really looking up and he had made a good save. After putting the gifts in his locker, he went to finish up his operative notes before his last surgery.

His last case of the day was a straight forward lobectomy of the upper lobe of a right lung. A two to three-hour surgery, and then he could get home before Kenna and set up a romantic dinner for them. He put on a mask and scrubbed in at the surgical sink before going into the operating room where a scrub nurse helped him don his surgical gown and gloves.

The surgery started out as expected, but soon took a turn for the worst. There were more adhesions than they had expected, and they had to switch from a thoracoscopic approach to an open approach. Once they opened the chest, they discovered the cancer was not only in the upper lobe, but also encroaching on the middle lobe as well. After a long four and a half hours, they completed the surgery.

Emmett went to the locker room to change and grab the gifts before running to beat Kenna home. He had planned on calling the sushi place on his walk to place the order for pickup. If he hurried, he could still make it work. He was reaching for the door handle on the stairway door when he heard someone call his name, so he stopped and turned. The head cardiothoracic surgeon for the hospital was walking towards him excitedly. He told Emmett that one of their patients on the transplant list had matched to a donor heart and it was on its way to the hospital now. They needed to prep for a long but exciting surgery.

"So are you coming?" he asked Emmett.

This surgery was likely the only heart transplant he would see during his residency, and it thrilled him to be given the opportunity to assist. His excitement and ambition outweighed the importance of their anniversary. "Yes, I wouldn't miss it. I'll change and be there in five minutes," he replied.

Emmett sent Kenna a text saying he was sorry that he would be working late and would miss their anniversary; he promised he would make it up to her. Then he changed back into scrubs and went to prepare for the biggest surgery of his residency.

CHAPTER 8
Losing the Spark

It was Saturday morning and normally Kenna would sleep in, but this morning she woke up early when Emmett got up promptly at five-thirty and jumped in the shower. She got up, putting on her robe as she went and followed him into the bathroom.

"Why are you up so early on a Saturday? Especially if you're not going for a run?" she asked, assuming he did not intend to run after showering.

"I have to go to the hospital for a bit this morning," he answered. He couldn't see her expression through the frosted glass of the shower door, but he was fairly certain that she was not impressed with him.

"But it's not your weekend to work." She knew he was supposed to be off this weekend.

"I know it's not love, but they need me to come in for a few hours to help out. I won't be there all day," he replied.

He was still in the doghouse after bailing on their anniversary for the heart transplant surgery. Kenna had barely said two words to him the rest of the week, and she sounded upset talking to him now. Concerned that Kenna would be even more angry with him after today, he knew he needed to make it up to her somehow. Being that it was a Saturday, tonight would be the perfect opportunity. Deciding he would make a reservation somewhere nice, he planned to wine and dine her into forgiveness tonight.

"Let's go out for dinner tonight and spend some time together. I'll get the details sorted out and you just need to be ready to go by six-thirty," he promised.

Her lips turned up in the corners the slightest bit as she replied, "I'll be ready." Smiling, she left him in the bathroom. Emmett had been working so much she was beginning to feel like she was married to a ghost. She was excited to spend some time with him tonight and go out for dinner, but she also didn't want to get her hopes up. After all, he had let her down so many times recently. The biggest letdown of all was their anniversary this week, and she was still scorned. She had bought him the watch she knew he had been eyeing for quite some time and had planned to give it to him on their anniversary. Hoping that he pulled through tonight, she decided she would give him the gift then.

Crawling back into bed, she was determined to enjoy a day off, starting with sleeping in. Ruby jumped up onto their bed. They usually did not let her up there, but Kenna made an exception today. With Ruby laying at her feet, she fell back asleep after a few minutes.

When she finally woke up, sunlight was poking through the curtains and she had overslept longer than she planned. Rolling over onto her back, she stretched her arms above her head and let out an exaggerated yawn. She got out of bed and started undressing out of her pajamas.

Seeing her reflection in the full-length mirror, she noticed she had put on some weight over the summer. Being down about their application denial, she hadn't had the motivation to work out as often as she should. It also didn't help that she had eaten her fair share of comfort food and quick dinners these past couple of months. Apparently, it was all catching up with her. Her love of wine probably wasn't helping, and she made a mental note to cut back.

She put on some shorts and a tank top, deciding to go for a run. After letting Ruby outside, she laced up her shoes and went out the front door, locking it as she left. Turning right, she started out at a slower pace; it had been a while since her last run. As she ran, she picked up her pace and it felt good. Girl power music was blaring in her ear buds and she kept pace with the beat. Breathing hard, she could feel her lungs burning as she pushed through it, determined to continue on.

After running for what seemed like forever, she had to stop for a red light. Putting her hands on her hips, she bent forward as she caught her breath. She realized she was on the edge of the East Side. She had run farther than she thought. Looking around while she waited for the light, she saw Becca getting out of her car up ahead. Curious to know what Becca was doing on this side of town, she started towards her so she could get a better look. She knew Becca didn't have any family that would live over there, so what was she doing?

Getting to the street where Becca parked her car, she stopped and looked to see where she had gone. She saw her heading deeper into the East Side and she followed her at a distance. After she walked a few blocks, she saw Becca round a corner and lost sight of her. Kenna quickened her pace, but when she turned to follow Becca, she was no longer in sight. Kenna stood at the corner searching the sidewalks for her friend but could not see her and could not figure out which way she went. Sighing, Kenna turned back the way she came and started for home.

When she got back home, she started the coffeepot before jumping in the shower. While in the shower, she shaved her legs and made sure her bikini line was well manicured for that night.

She was listening to music and singing along when she knew the words. All her thoughts of Becca had disappeared as she thought about a much needed night out with Emmett.

After showering, she threw on loungewear and grabbed coffee with a splash of creamer before heading out to enjoy the morning on the back deck with Ruby. As she sat drinking her coffee enjoying the morning sun, she threw the ball for Ruby, who retrieved it repeatedly. She thought about her and Emmett's relationship and how it seemed almost nonexistent these past few months.

When they started dating in college, they were both busy with full-time course work but still made time for each other. Despite the stress of studying for finals, boards, and planning their wedding in school, they supported each other and found fulfillment. She wondered why it was so different now and what had changed. Although they were both occupied with their careers, Emmett was much more engrossed in his work than she was. For the first time in their relationship, they didn't make spending time together a priority. Or at least, it wasn't a priority for Emmett.

Lately, it seemed like she was always angry with him, or at least disappointed. She knew how important medicine was to him and she respected his work ethic, but she couldn't help feeling like she was being abandoned. Would it ever end or get better? She wasn't so sure. Even after he finished his residency, he would still be a surgeon devoted to his work and she knew he would be absent often.

While going inside to get more coffee, she threw a load of laundry in the washing machine and started the dishwasher. She grabbed the book she had been reading for a few days and went back outside to her perch on the deck. It was a self-help book on using meditation and yoga to help relieve anger and frustrations. After trying some techniques taught in the book, she found herself more relaxed and more accepting. She hoped that she and Emmett could turn things around and tonight could be the start of that.

For the rest of the day, she did some various household chores and she took Ruby for a nice long walk to a park where they stopped to play frisbee. When they returned home, she looked over some of her financial spreadsheets for her business, and she was impressed with what she saw. She had been busy at work and was getting a steady stream of new clients. It was looking like her practice was going to be successful long-term.

Once it started nearing the time for their date, she decided to get ready. She curled her blonde hair into loose big curls and applied her makeup perfectly. Normally she didn't wear lipstick, but tonight she opted for a red color that she had bought a while ago on an impulse buy but had never worn. To match, she picked out red lingerie to wear under her dress. Her dress was black and simple, but had beautiful lines that hugged her curves in all the right places. Choosing a pair of strappy black heels, she checked her outfit in the mirror before heading downstairs to wait for Emmett.

As she sat there waiting for him, she couldn't help but have doubts arise that he would be late. Or he may not even show up at all. With these thoughts came feelings of anger and uncertainty flooded into her.

She got up and poured herself the rest of the Chardonnay that she had in the fridge from last night and tried to push the dark feelings away. She had her hopes set on tonight being perfect and she was trying to remain optimistic that her hopes would prove true. Turning on some smooth jazz music, she started to unwind while she waited for him to arrive.

Arriving home promptly at six, Emmett had even gotten her flowers. A dozen beautiful red roses. She put them in water while he ran upstairs quickly to shower and change. He came back downstairs twenty minutes later, looking dashing in dark gray trousers and a black button-up shirt.

"Hey handsome," she said, smiling at him as he reached the bottom of the stairs.

"Hello beautiful," he replied and stopped to

give her a kiss before they left for their evening out.

He had made a reservation for seven o'clock at an upscale Italian restaurant downtown. They arrived early and elected to have a seat at the bar while they waited for their table. She ordered wine and he started out with water before dinner.

"I'm so glad we finally made a date night work." She looked longingly into his eyes.

"Me too, love." He returned her gaze.

The hostess came to take them to their table shortly after they had ordered drinks and handed them menus after they were seated.

Flirting across the table, they discussed what they should order. Kenna felt excited to be out with him, like she had when they first started dating. They placed their food order with the waitress and Emmett ordered a whiskey neat.

"Do you remember our real first date?" Kenna leaned forward across the table.

"Haha yeah, it was a disaster," Emmett laughed, thinking about it.

"It was bad enough that you chipped your tooth on your beer mug, but then you locked your keys in your vehicle." She was smiling at the memory.

"And then it started raining. It could not have gone any worse," he said, finishing the story. He leaned forward across the table and took Kenna's hand.

"Well, at least it was memorable," Kenna replied.

"I miss us going on fun dates. I just miss spending time with you like we used to," Kenna said as she traced circles with her finger on the back of his hand.

"I miss that too." His brown eyes were focused intently on her face.

Kenna rubbed her foot along Emmett's leg under the table, and they continued to hold hands. Leaning over the table, trying to get as close to each other as possible.

"Maybe we could spend some time together tonight, like all night." She was feeling the effects of the wine, and her flirtatious side was coming out.

"Oh, I like the sound of that," Emmett said as he eyed her chest and bit his bottom lip.

"You look so sexy when you do that," she told him as she stared at his mouth.

Their food arrived along with Emmett's drink, interrupting their conversation. Everything looked fantastic. Emmett had gotten the prime rib while Kenna chose the sirloin and shrimp with a lemon butter sauce. They thanked the waitress and expressed their delight at the feast before them. Just as they took the first few bites, Emmett's phone buzzed. Kenna looked at him puzzled, as he answered his phone at the table, which he never did and considered rude.

"Okay, yeah I can," he said into the phone after

a while and then hung up.

He peered at Kenna with an apologetic look in his eyes. "I am so sorry Kenna," he started, "that was the hospital and they need me to come in to work. There was a multiple vehicle crash and several of the people involved need surgery so they are calling in more help."

Her face fell and her previous thoughts of anger and disappointment came rushing back, despite her attempts to keep them at bay. They had been having such a great time, and they needed it. Their relationship needed it.

"I understand," she replied, unable to mask the sadness in her voice.

They explained the situation to the waitress and she promptly took their food back to be boxed up for them and returned with the food and their bill a short time later.

Kenna was silent on the drive home. Emmett reached for her hand and apologized over and over on the drive. She was sad and angry, mostly angry at herself for getting so excited just to have her feelings crushed yet again when Emmett chose his work over her. He dropped her off at home and drove straight to the hospital without even getting out of the car.

When Kenna got inside, she decided she was still going to enjoy her dinner even if she was alone. She put the food on a plate, and it was still warm after the short drive home. After pouring herself more wine, she lit a candle and sat down to eat. This time she went with a Syrah that she thought would pair nicely with her steak. The steak and shrimp were to die for, but she couldn't quite enjoy it as much as she should.

As she chewed, she thought about Emmett and how their evening was ruined yet again. She couldn't help but let the anger and frustration build up within her. It was beginning to be a real problem. When she had finished her meal, she sat and drank her wine in the candlelight a while longer, contemplating her marriage and her happiness.

Tonight was the first time they had made a genuine connection in a long time. And for the short time they could enjoy themselves, she remembered what it was like when they were happy. She missed him, and she missed the way they were before their lives got too busy for each other. Or rather, his life had gotten too busy for her. Unsure of what she could do to change her situation, she just sat there feeling defeated and lonely.

She blew the candle out and let Ruby outside one last time before heading upstairs with her wine in hand. It was still early for a Saturday night, but she didn't feel like doing anything other than drinking her wine and watching a movie in bed. After she changed out of her little black dress and sexy lingerie, she slid into a pair of comfy pajamas before crawling under the covers with Ruby at her feet. She searched for something to watch and settled for a drama, one that would probably make her cry. But that's what she wanted, to be sad. Ruby, sensing her melancholic state, crawled up the bed to snuggle at her side. Kenna welcomed the warm snuggles and leaned into Ruby.

Emmett had gotten home in the middle of the night and poured himself into bed next to her. The next morning, she let him sleep in after she got up for the day. She went downstairs to make coffee and let Ruby out.

Today just felt like it was a cereal type of day and she poured herself a big bowl of her favorite peanut butter chocolate cereal. As she ate her breakfast and drank her coffee, she thought about what she wanted to say to Emmett when he woke up. She wasn't sure if she wanted to yell at him or if she wanted to cry and beg him to see how much he was hurting her. How much she missed him and needed him to be more present. He wasn't doing it intentionally and she knew that, but she could only take so much of this before giving up.

He woke up and wandered downstairs a little while later. Wishing her good morning, he poured himself some coffee and grabbed a couple of hard-boiled eggs from the fridge. When she looked at him, she forgot the speech she had played out in her mind. All the words she wanted to get across suddenly escaped her. So she just sat quietly, drinking her coffee and pushing her emotions down deeper within herself. They were in the same house, but Kenna felt like they were worlds apart. Spending the morning relaxing and being rather lazy, they sat on the deck as he read the newspaper and she read her book.

"What would you like to do today?" she asked, looking over at him, trying to break the silence.

"Well, I have some patient charting that I need to get done today," he said without looking up from his newspaper.

"I see," she replied, disappointed, but not surprised.

He must have realized her tone was apprehensive and so he put down the newspaper and looked at her. "Maybe we could take Ruby for a walk to the park and stop by the farmer's market to pick up some fresh food for a nice dinner at home tonight?" he asked.

"That would be nice," she answered with only half a smile. She supposed some time with him was better than nothing. But she would not hold her breath that it would work out.

They went on reading for a time and then got up to go inside. He worked on his charting while she did various things about the house before eventually going to shower and get dressed. The air had a chill that day. It was feeling like fall was closing in, and they both wore sweaters on their walk to the park.

"Starting to feel like fall, huh?" Kenna stated

to Emmett.

"Yeah, summer went by quick." He put his hands in his pockets.

"What do you want for dinner?" Kenna questioned, trying to continue the conversation.

"Whatever you want, love," Emmett responded, keeping his eyes forward as they walked.

They walked on and the silence created a space between them. Kenna wanted to talk to him about all of her frustrations, but she didn't know how to bring it up. She also didn't want to spend the little time she had with Emmett arguing, so she let it go and decided to just enjoy the day.

Emmett's phone got a notification and he looked confused as he read the message. They reached the park and while Kenna threw the ball for Ruby, Emmett could not rip his gaze away from his phone.

"Is something wrong?" she asked him.

"Not wrong per se, just perplexing," he replied without looking up from what he was doing. "A colleague just texted me about an unusual case he is dealing with today. He is stumped and asking for some ideas about what could be going on." He continued his research.

Kenna was annoyed and was having a hard time biting her tongue. After all, this was the first day they had spent together in weeks and she was already sour at him about last night. In her mind, she was yelling at him and pleading with him to be more present, but really she was just sitting next to him in silence. They made their way to get some produce and although he did eventually put his phone away, his mind was still elsewhere.

Returning to their house with fixings for a salad and salmon, they started cooking side by side in the kitchen.

"How should we cook the salmon?" she asked Emmett as she took the fresh fish out of the package.

"However you want," Emmet answered as he started cutting veggies.

"Do you need help cutting some of those?" she offered to help.

"No, I got it," he continued without lifting his gaze from his task.

"Would you like some wine?" she asked him with a mischievous grin.

"No, thanks." Again he didn't bother to break his gaze from his knife and cutting board.

Kenna turned and rolled her eyes. Typical, they had the day together and she can't get him to engage in conversation. His short answers were getting on her nerves. So she uncorked a white wine and poured herself an enormous glass.

His brief responses and lack of attention to her continued throughout dinner and while they were relaxing together before bed. He finally pulled out his laptop to continue trying to find the answers he was seeking. Later, she went to bed without him and she was fast asleep before he ever made it to bed.

CHAPTER 9
New Faces

Kenna was at the sink, brushing her teeth as Emmett showered before work. Her electric toothbrush splattered the mirror with her toothpaste, and she let out a sigh of annoyance. Downstairs, she started the coffeepot and grabbed a few things from the fridge to pack for lunch. As Emmett descended the stairs, Kenna gave him a side eyed glance and didn't acknowledge him when he approached the kitchen. She tapped her foot impatiently, waiting for the coffee to be ready so she could leave. He could sense that she was upset about something.

"Is something bothering you?" he asked as he opened the fridge.

"Ha," she let out a sarcastic laugh and looked at him like he was an idiot.

She walked towards to door, grabbing her work bag as she went. "I am just going to grab coffee on the way to work. I want to get an early start." And with that, she left as he stood there pondering why she had seemed so agitated.

Kenna walked towards work. There was a quaint little coffee shop on the way called Daily Cup and she liked their scones. As she walked, her thoughts circled around Emmett and his excessive work drive. She was getting increasingly irritated with him and it seemed to just keep building up inside her trying to get out. After their application got denied he didn't even seem upset. His lack of emotion angered her and she felt so alone in her despair. She shut him out and he didn't try very hard to get back in. Ever since, there had been a wedge driven between them.

Aware that her feelings were normal and appropriate, she also did not want to let them consume her. She just needed to figure out what to say to Emmett, to let him know how she felt without letting her anger get the best of her. One aspect of her job was to offer advice to clients on how to approach tough conversations, emphasizing the importance of communication in overcoming relationship obstacles. But now that she was dealing with her own relationship, all of her own advice was escaping her.

She reached the coffee shop and went inside. It was busy with the morning rush. Hoping they hadn't run out of scones, she got in line to order. There was a constant flow of people leaving the coffee shop and others entering to get in line. Looking over the pastries and muffins behind the counter, she could see they still had chocolate chip scones in stock. Occupied by her own thoughts, she was not really paying attention to those around her.

"Ma'am, can I take your order?" the young man with red hair behind the counter asked.

"Oh yes, I'm sorry." She hadn't realized she had reached the front of the line, "I'll take a chocolate chip scone and a medium roast coffee with sweet cream," she answered.

The young man rang up her order and gave her the total before turning around to grab her scone. As she reached into her work bag to grab her wallet, it wasn't there. She set the bag on the counter and started rummaging through it and moving everything around to see if maybe it was just in a different spot or maybe fell to the bottom. Although she hadn't noticed him, the man behind her was watching her struggle with concern.

"I am so sorry, but it appears I have forgotten my wallet today," Kenna told the barista with a disappointment but apologetic tone. She was really looking forward to her scone and coffee to start out her day.

"I'll get it for her," the man behind her said as he stepped to the counter, handing over his card for payment.

"Oh, you don't have to do that," she interjected, embarrassed. She reached for his hand to stop him from paying. Meeting his gaze, she smiled.

Looking back at her was a very well-made young man. He was tall with wavy blonde hair that he wore long but pushed back out of his face. His eyes were the most beautiful shade of blue, almost a deep cerulean hue. Wearing slacks and a button-up shirt with a brown leather messenger bag worn cross body, he looked to be a professional of some sort. She thought for a second that he looked like he belonged on a surfboard somewhere and not in dress clothes in the middle of the city.

"I'm happy to do it, honestly." He smiled back at her with her with a flirtatious smile.

She felt her cheeks getting warm as she got lost in his eyes. She noticed he had a dimple in his right cheek that showed when he smiled. Withdrawing her hand, she tucked a loose stand of hair behind her ear.

"Thank you so much, you're a lifesaver," she replied, accepting his generosity.

He finished paying for both of their orders, and they both went over to the pickup counter to wait for their coffees and scones. For a few seconds, they stood awkwardly, smiling at each other without saying anything.

Kenna finally broke her gaze away from his eyes that were so deep they seemed to suck her right back in every time she looked his way. She looked down briefly and cleared her throat.

"I really owe you one," she said to him. "This

coffee and scone is about to make my morning."

"It was my pleasure. Coffee and scones are the best way to start off a Monday," he joked.

Their orders were placed in front of them on the counter. They grabbed their drinks and breakfast and turned to leave the coffee shop. When they reached the door, he held it open for her. They stood on the sidewalk, looking at each other.

"Thanks again," she said, taking a sip of her hot coffee. "I never caught your name."

"Alec," he replied.

"Well, thank you Alec," she said with a smile as she turned to walk away.

"Aren't you going to tell me your name?" he asked her playfully.

"It's Kenna," she said, looking over her shoulder as she kept walking away with a smile still occupying her face.

She found herself smiling and thinking of her handsome stranger during the rest of her walk to work. When she arrived at her office, she saw Glenda had not yet arrived. Turning on all the lights as she went, she sat down at her desk with her scone and coffee. Thinking about Alec as she enjoyed her breakfast, she wondered where he was from and what he did for a living. But most of all, she wondered if he had a girlfriend. She knew he wasn't married, or at least he wasn't wearing a ring.

As she finished her scone and sat sipping

the rest of her coffee, she realized this was the first time since meeting Emmett that she had thought about another man. This realization left her confused, sad, and somewhat embarrassed. She knew she would never cheat on Emmett. Family was too important to her. Telling herself that her thoughts were just the result of an innocent crush and didn't mean anything, she got to work reviewing her client list in preparation. Thoughts of Alec plagued her mind the rest of the day and she continuously tried to push them away but was unsuccessful in her attempts.

A few days later, Kenna was getting ready to leave for work and she went downstairs to make coffee before heading out for the day. Reaching into the cupboard to grab a filter, she saw they were out of coffee beans. She decided she would just grab some coffee on the way to work.

Finding a pen and notepad in the drawer, she left a note for Emmett to let him know they were out of coffee and wishing him a good morning. He had worked an overnight shift so he had just gotten home a couple hours ago and was still sleeping upstairs. Hoping she would catch him after work for a few minutes to talk before he went in for another night shift, she signed her name on the note with x's and o's and left the house, grabbing her bag by the door as she went.

As she walked to work, she noticed the leaves

on the trees were just starting to turn colors. Fall would soon be upon them and although she enjoyed the season, she was sad to see the warm sunny days coming to an end. She took her time walking to work, enjoying the nice weather and watching the start of the morning bustle.

Approaching the Daily Cup, she suddenly had images of Alec running through her mind. If she was being honest with herself, she would know that she was hoping to see him there. As she reached for the door, it opened, taking her by surprise. The gentlemen who was leaving apologized for scaring her and held the door for her as she ducked inside.

When she entered the shop, a smell of fresh coffee and pastries filled the air, making her mouth water and her stomach growl. She scanned the room as she strolled to the counter. Seeing that Alec was nowhere to be seen, she was disappointed but tried to convince herself she was indifferent. The menu was a blackboard with colorful chalk listing the drink options and the pastries available for the day. There were a couple of people in front of her and as she moved forward with the line, she heard someone clear their throat loudly behind her. She turned around to see who it was and saw Alec's piercing blue eyes staring back at her. Her eyes lit up and she tilted her head while giving him a flirtatious half smile.

"Fancy seeing you here," she greeted him.

"Indeed, I am surprised to see you, too," he replied.

"Well, now I can repay your kindness with breakfast," she said.

"There is no repayment necessary. I would gladly do it again," he had his eyes locked on hers as he answered.

"I must insist on paying you back, and will not hear of your refusals," she joked.

"All right. If you insist, I will oblige," he said with an exaggerated bow.

Soon they were next in line and stepped up to the counter to order. Kenna paid for them both before they stepped aside to the pickup counter. Their order was done quickly and as they both grabbed their items, she found herself sad their encounter was coming to an end so soon.

She turned to bid him farewell, but he interrupted her before she could get her words out.

"Why don't we sit down and eat breakfast together?"

"Okay, that sounds fine." Flattered by this request, she accepted without really thinking about it.

He chose a small table in the front corner, away from the line of people and their chatter. When she sat down and saw him sitting across from her, she felt excitement but also a sense of uneasiness. It felt like she was doing something she shouldn't. They unwrapped their pastries and sipped their coffee, looking out the window at passersby.

"So Kenna, tell me about yourself. What do you do?" Alec asked with genuine interest.

"There's not much to tell. I'm afraid I'm quite boring," she answered between bites.

"Oh I doubt that very much," he replied in a smoldery tone.

She stared back at his sensual as she answered, "We moved to Thayes when I was a child and I have been here ever since. I am a psychologist and have my own practice close to here." She sipped her coffee. "What about you?"

"I moved to Thayes about a year ago. Originally I'm from Region Three, and I am actually a Professor of psychology," he replied matter-of-factly.

"No way. What a coincidence," she exclaimed. "Where do you teach?"

"GreyStone University," he elaborated, leaning forward to hear her better.

"That's where I went to school," she told him, surprised.

"Small world," he replied. Not surprised that she had attended GreyStone as it was in Thayes and was the largest university in Region Four.

"What do you specialize in, at your practice?" he asked inquisitively.

"I dabble in a little of everything, actually. Grief counseling, your run-of-the-mill depression, bi-polar, and all the usual disorders. I am hoping to get into addiction medicine soon as well." She lit up while talking about her work.

"Sounds like you keep busy," he replied, interested in keeping the conversation with her going.

"Yeah, my practice is really taking off. Even more than I anticipated it would," she answered as she took the last bite of her danish, the buttery pastry melted away in her mouth.

"I'm sure you're busy because you are good at what you do," he complimented her.

"Thank you," she said, blushing slightly.

"I would be delighted if you would be a guest speaker to one of my classes sometime," he said invitingly.

"Me? Be a guest speaker? I guess I had never really thought about giving lectures or teaching," she answered him hesitantly.

"I bet you would be great at it. And the school likes when Alumni come back to lecture," he encouraged her.

"I'll have to think about it. I don't even know what topic I'd want to discuss," she said, considering his proposition.

"Let me know what you decide." He slid one of his business cards across the table to her.

"I will." She grabbed the card and placed it in her wallet. "I should get going, otherwise I'll be late before my day even starts." She got up from the table, draping her bag over her shoulder and picking up her coffee. "It was nice to meet you,

Alec."

"Thank you for breakfast, I thoroughly enjoyed getting to know you Kenna." He looked at her intently, his eyes looking deep within her. Awkwardly, she stuck her hand out and he graciously took it. Shaking her hand nice and slow as he continued boring a hole through her soul with his eyes.

Her cheeks flushed. She realized she was biting her bottom lip and quickly stopped. Tearing her eyes away from his powerful gaze, she started toward the door. When she got outside, she realized her heart was racing and her skin was tingling with excitement. Trying to brush off these uninvited feelings, she walked toward her office.

CHAPTER 10
The Confession

Kenna had just arrived at work for the morning and she was following her normal morning routine, preparing for a busy day ahead. While reviewing her list, she saw Becca's name. She was her last client of the day. It had been a couple of weeks since they had last spoken, and she was looking forward to catching up with her. They had really connected when they went out for dinner. Admittedly, Kenna had also been fairly lonely lately and did not have many other friends to confide in. Although she had made up with her sister, she was still avoiding spending much time with her because she could not control her jealously yet.

Thinking of Becca brought up memories of her own application getting denied months ago. She knew what Becca was going through but could't imagine being denied four time. To experience that gutting heartbreak every year for four years. Her heart went out to her friend.

Thoughts of her own denial brought with them thoughts of Emmett and his absence throughout the grieving process. She had basically went through it alone. At least Becca had the support of her husband to help get her through.

To get through it she focused on work. She was working hard at building up her practice and had done some continuing education on addiction and pain management so she would feel comfortable expanding her client base.

When she had graduated from school and was starting her own practice, she was ambitious and hungry for success, but her priority was having children. That was her main focus and she had given little thought to how she could branch out and strengthen her career. Now, she had to wait a year to reapply to have a child, and for the first time, she was pouring everything she had into her profession. She was gaining more confidence in herself as a professional and was even considering Alec's offer to be a guest speaker for one of his psychology classes.

Her first appointment arrived for the day, and she put her thoughts aside to focus on the needs of her client. A young man in his thirties with black curly hair and brown eyes entered her office and sat on the sofa by the window. Kenna stood from her office chair to welcome him and then sat in the chair near him, grabbing her notebook off her desk as she went. He had been coming to see her on a biweekly basis for several months to help work through his depression.

Earlier in the year, his boyfriend left him for another man and he was having a difficult time moving on. In the beginning, his depression was so bad it was affecting his work life and so he also lost his job. When he first started seeing Kenna, his outlook on life was bleak and he was not motivated to continue his life. Now, he was working again and enjoyed his job thoroughly. He had reconnected with some of his friends and was finding joy in life again. Kenna was excited for him and enjoyed seeing him flourish in his new life.

Sometimes her job was not as fulfilling. There were some clients that just didn't get better. Clients that committed suicide or attempt suicide. She felt deeply for these people and sometimes had a hard time leaving her feelings at work, not bringing them home with her. Although she was improving with this as she became more seasoned, she doubted she would ever completely be able to detach when she left work for the day.

The rest of her day continued on. She listened to people from all walks of life tell her about their sorrows and triumphs. Finally, at the end of the day, Becca had arrived for her appointment and Glenda sent her back to Kenna's office. Becca entered wearing a floral summer dress and her untamed curls were hanging freely down her back and shoulders. She sat across from Kenna, crossing her legs once she was seated. They exchanged greetings and made small talk before diving into a deeper discussion.

Kenna couldn't quite put her finger on it, but something was different about Becca. She was smiling and talking candidly, using her hands to make gestures. Even her posture was different today. She was sitting up straighter in contrast to her normal slouch. Her demeanor was bright and infectious, very different from the defeated woman she had first met.

"Last time we talked, you and your husband were having some difficulties and you were starting back at school after summer break. Let's discuss how that is going," Kenna started.

"Fletcher and I are doing great. He is being super supportive and he's just been amazing, really. Going back to school is always exciting and a little exhausting, but it went well and I've been adjusting to full-time hours again," Becca replied.

Kenna wondered to herself if Becca's carefree attitude was the aftermath of getting back to a normal routine and being in her classroom that she loved. She had certainly made a drastic turnaround in her depression and, although Kenna was happy to see her doing well, she was surprised at her speedy recovery.

"That is good to hear. Let's talk about how Fletcher has been helpful to you. In what ways has he been supportive?" she pried deeper.

With this, Becca fumbled a bit, coming up with examples of his behavior. "Well, he has been doing more around the house since he knows I am working full time again...Oh and he uh...I don't know, he supports my decisions, I guess."

"What decisions has he been supportive of?" she asked.

"I can't think of any off the top of my head," Becca replied. "I wanted to come see you today to let you know I am doing well and that we can stop having sessions."

"I am glad to see you are doing so well. I know we discussed that because of our friendship, it is not professional for me to continue seeing you as a provider. However, I can certainly refer you to someone else to continue your care."

"I don't think that will be necessary. I feel like I'm back to my normal self," Becca said.

"Have you decided to reapply for a child when you are able?" Something just didn't seem right to Kenna and she wanted to get to the bottom of it.

"Well, no," Becca replied.

"Have you come to terms with the possibility of never having a child? I am just curious how you were able to make such a quick recovery from your depression," Kenna asked bluntly.

Becca looked down at her hands in her lap while she picked at her nails. She tapped her foot nervously. She then looked around the room as though she was studying it, with her brows scrunched together and her mouth twisted in contemplation.

She then met Kenna's eyes and asked her, "We have provider to patient confidentiality, or whatever it's called, right?"

"Yes," Kenna replied, wondering what Becca was up to, "as long as you are not planning on harming yourself or others."

Becca was wringing her hands and tapping both feet now. She went back and forth from looking at her hands and looking at Kenna. She was trying to decide if Kenna could be trusted.

"I am so happy because we have decided to have a baby," Becca stated.

Kenna tilted her head quizzically, a look of puzzlement across her face. "What do you mean? You mean you're going to try applying again?"

"Not exactly," Becca replied hesitantly, "we have decided to go another route."

"What does that mean 'exactly'." She used her fingers to signify air quotes. Kenna was tired of playing cat and mouse and was eager to know what was going on.

Becca let out a loud sigh, her chest rising and falling before she spoke, "We have heard of this woman, a doctor that helps couples like us. She does this in secret, working out of the East Side."

Kenna realized Becca must have been meeting with this woman when she saw her on the East side that day. "How does she help?"

"She removes the uterine implant," Becca said, looking Kenna square in the eyes. Her demeanor was unwavering and she seemed determined.

"That's crazy, not to mention illegal!" Kenna blurted out before she could control her thoughts. "How do you know you can trust this woman? And how do you know that going to her will be safe and sanitary?"

"I don't. I have no idea if I can trust her or if I'll make it out alive, but that is a risk I am willing to take to be a mother. This is my last hope to ever have a child. My application will never get approved, no matter how hard I try. If I can never have a child, what would be the point of living? This procedure will save my life." Becca was not nervous or anxious anymore. Her voice was firm and her thoughts were clear. She was going to do this.

"How much is this going to cost you? Besides possibly your life and freedom?" Kenna was not sugar coating the situation and, as a friend, she was not hiding her disapproval of Becca's decision.

"Five thousand dollars, but we have been building up our savings for a while and have enough to cover it. Then we will need to move somewhere new and start over, which will probably drain the rest of our savings. But none of that matters to me. I would give everything I have for a child and I know it will be worth it all in the end."

"I think you need to consider all the consequences that this will bring with it," Kenna said.

"I have, and I am not changing my mind," Becca said sternly, crossing her arms across her chest.

Kenna sighed heavily, her shoulders falling as she looked at Becca and shook her head. "Our session is over, but I really do not want to leave this conversation hanging. Do you think we could meet up outside of my office sometime so we can talk about it more, just as friends?" Kenna asked.

"You can come over for supper tomorrow night. Fletcher is making his famous homemade pizza. We would love to have you over, but you will not change my mind," Becca replied, her gaze unwavering.

"I will see you then," Kenna said.

Kenna escorted Becca out of her office and then helped Glenda tidy up and turn off all the lights before leaving and locking the door behind them. On her walk home, her head was swarming with questions about what Becca was about to attempt. Who was this doctor? What would happen if they got caught? How will she receive prenatal care or deliver the baby while trying to keep it a secret? How will she hide it at work? There were so many elements that needed to be considered and so many opportunities for things to go wrong. She was worried that her friend was biting off more than she could chew.

The following day after work, Kenna got home to let Ruby out and feed her. She then changed into some casual clothes and texted Becca, asking for her address. As usual, Emmett was nowhere to be found. Absence had become his new normal. She took Ruby out for a quick walk to stretch her legs and afterwards she grabbed her things to leave. After she wrote Emmett a note letting him know she was having supper with a friend and would take the vehicle, she started off towards Becca's. It was a short drive and normally she would have just walked, but she didn't want to have to walk home alone in the dark later.

She knew the general direction in which Becca lived, but she used her GPS anyway and found it with ease. Parking was much easier to come by in this residential neighborhood and she got a spot right in front of their house. The house was small, but charming. It was an olive green craftsmen style home with a small cedar front porch and matching shutters. There were large planters by the stairs to the porch and they were bursting with wave petunias in all different shades.

She climbed the few steps up to the porch and rang the doorbell. As she waited, she noticed a hanging porch swing to her right and she imagined Becca and her husband sitting there in the evenings, talking about their dreams of having a family someday. The thought of it made her heart ache for her friend. Just then her thoughts were cut off by Becca opening the door to welcome her inside. A young tabby cat slipped out of the door as Kenna was entering.

"Come in! It's so great to have you over for supper and I promise that Fletcher's pizza is to die for," Becca said while motioning her inside. "Don't worry about our cat, Lucky always comes home after he's out prowling."

Kenna took off her shoes upon entering and set her purse on the bench in the entryway. There was a magnificent scent coming from the kitchen consisting of fresh bread with a mixture of basil and oregano.

"You can have a seat at the table and I'll grab some wine. Do you want white or red?" Becca asked.

"You can choose. I'm not picky," Kenna replied.

The tall man with a friendly smile that Kenna had seen months ago at the application review office peeked his head around the corner. "Hey! You must be Kenna, I'm Fletcher and I'm glad to finally meet you. I'd shake your hand, but mine are covered in pesto at the moment."

"Well, I'm happy to be here, and your famous pizza I have heard so much about smells amazing," Kenna praised.

Becca returned to the small dining room with a bottle of red and three glasses. She poured Kenna and herself generous portions and winked at Kenna as she took a sip. There were already three place settings arranged at the small dining table that could seat four people comfortably. Fletcher emerged from the kitchen, looking victorious with a large pizza in tow.

"Ladies, dinner is served," he grinned, giving a dramatic bow as he set down the pizza. The crust was thin and cooked to perfection. It was topped with fresh mozzarella, Roma tomatoes, and pesto.

Kenna's mouth was watering and she realized she hadn't eaten since breakfast that day. She took a large slice and dove right in. The highly talked about pizza did not disappoint, the warm mozzarella melted in her mouth and the pesto gave the perfect touch of flavor with the tomatoes. Chatting as they ate and sipped on their wine, they conversed easily as if they had all been friends for many years. She learned that Becca and Fletcher had met shortly after college and had already been married for ten years. As Becca and Fletcher talked and teased, they looked at each other with such playful admiration. Frequently touching each other's hands or legs as they were drawn closer together. Anyone who saw them could see how in love they still were.

She felt a pang of jealousy as she watched them interact together. She and Emmett used to look at each other like that and she missed it. Even though they lived under the same roof, she missed him all the time. Longing for the days when they couldn't get enough of one another. The past few months had been the most difficult time in their relationship and in her life. It was exhausting emotionally, as she constantly analyzed their relationship and wondered how she could change the way things were. She wasn't even really sure how they got to this point, and she hoped they could turn it around before it was too late.

They took their plates into the kitchen, continuing their conversation as Fletcher did the dishes. The girls poked fun at him while they laughed and drank. Kenna was genuinely enjoying herself for the first time in a while and she was thankful to have made a friend in an unexpected circumstance. She did not want to ruin the evening by bringing up the topic she had come there to discuss, but she was worried about Becca and felt an obligation to talk some sense into her and Fletcher.

"Don't look at me like that," Becca said to Kenna.

"Becca, if I am looking at you like a worried friend, it's because I am. You're not thinking sensibly about this," Kenna replied cautiously.

Fletcher was looking at Becca with understanding on his face. He then shook his head and switched his focus to Kenna. "Look, I know it sounds like a crazy plan. Don't you think we know that? But this is our only option, and I support Becca in this because I know that if I don't, she will be miserable for the rest of her life."

"What if you get caught? What then?" Kenna asked them both.

"If we get caught and have to face those consequences, at least I will know that I did everything I could to become a mother. I can't go on living and waiting for something that will never happen. We are taking matters into our own hands." Becca poured herself another glass.

"I understand that you're hurting and that you want a child more than anything in this world. Believe me, I understand, but I can't let you go through with this reckless plan," Kenna pleaded.

"Will you try to stop us?" Fletcher asked her.

"No, I will not speak a word of this to anyone else. But I can no longer see you as a client or I will be required to report it. And I am afraid I can't be involved as your friend, either," she said, looking at Becca with sadness in her eyes.

"I understand," Becca replied. "Thank you for coming to dinner. I think it is time that you leave," Becca said as she stared at the floor. She was afraid if she met Kenna's gaze that she would cry and she was trying to hold it together.

"I will let myself out." Kenna turned to Fletcher. "Thank you for the pizza and wine. It was amazing." She forced a smile with teary eyes and left them standing in the kitchen.

As she drove home, Kenna thought about Becca's plan and how difficult it would be to pull off. She was sure that her friend would fail in this endeavor and would get caught. Aware that it would be inappropriate for her to be involved in illegal activities with one of her clients, she knew she had to distance herself from this situation. Furthermore, she could not be supportive of her friend when she was willingly putting her life at risk. And for what? Surely, if her mission was successful, she was only setting herself and her family up for a lifetime of lies.

Kenna was going through all the possible outcomes in her head as she drove. Worst-case scenario would be that Becca die on the table and she would forever blame herself for not stopping her friend or reporting her to the authorities. Best-case scenario would be that Becca survives getting the implant removed and somehow survives child birth with no medical care. But even then, she would need to flee with her family and start fresh somewhere new. Any way Kenna looked at the situation she was losing her friend.

Arriving home to her empty house just solidified her loneliness. In her mind, she had just lost the only friend she had made a real connection with in a long time. She crawled into bed and picked up her book from her bedside table. After several attempts at reading, she gave up as her mind was too busy and it was a lost cause. Staring at the ceiling, she dared to imagine if she herself would do the same if she were in Becca's shoes.

She understood her friend's motive, but she knew she could not fathom the desperation and the devastation her friend had endured after being denied so many times. After contemplating this for several minutes, she concluded she would do the same thing. If it was the only way she would become a mother, she knew she would risk everything and give up her current life to go through with it.

Turning off the light, she rolled over in bed and thought of her friend one last time before falling asleep. What she felt wasn't anger, judgement, or even jealousy. It was empathy and understanding.

CHAPTER 11
Chasing Hope

Becca and Fletcher ran from their house toward her car with their hoods pulled over their heads, trying to avoid the rain. When they reach the car, they both jumped in and slammed the door behind them, taking down their hoods and shaking the rain from their heads. The windshield wipers squeaked across the windshield, clearing away the drops as Fletcher pulled away from the curb.

As they drove through dips in the road, the water rushed out from their tires, flooding the curb briefly. Pulling to a stop at a red light, the sounds of the raindrops made plopping noises as they landed on their windows and roof. They did not see many people on their drive, and the people they saw were hurrying to their destinations, trying to get in from the rain. She glanced out the window at the gray and cloudy sky. There was the occasional flash of lightning far off in the distance and the much delayed sound of thunder coming behind it.

"Are you absolutely sure you want to do this, Becca? "Fletcher asked, looking at his wife. "We can turn around right now and go home. You just say the word and we can go."

"I've never been more sure of anything in my entire life," she replied, meeting his stare with her light brown eyes. She had made up her mind and there was no one on this earth who could talk her out of it at this point. Even the dreary, ominous day would not deter her from her mission.

Fletcher nodded his head in understanding and continued the drive onward. He wanted nothing more than for his wife to be happy, and he knew she would never be truly happy and content until they had a baby and completed their family.

He had a feeling of unease that was gnawing away at his stomach. They were not the type of people that broke the law. And although he was prepared to do it for Becca, he was not thrilled at the idea of sneaking around or getting caught. But he would not stand in the way of her only chance to become a mother. He would not be the cause of her continued unhappiness.

At the full-service repair shop where he had worked for over a decade, he had become the lead supervising mechanic because of his hard work. Knowing that he was risking his career and blowing most of their savings had kept him up at night for the past several weeks. But when he looked over and saw Becca looking out the window, daydreaming about their future child with a hopeful smile on her face. It was all the motivation he needed to continue their quest.

"Do you think we will have a boy or a girl?" Becca asked him with a light in her eyes. She had been thinking about babies nonstop since she found a way to make it happen. Making lists of baby names, picturing how the nursery would look, she had even bought a few baby outfits. She couldn't resist.

"Well, first I think we should take one step at a time. We are going to have to be very careful and plan everything just right so we don't get caught," he said smartly, "but I hope we have a girl." He smiled at Becca. "And I hope she looks just like you." Despite his feeling of unease, he was still excited at the prospect of completing their family.

Months earlier, after their application was denied, Becca went into a deep depression. It seemed like weeks had passed before she was able to drag herself out of bed to be a functioning human being again. In her mind, all hope was lost and the prospect of having their application approved no longer seemed like an obtainable reality. Fletcher kept a close eye on her. He was worried she would become suicidal. Every day when he left for work, he hoped she would still be there when he got home. For weeks he had been trying to convince her to go to therapy, and she had finally agreed.

"You're looking better," he said, handing her some coffee as she plopped down on the couch. It was the first time she had left their room in days.

"I still feel like shit," she answered sadly.

"I'm so sorry. I wish there was something else we could do." He rubbed her upper back.

"If there was, I would do it." She took a drink of her steaming coffee.

"Me too." Emmett leaned down to kiss her forehead before leaving for work.

"It would be good for you to get some fresh air today, and a shower wouldn't hurt," he said as he opened the door to leave, "and remember, you have that appointment tomorrow."

She nodded in understanding over her coffee. Tomorrow was her first therapy appointment and she was already dreading it. To please Fletcher, she had agreed to a few sessions.

Over the past few days, she had started thinking of alternative ways to have a child without applying again. First, she did some research online and had discovered that there were several cases of woman having their heranons removed illegally. This sparked hope and she eagerly combed the web for any information she could use to her advantage.

As a result of her searching, she happened upon some chat groups online that discussed where and how to successfully remove the heranons. These chats were hard to find and when she could find them, it was hard to follow the codes and secret messages that made up the conversations. Day after day, she remained glued to her computer screen, attempting to decode the secret language, only to find the chat room had gone silent and moved when she returned.

Her first therapy session was upon her and even as she got ready to go to it, she was contemplating canceling. But she wanted Fletcher off her back about it, so she went. Afterwards, she was pleasantly surprised. It wasn't as bad as she thought. The shrink was kind and Becca felt almost comfortable with her by the end of the session. She planned to go back the following week. When she returned home from her session, she immediately got to work on her computer, trying to find a way in.

Finally, after a couple of weeks, she discovered a chat group with the name R4TTCI, and her heart skipped a beat. This name was code for Region 4 Trying To Conceive Illegally. She quickly entered the chat and observed a conversation going on between two others. It appeared they were arranging a meeting.

"Come to E tomorrow," wrote someone with the user name want4bb3000.

And with that, the chat went dead. Becca sent the user a message in a private chat, "Hi, interested in TTC. Please provide info." Waiting for a reply for what seemed like hours, she called it a night and go to bed. As she lay in bed, she thought about the chat and what the codes would mean. Where was E? Was it a building? A town? Sleepily, she wrote down these ideas on a pad of paper she kept on her nightstand as Fletcher snored away.

The next morning was Sunday, but Fletcher had left early to help a friend work on his truck at home. After she got out of bed, she glanced at the notepad and started brainstorming. There were three towns in Region 4 that started with the letter E, however, these were smaller towns and seemed like unlikely places for this type of back alley operation. There were few businesses in Thayes that started with E and none of them seemed like a potential meeting place for illegal activity. Sitting back in her computer chair crossing her arms with a sigh, her eyes searched the map on her screen for answers. In the corner of the map, an E caught her eye. It was the compass!

"East," she whispered to herself, "it's the East Side."

It made sense. The East side was the poverty-stricken side of town and where a majority of crime went down. Not sure what to do next, she threw on clothes and grabbed her bag to leave the house. As she made her way toward the East Side, she kept her eyes peeled for activity, but she didn't really know what she was looking for.

Parking a few blocks away, she walked the rest of the distance to the East Side.

Once she arrived, she realized she had never truly entered this part of town. She had no reason to. Immediately, she noticed the difference in her surroundings. The roads were full of potholes and the sidewalks were littered with trash and partly overtaken by weeds growing up through the cracks. Buildings were in rough shape and many had signs that read *condemned*. People of all shapes and sizes sat on their steps outside or on benches along the street. They talked with others nearby and laughed with their friends. Despite the shabby surroundings, the general sense of the neighborhood was joyful.

Becca first went into a corner store and got a bag of chips and a soda. There were no healthy eating options to be found. Snacking on her chips, she sat on a bench near the sad excuse of a park down the street. There were no children playing and the rusted playground equipment looked sad and out of place.

For a couple of hours she sat, just looking around waiting for something to happen. But nothing did. Sighing, she got up from her perch and started walking back. She realized how unlikely it was that she would find what she was looking for. The East side was large, and she didn't even know what area she needed to be in. She didn't know if she was looking for a house or a storefront. Finally, she gave up and went home.

After supper that evening, she returned to her computer while Fletcher tinkered on their lawnmower in the garage. Full of angst, she checked her chat messages. They were empty. Still no reply from the mysterious user from last night. She searched for the new chat location but was unsuccessful. Feeling defeated, she went to bed.

Normally she fell asleep soon after her head hit the pillow, but that night she could not turn her mind off enough to fall asleep. Eventually, she got up and wandered down to the kitchen for some tea. When she opened up the cupboard, she found the chamomile and lavender tea she was looking for. Hoping the tea would make her sleepy, she started the teapot and waited.

Drumming her fingers on the cool granite counter tops, she replayed her trip to the East Side over in her head. Getting connected with the right people for illegal heranon removal seemed harder than finding a needle in a haystack. The loud shrill whistle of the teapot startled her from her thoughts. She jumped and grabbed it off the stove so it wouldn't wake Fletcher.

Taking her tea with her, she grabbed her laptop and went to their four season porch. The heat from her mug warmed her hands and she gently blew on the tea to cool it as the steam rose in wisps from the sweet smelling liquid. Summer was ending and the chill of the night was cooler than she had expected, so she reached for a flannel blanket sitting next to her.

As she looked out at the darkness of their backyard, she continued to wrack her brain, trying to understand all the clues she had been finding. Try as she might, her mind continued to come up blank.

Frustrated, she propped her lightweight laptop on her lap and began to search for chat rooms. She was getting better at knowing where to look and interpreting the lingo. Suddenly she inhaled sharply in surprise as she saw a familiar user name want4bb3043. It was the same as before, but the number had changed. Quickly she engaged in a chat with them.

"Want bb, need info." She typed and waited. Three little dots appeared to let her know the user was responding.

"R?" wantbb3043 replied. Becca knew this meant region from her research.

"4," she responded.

"mm at E tom," the user typed.

"Meet at East Side tomorrow," Becca whispered to herself. "Okay, but where?" she asked herself. Thinking quickly, she was afraid if she did not reply fast or said the wrong thing, the user would disappear again. She was trying to think of a coded response to ask were when she saw the three little dots again.

"The mother weeps for her son. 9." Suddenly the user left the chat.

Becca knew she had until nine o'clock the next day to figure out where they were supposed to meet. Not sure if the user meant a.m. or p.m. she decided she'd get to the East Side bright and early so she didn't miss her opportunity.

On her computer she pulled up a map of the East Side and zoomed in so she could read the names of all the businesses. She put together a list of potential places the meeting could be. On her paper she had written school, daycare, and cemetery. But none of these seemed right as she stared at the list.

This could be her one and only shot to get connected with the people that could help her, and she did not want to miss it. Her tea had gone cold, but she drank it anyway, wishing she had chosen a tea with caffeine to help waken her brain so she could continue searching. Switching from the map view to the street view, she looked at the storefronts for clues. Moving too fast, she caused her screen to freeze and a distorted image of the old catholic church was stuck on the screen.

She stared at the image for a minute, annoyed that her computer was slowing her down. Her eyes were drawn to a statue of a woman outside of the main church doors. The virgin Mary.

"That's it!" she shrieked delightfully. Instantly, she knew it had to be the place she needed to go. Everything was finally clicking and for the first time in months, Becca had hope again.

Early the next morning, after Fletcher went to work, Becca called the school feigning an illness. She felt guilty calling in sick since it was the first week back at school, but she knew she had to take her chance now. The need to have a child was outweighing everything else in her life, including work.

Searching her closet for something to wear, she threw on black jeans, a black short-sleeve shirt with a baggy gray cardigan and a worn baseball cap. Completing her outfit with some white sneakers and aviator sunglasses, she looked unassuming and could blend in anywhere. When she got into her car, she looked at the time and knew she would be early. Her plan was to park a few blocks away from the East Side and to get coffee from a coffee shop before walking over, hoping to blend in.

Now that it was really happening, she felt a wave of excitement mixed with equal amounts of unease. She hadn't done anything illegal since she was a teenager. Once she crossed this line, she knew there was no going back, and one way or another her future could change forever.

On her drive to the East Side, Becca drove past Kenna's office. As she looked at the old building, she had this urge to tell Kenna everything she was doing, wanting to confide in her friend. She realized that was stupid and no matter how close they had gotten over the past couple of weeks,

Kenna would never support her in this. Or would she? Since Kenna herself had also been denied and knew the sting that such a refusal could inflict, maybe she would understand.

Parking in front of a coffee shop she like called The Roasted Bean, she threw her black leather cross body purse over her shoulder and went inside. Immediately, she was hit with the scent of freshly brewed espresso and the sound of a coffee grinder buzzing. There were a few others in line, but the morning rush was clearly over.

She ordered an ice coffee and a buttered croissant. Scarfing down the croissant faster than usual, she realized how nervous she was. She had a habit of binge eating when stressed. Exiting the coffee shop, she started toward the East Side trying to sip her coffee as she went but ended up spilling some down her chin instead.

"Calm down Becca," she whispered to herself, "you've got nothing to lose."

Once she reached the East Side, she looked at her watch and saw the was about a half hour too early. She didn't want to draw attention by standing outside the church waiting for too long, so she sat on a bench nearby and waited. There were few people around, a stark contrast to her visit here yesterday. A few run-down cars drove past her carrying their passengers to work for the morning. Anxiously, she kept looking at her watch, waiting for the time to go by, but it seemed to drag on and it felt like the longest half an hour of her life.

Finally, her watch struck nine and she started toward the church. The old brick building towered over her with pointed spires reaching to the sky. Gargoyles perched on ledges and above the door seemed to be staring at her. Outside, she saw the statue of Mary with tears streaming down her face, and she knew without a doubt she was in the right spot. She walked up the concrete steps and opened the large wooden door as she looked over her shoulder to make sure she wasn't being watched. Paranoia was starting to kick in, but she wouldn't turn back, not now when she was so close she could taste it.

The church was empty and the sound of her sneakers on the old tile floors echoed throughout the grand space. There was an elaborate mural painted on the ceiling depicting Jesus with cherubs that was now chipped and faded. Stained glass windows colored the sun's rays as it filtered through the windows, some of them broken and held together with duct tape. Slowly, she walked up the side aisle, looking around for someone as she went. Stopping at the altar she stared at the large cross on the wall.

Christianity was becoming less and less prominent in the country, especially in the other regions, and she had only been in a church twice when she was younger. It was a miracle this old church was still standing and she knew that in a few years, it might not be.

Feeling slightly uncomfortable in her surroundings, she took a seat in the front pew off to the side and waited. Five minutes passed as she tapped her toe nervously. As another ten minutes went by, she wondered if they had meant nine o'clock p.m. Checking her watch again, her mind turned and she was fearful that she was being set up and soon the police would rush through the door to arrest her. Yet she sat and waited.

After what seemed like forever, a small wooden door next to the altar creaked open and a plain-looking woman with a short stature and kind eyes peeked her head through. She nodded her head at Becca, and she obediently rose to follow the woman. They went down a dark stone staircase to the church basement.

The space was dreary and smelled musty and damp. In the center of the room, there was a small folding table and chairs. Another woman with ebony hair that ended just below her jawline and high cheekbones sat in one chair, staring at them intently with her piercing green eyes. Becca sat across from her and folded her hands in her lap. The short woman left them to keep watch at the top of the stairs.

"Why have you come today?" the woman asked, her face serious.

"I want to have a baby," Becca replied, trying to sound confident. Although she felt very small.

"And you think we can help with that?" the

woman said.

"I hope you can," Becca said pleadingly.

The mysterious woman let her demeanor soften slightly. "Do you fully understand the implications that come along with doing this illegally?"

"Yes. I have thought about this long and hard and I will go to whatever lengths are necessary to become a mother. After applying four times and being denied, I know this is the only way to accomplish that." Becca shifted slightly in her chair.

The woman nodded in understanding. For the next half an hour, the woman explained the process to her, without going into too much detail.

"There is a doctor we work with who can remove your heranon, but you need to understand she does this with minimal equipment and resources, so there are risks. If you conceive (she put an emphasis on "if,") the doctor will need to replace the heranon after your child is born. We will get you in touch with someone who can get you new documentation, if that is what you desire. This process will cost you five thousand dollars cash."

Becca had so many questions and she was trying to process what she was hearing.

"What about prenatal appointments and birth?" she asked, concerned.

"There will be no prenatal care, no

ultrasounds, etc." the woman said cooly. "I will help you with delivery along with my assistant at your home, but you need to understand this also carries substantial risk," the woman let Becca know that not only her freedom but also her life could be in danger by going through with this.

"I understand the risks, and I would like to proceed. If I can never have a child, there is no point to go on living. It is worth the risk to me," Becca replied honestly.

"Is your partner on board?" the woman asked as she arched her brow.

Biting her lip nervously, she thought about Fletcher. She had not yet confided in him about her plan and she knew he would be angry with her for entertaining something illegal. She had to make him see how important this was to her so that he would go along with it. They would have to leave their home along with their friends and family to go into hiding. He would lose everything he had worked for in his career, not to mention they would probably spend all of their savings in the process.

"He is," she lied to the woman.

"Alright then." The woman handed Becca a burner phone. "We will be in touch. Have your money ready."

Back at home, Becca knew she had to tell Fletcher right away. It would take a lot of convincing to get him on her side, and she didn't know how much time they would have before they got the call they were waiting for. As she was trying to prepare her speech to him in her head, she wandered around the house tidying up and cleaning to keep herself busy. After the house was picked up, she started on supper-lasagna, which was Fletcher's favorite. Paired with a bottle of red wine that they enjoyed.

When Fletcher arrived home from work, the intoxicating scent of homemade lasagna and garlic toast greeted him at the door. Becca was setting the table in the dining room. She looked lovely in a yellow sundress with her auburn curls hanging long down her back.

"Wow! What's the occasion?" he asked with a wide grin filling his face.

"There doesn't have to be a special occasion to make your favorite meal, honey," she replied to him with a mischievous smile on her face.

"I'm so glad to see you coming out of your cocoon," he said as he took a seat next to her at the table.

As she poured them both some wine in stemmed glasses, she asked him about his day. The fragrant aroma from the wine was fruity yet smoky and paired well with their meal. They engaged in their normal small talk as they ate, discussing work and projects they had planned to do around the house.

After they had finished eating, they sat at the table drinking their wine for some time.

Reaching for Fletcher's hand, Becca's eyes met his, and she knew she had to get it over with.

"I have something to tell you," she stated seriously as she held his hand and tried to steady her breathing.

"Shoot," he replied, intrigued.

"What if I told you I found a way for us to have a baby?" she asked.

"How would that be possible?" He answered with a puzzled look.

"It isn't exactly legal," she said with her eyes wide.

"Becs," he sighed, "we aren't going to do anything illegal. You wouldn't even know how to go about it."

"Wanna bet?" she said as she raised her eyebrows.

"You didn't." he said with a look of shock on his clean-shaven face.

"I did," she replied nodding.

"When?" he asked

"I have been doing research for weeks trying to get in contact with someone that can help us, finally today I met with them," she admitted while wringing her hands in her lap.

"I cannot believe you have been keeping this from me and sneaking around behind my back, planning all this. Not to mention lying to me about going to work today," he scolded with more disappointment than anger in his voice. He did not appear as surprised as Becca had anticipated.

"I'm sorry that I lied to you and didn't tell you what I was doing," she apologized, "but you know how important this is to me," she said, pleading with him.

He rubbed his palms into his eyes and sighed heavily. "This is crazy Becca. It could ruin our lives."

"Or it could make our lives worth living," she said softly.

He knew she wanted a child more than anything else in the world and his love for her was outweighing his common sense. Seeing her go into a deep depression after the last denial was so hard on him. The woman he loved was wasting away in front of his eyes and he was concerned he might lose her. Wanting nothing more than to make his wife happy, he knew what he had to do. It was crazy and they could end up losing everything, but he would do it for her. He would do anything for her.

Becca and Fletcher parked her car a couple blocks away from the East Side. He gave her one last questioning look, and she squeezed his hand in reassurance. As they started walking toward their destination through the rain, holding hands, she wished she would have brought an umbrella. Swiftly they crossed through the park and made their way deeper into the East side. The farther they went, the more run down the houses and apartment buildings became. After a while, they reached their destination. An old brick apartment building that was crumbling and had a big yellow sign on the door that read *CONDEMNED DO NOT ENTER*.

"This can't be right," Fletcher said. "Are you sure you have the correct address?"

"Yes, this is it," Becca said as she double checked the directions given to her on the burner phone.

They withdrew cash in small amounts from their savings account until they had five thousand dollars cash in the black backpack Fletcher was carrying. She ducked under the warning sign and easily pushed the door open. The hallway was dark, with only a small light at the end to guide their way. A putrid smell of decay filled their noses from the mold growing on the walls and as they continued on, they stepped on moss growing on the old thin carpet. Near the end of the hall there was a staircase and they took this up to the third floor to room three thirty-three, following the directions given to them via the burner phone.

With one last worried look at each other, they knocked on the door.

"Pass code?" a female voice asked from behind the door.

"Mary had a little lamb," Becca repeated the phrase that had been sent to her.

Then the door opened and a short woman

dressed in blue scrubs with a surgical cap and mask allowed them entry. The apartment was tiny and was empty other than the limited equipment they had set up. Spider webs clung to all the corners in the room and the windows were boarded up with plywood. In the center of the main room, there was a padded table with a crisp white sheet on it. Bright white light was coming from a portable lamp perched over the table.

"Do you have the money?" the woman asked.

"Yeah, it's all here," Fletcher replied, handing over his old tattered backpack.

Another woman appeared from the narrow hallway in the apartment. She was tall and slim and was also wearing a surgical cap and mask but had a surgical gown over her scrubs. In her arms, there was a blue package that she set on an end table. Removing one flap at a time and opening them away from the center, she slowly uncovered the contents inside. Becca suddenly felt queasy as she eyed the metal instruments in front of her.

Finally, after the setup was complete, the woman in the surgical gown turned toward them.

"They call me Dr.J and I will perform your heranon removal." Her graying hair and wrinkles around her eyes revealed she was likely in her sixties or older. "There will be some discomfort, but it will be over relatively quickly, as the procedure only takes around fifteen minutes. Do you have any questions before we get started?" Her eyes darted between Becca and Fletcher.

Fletcher pulled Becca into an embrace. "I'll be here with you the whole time."

She breathed in his scent of fresh aftershave and evergreen deodorant before breaking away. "I'm ready."

The others turned their backs while Becca removed her pants and underwear. She then laid on the table with a white sheet over her bottom half. The assistant positioned her legs so her knees were bent up and spread apart. Suddenly she felt the shock of cold metal entering inside her and she gasped in pain as the speculum opened wider. Fletcher was at the head of the bead holding her hand and telling her to breathe.

"This is the painful part when we dilate you cervix, try to breathe through it," instructed the doctor.

Becca yelled out in agony as the shearing pain ripped through her pelvis. She almost crushed Fletcher's hand she was squeezing it so hard.

"You have to stop!" yelled Fletcher.

"No, don't stop. Just get it over-with!" Becca screamed through gritted teeth.

"Just a bit more. Keep breathing through it," Dr. J instructed as she worked quickly. "There, the hardest part is over."

Becca was relieved the hard part was over. She

wiped away the few small tears she had shed in pain. "See, that wasn't so bad," she uttered sarcastically to Fletcher.

Fletcher shook his head. He couldn't wait for this to be over so he could get her out of there and back to the safety of their home.

Once they had finished with the dilation, the pain lessened to a dull, cramping pain. A long metal tool with a sharped tooth grabber on the end of it was then used to grab the tiny heranon positioned at the superior aspect of her uterus. This took several minutes, but at the end the doctor triumphantly pulled the little bar out and showed it to Becca.

"I'm free," Becca said calmly, now that the pain was gone. "Thank you. This means everything to me."

"Don't mention it," Dr. J replied, and she meant it.

Fletcher did not thank the doctor. In fact, he wanted to exchange a few heated words with the doctor, but he held his tongue for Becca's sake. If he would have known how painful the procedure would be and how unsterile their workspace was, he never would have agreed to it. And now he just wanted to put it behind them.

The doctor and her assistant left Becca and Fletcher and went down the narrow hall of the apartment. Becca sat up and wiped herself off, bright crimson blood stained the once white sheet. Feeling light-headed, she sat for a few minutes on the table to steady herself. Once she had regained her strength, she reached for Fletcher's hand and they left the building together the way they came.

Back in their car, Becca leaned her forehead against the cool glass of her window as Fletcher drove. After arriving at their house, she immediately took a pain reliever and curled up in bed for the night. Fletcher brought her water and crackers with cheese a while later. While she ate and drank, she perched on the foot of the bed with Fletcher watching her. Although she was tired from the endeavor, he could tell that she was excited and hopeful about the success of her mission. He was glad for her, but he did not feel the same excitement as she did. He felt there was now a dark cloud over them and he would do everything he could to protect them from it.

CHAPTER 12
Playing with Fire

It had been several weeks since Kenna and Becca had their falling out and Kenna was still feeling down about it. They had become close friends quickly and now that they were no longer talking, Kenna felt like she had no one to confide in. Kassie was showing now, and Kenna could hardly stand to be around her. Emmett was working his life away and she felt like she hardly ever saw him, let alone had meaningful conversations. Victoria was busy with her campaign and was traveling all over the region, rallying her voters. This feeling of loneliness had plagued her too often lately and she was getting rather sick of it.

It was a weekday but she had taken the day off for a mental health day. After waking up and doing some yoga on the patio, she settled on the couch in her leggings to drink her coffee and watch a few of her favorite shows.

After watching several episodes of her show,

she decided she should probably get off her ass, so she jumped up from the couch and threw on her long gray trench coat and left the house to go for a walk. The cool air energized her as she walked toward the hospital with her hands in the pockets of her coat. Once she arrived at the hospital, she had to ask for directions to the OR, since she had never visited Emmett at work before. She arrived at the OR waiting area and asked the young man behind the small desk to page Emmett.

"You mean Dr. Foster?" the young man asked. "Who should I say is paging?"

"His wife," she replied.

Finding a seat in the waiting room, she mindlessly flipped through a garden magazine that was on the end table next to her. After about ten minutes, Emmett appeared through the doors with a distressed look on his face.

"Kenna, is everything alright?" he asked worriedly as he rushed over and reached for her.

"Everything is fine. I wanted to surprise you for lunch, that's all," she replied with a smirk.

"Oh Kenna, I was worried there was an emergency," he said, letting out the air he was holding in. "I would love to get lunch, but I am in between two cases and I won't have time. I was literally just about the grab a sandwich from the fridge in the doctors 'lounge."

"Sure. You're busy. I get it," she said, trying not to sound like a needy teenager. "I'll see you at home then."

"I should be done at a decent time. How about we order takeout?" he said as a consolation.

"Sounds great," she said with a forced smile. Her shoulders slumped as she turned to leave. Tears welled in her eyes, and she was annoyed at herself for letting it bother her. It seemed the more she tried to reach out to Emmett, the more rejection she was subjecting herself to. She was losing her drive to keep their marriage going and was questioning if it was worth her efforts.

As she walked back home, she decided to stop at the Daily Cup to grab a sandwich for lunch. The bell on the door clanged as she walked in, and the quiet chatter from the other lunch guests greeted her. As she walked to the counter, she scanned the room and was disappointed when she didn't see Alec's face, although she didn't admit that to herself.

From the kitchen wafted a mesmerizing smell of tomato and fresh basil that made Kenna's mouth water and her stomach squeeze in anticipation. She ordered the soup of the day with grilled cheese and grabbed a booth near the back. After only a few minutes, they delivered her food to her table, steaming.

Once she had finished her meal, she sat for a while and thought about Alec's business card in her purse. Taking it out of her wallet, she fingered the thick white paper with neat blue text, turning the card over in her fingers again and again. The thought of giving a lecture at the college excited Kenna, and she knew it could be just the distraction she needed.

In her brief moments with Alec she felt noticed again, and it was exhilarating. She couldn't help but want the attention. Debating whether or not to call him for a few minutes, she finally gave in and went for it. After dialing the number on the card, she waited to hear his voice but got his voicemail instead. She left a brief message for him to call her back and left the coffee shop to go home.

As she slowly walked home, she breathed in the crisp air. All along the streets, the trees were vibrant reds and oranges, contrasting against the concrete roads and sidewalks. Fall was in full swing, and it was breathtaking. It was Kenna's favorite season and she wished it wasn't so short. Soon winter would be upon them, along with several feet of snow piled on all the sidewalks and icy roads. Winter was her busiest time of year for work. People are just happier in the summer. She didn't mind being busy and maybe it would take her mind off of her marriage problems.

When she reached their front door, she was digging for her keys at the bottom of her bag when her phone rang. Her heart skipped a beat when she saw Alec's number flashing across her phone screen. Forgetting about the search for her keys, she quickly grabbed her phone and answered.

"Hello," she answered, trying to sound casual.

"Hi Kenna, I just got your message. You ready to come lecture one of my classes?" Alec asked, intrigued.

"Yeah, I'd like that. That is, if the offer is still open?" she answered coyly.

"Oh, it is definitely still open," he replied a little too enthusiastically.

"Great! When would be a good time?" She bit her bottom lip.

"Would two weeks work for you? Give you enough time to get your lecture together?" he asked.

"That works for me. I'll see you then." She was smiling to herself.

"I'll text you the details. I'm glad you called, Kenna. See you in a couple of weeks," he said and ended the call.

When she hung up, she finally found her keys she was fishing for and went inside. Ruby ran to greet her with her tail wagging happily. After she hung her coat up on the coat hook in the hallway, she took Ruby out back to throw her ball for a few minutes. In their backyard, the maple tree was now a fiery red and she took in its beauty while playing with Ruby.

She went back inside and got to work on the slides for her lecture at the college. Wanting to discuss a topic she was passionate about, she chose to talk about addiction medicine. After a few hours of putting her materials together, she called it good and ordered some takeout. Emmett was nowhere to be found, but that didn't phase her today. She had a new focus.

On the morning she was going to GreyStone for her lecture, she had tried on ten outfits before deciding what to wear. She wanted to look professional and desirable, which was proving difficult. Choosing a form fitting black pencil skirt with a white button-up shirt, she paired it with a thin black leather belt and black pumps. As she assessed her outfit in her full-length mirror, she liked what she saw. Finishing the look with a pearl necklace her grandmother had given her years ago and diamond stud earrings, she felt like she could rule the world. Her gold locks fell in loose curls around her shoulders as she applied her lip gloss with her mouth forming an O. She grabbed her black leather briefcase and tied a bright silk scarf around the handle.

GreyStone was located on the North Side of town across the river from downtown. The bridge was a large one made of metal and concrete with intricate metal archways that had been preserved even after the bridge had been updated many times. As she drove over the enormous bridge, the golden glow of the morning sun was glinting off the metal bridge, causing it to sparkle. The slow alternative rock song playing softly from her car sound system was familiar and helped to calm her nerves.

Although the college was not very far from her home, she had not been there since graduation. She never needed to go across the bridge to that part of town, and it seemed strange to be going back there now.

She parked her car near Tawny Hall, which was where most psychology classes and psych professors' offices were on campus. As she glanced across the road, her eyes fell upon the medical school building and she remembered meeting Emmett in this exact spot over eight years ago. The memory brought a smile to her face and a trace of happy tears in her eyes. Clearing her throat, she gripped her suitcase and walked inside her destination.

The musty smell of the old building and the sound of students' feet slapping the steps were exactly as she remembered it. She peeked in one of the empty lecture halls. It was a small fan shaped room with tiered seating at old wooden desks that were original to the college. Remembering her time there was bittersweet as she was both glad to be done with school and sad that chapter of her life was over. When she was in school, she was so driven and focused on doing her best. Now, looking back, she wished she had tried to have more fun and make more friends.

"Hey you," she heard Alec's charming voice

from behind her.

"Hey." She turned to see him, her lip turned up in the corner in a flirty half smile.

"We have some time before my next class. Let me show you my office and you can tell me about your lecture," he said, motioning for her to follow him.

Following him down the narrow hall where the professors 'offices were held, they stopped along the way to see one of her favorite professors, Dr. McColfax. She was sitting at her desk wearing her signature black thick-rimmed glasses with her hair in a short pixie cut and she looked like she hadn't changed a bit. Rising from her chair, she crossed her office to give Kenna a hug with her slight frame.

Kenna looked up to Dr. McColfax as a role model and was glad to see her again. She was a known feminist and political activist, and Kenna often wished she had the confidence and vivacity that Dr. McColfax radiated. They exchanged contact information and vowed to keep in touch. Kenna was getting excited at the prospect of lecturing at the college again in the future. She even entertained the thought of working there someday.

Alec's office was small but tidy, with one small window looking out on the campus. A half-full bookshelf stood on one wall, while a small wooden desk and a brown leather office chair were on the opposite wall. There was also a chair for visitors. She took a seat across from him at the desk and opened her briefcase to grab her laptop. After she gave him a general rundown of her lecture, he sat back in his chair with his hands behind his head, relaxed.

"It's really great to see you again, Kenna." Alec was eyeing her curves in her tight skirt.

"I'm really glad I called you," she replied as she leaned back in her chair.

"Maybe we should get together sometime, outside of work." He raised his brow questioningly.

"Alec, I'm a married woman," Kenna said, blushing as she looked away from him.

"I wish you weren't," he said seriously.

"We shouldn't be talking like this, Alec. It's not appropriate," she scolded him, but she didn't want the conversation to end.

He glanced at his watch. "It's almost time for your lecture. I'll show you where to get set up."

She was glad for the interruption and stood to follow him out of his office. They walked to the lecture hall together and she had a few minutes before class to get set up. It was the room she had looked in when she first walked into the building, and she was a little relieved that it was a smaller hall for her first lecture. The students started filing in to take their seats, and the room was filled with their casual chatter. Kenna was surprised at how young they all looked and it was hard to believe she had been in their place a few short years ago.

Once the clock was at the top of the hour, Kenna began her lecture. She started out nervous and a little quiet, but as she found her stride, she gained confidence and she kept the students captivated for the entire hour. Alec sat in the back row, off to the side. She met his gaze occasionally and he gave her an encouraging nod. After she was finished, several students asked questions. She was thrilled they had paid attention and were interested. Once the students cleared out, Alec made his way down from his perch.

"That was great! You will have to do it again sometime," he praised her.

"Thank you. It felt fantastic being up there. I'd definitely be interested in doing it again," she replied, elated.

"What are your plans for the rest of the day?" He leaned casually on the podium drinking her in.

"Well, I don't have any clients until the afternoon, so my morning is free. No plans other than to get lunch somewhere," she said as she packed up her computer.

"I have a class right now down the hall, but if you feel like sticking around, we could grab lunch at the food court in the union after," he asked hopefully.

She wasn't sure what to say. The morning was going great and she wanted to see Alec lecture, but she felt a little wrong about having lunch with him. She bit the corner of her lip while she internally argued with herself on the matter. It was just lunch at the union, not like they were going out on a date. His deep blue eyes burned into hers as he waited for an answer.

"Sure, why not?" she replied against her better judgement.

"Sounds like a date." he replied enthusiastically. "Let's go to my next class."

The lecture hall they entered was spacious and had cinema-style seating, with small desk tops attached. The front of the room was raised, almost like a stage for a performance. When they arrived, Kenna took a seat near the front, but close to the wall on the far left side. The buzz of conversation hummed in the room, but as Alec took the stage, everyone went quiet. As he taught, he walked along the stage and used his hands as he talked. Everyone was captivated, including Kenna. Students were writing notes and some just sat back and tried to absorb the information. Every so often, his eyes would meet hers and she could feel heat rising from her chest and abdomen. She was acutely aware of her attraction to Alec and tried to remind herself that it was just a silly crush. But then why did it feel like so much more than that? She knew she shouldn't feel this way about him, and her conscious reared its head every time she smiled at him. It was getting harder to control her physical reaction to his charm.

"Why does he have to be so damn good looking?" she whispered to herself.

After he had finished with his talk, a handful of eager students gathered near him to ask questions. He was always helpful to students and appreciated when they were interested in learning. Walking up the side aisle toward her, he put his hands in the pockets of his khakis and winked at her.

"Did you like what you saw?" he asked flirtatiously.

"Your students really like you and I can see why. I didn't see even one sleeping kid in the whole auditorium," she teased lightly, trying to keep the conversation appropriate.

"Ready for some lunch?" he asked.

"Absolutely," she replied

They walked a couple of short blocks on the crowded sidewalks to the union, as there were not many parking options on campus. The union was the largest buildings on campus and was the hangout spot for study groups and all nighters. Once they reached the union, they went down the large staircase into the food court. The place smelled of fresh pizza and Chinese food. It was still a little early for lunch and they had beaten all the lines for food.

"What are you in the mood for?" he asked.

"Chinese for sure," she answered. She had regularly frequented the Chinese restaurant here while she was a student and she knew the food was to die for.

Their food was ready within a few minutes, and they took it over to a small table with two chairs. Over their lunch, they discussed teaching and how it differed from her private practice. She could see herself teaching at least part time someday and it made her glad she took a chance and came today.

Her foot briefly brushed Alec's leg and she felt like white lightning had shot through her body with his touch. She tried to act natural and let her emotions show, but the redness in her cheeks was giving her away.

"Kenna, what brings you here?" she heard a familiar female voice approaching their table.

When she looked up from her food, she discovered her mother standing beside their table.

"Mom!" she exclaimed, surprised to see her, "I was a guest lecturer for a psychology class here today" she explained rather proudly.

"That is wonderful. What a great opportunity for you," Victoria replied.

"Why are you here, mom?" Kenna asked.

"I'm here because they did the grand opening for the new library and I cut the ribbon," Victoria divulged. She was in full-blown campaign mode now and was attending public events and photo ops daily.

Victoria extended her hand out to Alec.

"Hello, I'm Mayor Carson, Kenna's mother."

"Nice to meet you. I'm Alec Kingston, psychology professor," he said, taking her hand into a firm shake.

"I best be going but Kenna, we should get together for lunch soon," Victoria said, eyeing her daughter and her lunch date.

"That'd be great mom," Kenna replied. Victoria left them to finish their lunch.

"So your mom is the mayor?" Alec said. "My dad is in politics too."

"Yeah, she's running for Region Four Chair this election," Kenna replied.

"She probably knows my dad then. He is Region Four Treasurer," Alec stated between bites.

After figuring out they had something in common, they talked about their childhoods and what it was like having parents in politics. Late nights without them at home and having to parade around at public events. Alec's parents divorced when he was a kid and he moved to Region Three with his mother. He had escaped the political circus for the most part.

Once they had finished eating, they dumped the remaining contents of their trays into the garbage and placed the trays on top of the trash bin. As they walked back to Tawny, her feet were hurting from her pumps, and it reminded her why she didn't wear heels often.

"Here I am," Kenna said as they approached

her car.

"Again, I am really glad you came today, and I hope we can do this again," Alec said imploringly.

"Definitely. I'll keep in touch," she replied as she reached for her car door.

"Kenna, I have a confession. After we met at the coffee shop, I went back there for days hoping to see you again," Alec said somewhat foolishly.

His confession made her go weak at the knees, and she gripped the door handle tighter to keep herself from stumbling. Wracking her brain for a response, she just stood there staring into those mesmerizing blue eyes.

"It was good to see you Alec," Kenna responded after what seemed like several seconds. She knew she needed to get out of there before she said or did something she shouldn't. Needing to put some space between their charged bodies, she took a gingerly step back.

Without saying another word, she hopped into her car and drove off. Not daring to look at him, for fear she might get trapped. When she was at a safe distance, she peered in her rearview mirror and saw him in the middle of the road, watching her as she drove away.

CHAPTER 13
Dangerous Line

Since Kenna had left last week, there was scarcely a moment when she did not occupy Alec's thoughts. As he sat in his office trying to grade papers, he kept getting distracted thinking about her contagious smile and the way her skirt hugged her body, accentuating every desirable curve. He imagined being with her, his skin touching hers. He was getting aroused and he pressed the palms of his hands against his temples and tried to push his thoughts to the back of his mind so he could focus on his work.

A knock at the door startled him and brought him back to reality. The door was cracked and someone was pushing it open the rest of the way. In front of him stood a young woman with shoulder length black hair and pouty lips. She was wearing a denim miniskirt and a white tank top. He noticed she was not wearing a bra and her perky nipples pressed through her shirt. After closing the door behind her, she turned to face him with her icy blue eyes.

"Can I help you?" he asked her, finally able to pull his eyes off of her breasts.

"My name is Asha and I'm in your intro to psychology class," she explained.

"What do you need?" he asked, leaning his elbows on his desk.

"Well, I didn't do very well on the first quiz, and I was wondering if there was anything I could do for extra credit," she answered as she twirled a strand of hair around her finger and leaned seductively against the door frame.

"Um, yeah, we can work something out," he replied, watching her as she moved across this office closer to him.

Sitting herself on top of his desk in front of him, she reached out and ran her fingers through his hair. Her fingers felt like electricity caressing his scalp and he didn't stop her.

"What did you have in mind?" he asked as he eyed her bare legs in front of him.

"This," she replied unabashedly as she leaned down and placed her lips against his, slowly opening her mouth and rubbing her tongue along his bottom lip.

Reciprocating, he parted his lips to allow her tongue entry as he reached up and touched her thighs with both hands. Their kissing quickly became intense and they were both hungry for more. He stood and pulled her closer to him with her legs around him and slipped his hand up her shirt. Groaning, she reached out to stroke him over his pants as he moved his lips down her neck.

He pushed her skirt up around her waist, and he started to take off her panties. She undid his belt and pants, revealing him to her. Pulling him closer as he entered her, she wrapped her legs around him as her nails dug into his back. They tried to be quiet so people in the nearby offices wouldn't hear, and the rush from the possibility of getting caught was exhilarating.

When they had finished, he handed her a box of tissues on the bookshelf so she could clean herself off as he pulled up his pants and did his belt. She hopped off the desk, pulling her skirt back down around her legs. After she straightened out her top and ran her fingers through her hair, she looked at him slyly.

"So, what about that extra credit?" she asked, with her head cocked to one side.

"Consider it done," he said as he tucked in his shirt.

And with that, she left his office, giving him one last flirtatious look over her shoulder as she left. After she left him, he sat down in his chair and let out a gigantic sigh. Disappointed in himself for doing something so stupid, he stewed for a few minutes. In the past he had been promiscuous with younger women, but he knew here he would need more self-control. It was definitely frowned upon for a professor to be sleeping with one of his students, and a freshman at that. Determined not to let it happen again, he pushed the girl out of his mind and tried to get his work done.

The following day he arrived a few minutes late to his intro to psychology class in the large auditorium, only to see her sitting in the front row. Wearing black leggings and a crop top, she was licking a sucker. When he looked over at her, she gave him a small wave and a seductive smile. Trying to ignore her, he went about setting up for his lecture.

As he walked along the stage talking to his class about the stages of grief, she watched him intently with her elbow resting on the desk and her chin in her palm. Once he had finished his talk, there were a few students that had questions, and she lagged behind them. Everyone was leaving the auditorium as she approached him.

"Hey," she said as she swung her backpack over her shoulder.

"Hi Asha. Look, about yesterday, what we did cannot happen again," he told her sternly.

"I don't understand. Didn't you like it?" she asked with a puppy face.

"It's not that I didn't like it. It's inappropriate," he replied, keeping his voice low.

"Professors sleep with students all the time. It's not that big of a deal," she said, trying to convince him.

"It was a mistake and I won't let it happen again," he stated, staring at her seriously.

"You don't mean that," she said as she reached for his arm.

He pulled away from her and she looked hurt. "You used me!" she accused him.

"I used you?" he said sarcastically. "You are the one that came on to me and it was clear that was your plan all along when you came to my office."

"That's not true. I thought we had a mutual feeling," she said, sounding wounded.

"From now on, our relationship is strictly that of a professor and student. Nothing more," he said.

Rolling her eyes at him, she turned on her heel and left the building. He let out a sigh of relief that she was gone. He hoped she got the hint and wouldn't be a problem for him.

Later that week, he was sitting at the bar at The Court, a sports bar near campus, when he saw Asha enter with two friends. She was wearing jeans and a red top with a black leather jacket overtop. The bar was fully of tipsy young people looking for someone to go home with. When she finally saw him, she waved her friends off and approached him. After a few drinks, he was feeling the effects of the alcohol and his determined demeanor from their last conversation was gone.

"Hey," she said, leaning against the bar.

"Hey," he replied as he stared at her cleavage in her low cut top. "Are you even old enough to be here?" he jested.

"My fake ID says I'm old enough to be here," she answered boldly. "Are you going to buy me a drink or what?" she teased him back.

For the next hour, he continued to playfully dig at her and she mocked him back in turn. Soon he was a few too many whiskey drinks in and she had an equal amount of vodka sodas. She slipped off her stool and stumbled, but he held out his arm and she grabbed it, steadying herself with a drunken giggle.

"So, are you going to take me home or what?" she asked him playfully.

"Yeah, you don't have to twist my arm," he said as he leaned down and kissed her.

She put her arms around his neck and they stood in the middle of the bar, kissing unsteadily on their feet. Too drunk to care, he was oblivious to the crowds of college kids around them. He took her hand and lead her out of the bar with her leather jacket in his other arm. They walked the few blocks to his apartment, stopping occasionally for drunken make out sessions leaning against random apartment buildings.

When they reached his apartment, they took the elevator up four floors to his large studio. He had a spectacular view of the downtown lights sparkling off of the river, and it was serene. Alec locked the door and tossed both of their jackets over a brown leather armchair as he crossed the room toward her.

From behind her, he wrapped his arms around her waist and leaned down, planting hungry kisses down the side of her neck. She closed her eyes in ecstasy and raised her arm up, lightly grabbing his hair with her hand. His hands traveled up her shirt and down her pants as he licked her ear. She turned around to kiss him and he grabbed her, lifting her up with her legs wrapped around him.

He carried her to his bed and laid her down gently, leaving kisses down her chest as he stood to remove his clothes. She crossed her arms, grabbing her top and took it off in one graceful movement, exposing her perfectly round breasts and erect nipples. Slowly, she lifted her hips up off the bed so he could remove her jeans and underwear.

The night was a blur as they fell into each other again and again, hungrily exploring each other's bodies until the early hours of the morning. Afterward, they collapsed next to each other in bed naked and slept hard for several hours.

Awakened by the brightness of the morning sun, Alec turned over in bed to hide from the light and laid eyes on Asha, sleeping naked beside him. Her olive skin contrasting his white sheets alluringly as her bare chest rose and fell with each breath. She was bewitchingly beautiful and highly intelligent. He had come to find out. If it wasn't for their age gap and his interest in Kenna, he might have allowed himself to like her. Letting her sleep, he quietly snuck out of bed and made some coffee before jumping in the shower. It was Saturday and he didn't have any plans for the day except for catching up on laundry and grading papers.

The smell of freshly brewed coffee woke Asha from her slumber and she stirred out of bed, stretching as she went, with her naked body on full display. It took all of his control not to go to her and ravage her body with his mouth. She grabbed his worn t-shirt off the floor and slipped it on along with her lace thong panties.

"Mmm coffee," she cooed as she poured herself a cup. "Do you have any Tylenol? My head is killing me."

"Yep," he grabbed the bottle out of the cabinet above the coffee machine and tossed it to her.

"What are you doing today?" she asked, yawning sleepily.

"Not much, just laundry," he replied.

"Want some help?" she asked.

"Sure," he answered with a small shadow of a smile. He was warming up to her now that he had gotten to know her more.

After throwing on her jeans, she sorted his clothes and put them into baskets to take to the laundry room in the building's basement. They each grabbed a basket and went to the elevator that would take them to the basement. Over the next few hours, they washed clothes and folded them as they chatted about life. It was nice and relaxed.

"Where are you from?" Alec asked as he folded a pile of t-shirts.

"Region Two. How about you?" she returned as she pulled herself up to sit on the washing machine.

"Region Three, but I came here a lot as a kid to visit my dad," he explained while he continued to fold. "Why did you decide to go into psychology?"

"Because the human mind fascinates me and I want to learn everything I can about it," she said, leaning forward, bringing her face close to his.

"Yeah, it's wild," he agreed with a smile before playfully pecking her on the lips.

Once they had finished, Asha decided she should probably go home and shower and get some new clothes, so she left.

Alec was sitting alone in his studio watching TV and drinking a beer when his phone vibrated, signaling he had a message. He grabbed his phone, hoping to see Kenna's name flashing across his screen, but he saw a text from an unknown number.

Unknown: Hey it's me.

Alec: Who is me?

Unknown: Asha, who do you think?

Alec:How did you get my number?

Asha: It was on the syllabus.

Of course, he had almost forgotten she was his student after their time together that morning. They exchanged texts until late into the night. He wanted to invite her over that night for round two, but he was trying to have some self-control.

CHAPTER 14
Signs of Change

After the traumatic experience of having her heranon removed, Becca had taken a few days off at home to decompress. Surprisingly, she recovered from the ordeal quickly and she returned to school with a newfound joy and hope. She and Fletcher continued their normal routine of work and home life. The secret they shared between them was always on their minds. At night, as they laid in bed, they discussed plans for their future once they had the child they desired. They knew there were going to be challenges and they had a lot of planning to do and arrangements to make, but they had plenty of time to get that all sorted out.

Becca was at the school weeks later, ready to start her morning with her first grade kids. She instructed them to grab their reading books and head over to the reading nook in the corner of the room. As she sat down in the large beanbag chair, her students gathered around her in a semicircle, sitting on the carpet with their legs folded like little pretzels. When she read to her class, she did special voices for different characters in the book and the kids loved it. Soon they were watching her with wide eyes as she talked about a horrible witch and then burst into giggles when the witch was squished by a flying house.

Usually, story time was Becca's favorite, but today she was feeling a little ragged. She was abnormally tired and when she tried to drink her coffee, it just didn't taste right. Even the smell of it made her stomach turn. Having struggled with stomach issues in the past, she didn't think much of it and grabbed a couple crackers for breakfast on her way out the door that morning.

Once she had finished the story, she got up from the beanbag and immediately felt light-headed. Quickly, she reached for a bookshelf nearby to steady herself as a wave of nausea hit her. Taking deep breaths, she put her hand up to her mouth as if that would somehow stop it. Slowly, she walked back to her desk at the front of the room and sat down. Opening her top drawer, she pulled out a mint and plopped it in her mouth, hoping that would help.

It seemed to ease up a bit and she was able to tell her class to get their math books out and start teaching the lesson on the touch board at the front of the room. During her demonstration of addition problems, she felt another wave of nausea. This time it was more intense and she knew she could not hold it back. She ran to the bathroom at the back of the classroom and shut the door so the students wouldn't hear her vomit. Over and over, she wretched until there was nothing left and her body shook as she dry heaved.

When it finally stopped, she washed her hands and splashed cold water against her face, rinsing out her mouth. As she opened the door to the bathroom, she saw her kids were all turned around in their chairs, watching her with concerned faces. She put on a smile and calmly went to her desk to call the office, trying not to alarm them. The school secretary answered and Becca informed her that she had some sort of stomach bug and would need to go home for the day.

Walking out to her car, she instantly felt a little better after being in the cool, fresh air. After she left school, she drove through a fast food place for a coke which usually helped ease her stomach. Taking a few sips as she drove home, she realized she felt almost completely better already in such a short period of time.

With her car idling in front of her house, she thought to herself how peculiar it was. Then the thought crossed her mind that maybe she was pregnant. Could it be? It would be unlikely to happen so soon. It had only been a few weeks since her heranon was removed. She knew it was probably wishful thinking, but she pulled away from the curb and went to buy a pregnancy test.

When she got to the corner drugstore, her nerves begin to set in. What if someone saw her buying the test and ratted her out? She told herself she was just being paranoid, but she threw on a baseball cap from her backseat and her large dark sunglasses that covered most of her face. In the store, she tried to look inconspicuous walking around and looking at various items.

Finally she approached the checkout with the test, a lip gloss, and chewing gum. She wished they had a self-checkout so the cashier wouldn't see what she was buying. Behind the counter stood a young woman who appeared to be just out of high school. She was wearing trendy jeans and a white T-shirt and had piercings going all the way up both her ears. As she rang up the items, Becca was holding her breath and watching her intently. The girl didn't even seem to recognize the test, and Becca quickly paid and left the store, relieved.

When she got home, she immediately went to the bathroom to take the test. There were two in to box and she saved one for later, so she wouldn't have to go through the whole ordeal of buying another one later. She quickly skimmed the directions and peed on the stick as directed. While it sat on the bathroom counter, she kept looking at the timer on her phone. Finally, after the long three minutes, she peeked at the stick hopefully. There was only one little pink line. It was negative.

Her heart sank and she was angry at herself for getting her hopes up so soon. Of course, she wasn't pregnant already! How stupid could she be? She thought to herself as she threw the negative test in the trash.

When Fletcher got home from work that evening, she told him all about her day.

"I puked at school," she informed him.

He looked at her worriedly. "Are you okay?"

"I'm fine now. I just…I thought for a moment that we might be…you know."

"Isn't it too soon for that?" he asked.

"It must be, because I stupidly went to the store and bought a test, and it was negative," she divulged with a frown and drooping shoulders.

"I'm sorry you had your hopes up just to be disappointed." He hugged her, running his big powerful hands across her shoulders and down the small of her back. "It will happen eventually, baby. We just have to be patient." He kissed her and squeezed her tight. They had supper and went to bed, but she was still disappointed.

A week later, Becca was getting ready for school and she had just started brushing her teeth. She kept gagging on her toothbrush. The sensation was just weird in her mouth, causing her to be nauseous. As she continued brushing, it happened again, and she gagged. This time, she vomited and quickly spun around to make it to the toilet. She thought it was strange. She had never had this issue before. Again, she thought maybe she could be pregnant.

Trying to focus, she thought back to when she last had her period. It had been before the heranon was removed, but she wasn't sure if having it removed had disrupted her normal cycle. Hesitantly, she took the box with the remaining pregnancy test out of the drawer. Her mouth pursed and twisted as she considered taking another test. Feeling foolish for testing again so soon, she went for it anyway and peed on the stick. She set the timer and anxiously waited for the results.

Now that she had been dilly dallying this morning, she was running late, so she set the test on the bathroom counter and went to pour her coffee and get her bag ready. Once she was ready to leave the house, she ran back upstairs to the bathroom to check the test, fully expecting it to be negative again. She glanced at the test and her mouth twisted in confusion. There were two little pink lines. When the realization finally set in, Becca beamed from ear to ear as happy tears fell from her eyes and streamed down her cheeks.

She wanted to let Fletcher know right away, but he had already left, and she didn't want to do it over the phone. As she left for work, she came up with a plan to surprise him with the news that night at supper. He would be so thrilled! At least she hoped he would be.

That evening when Becca got home from school, she placed the pregnancy test in a small box and wrapped it with plain wrapping paper to give to Fletcher. It was nothing fancy, but it would work in a pinch. After they finished eating, she eagerly turned to him with the box in hand.

"I have a surprise for you," she said, handing over the box.

"What is it?" he asked as he took the gift and started tearing off the pale blue paper. He suspected what it could be, but he thought it was too soon. So he pushed the thought out of his head.

"Just open it!" she said excitedly.

He opened the box and pulled the stick out, examining it. "Is this for real?" he asked her with wide eyes and she nodded her head yes in return.

"Holy shit," he said.

"Holy shit is right," she replied with a huge grin on her face and they embraced each other, smiling and crying together.

They stayed clung together for several minutes, happy tears staining their skin. He had is strong arms wrapped around her small shoulders and she was hugging him at the waist. When she pulled her head away from his broad chest and looked up at him he had a look of concern. The weight of what they were about to embark on hit her. The joy she had felt just minutes before was clouded with fear of the unknown.

"I'm scared," she admitted to him in a whisper.

"Me too baby, me too," he squeezed her as she rested her head back on his chest with a small sob escaping her throat.

CHAPTER 15
In Friends, We Trust

One night as Kenna was getting ready for bed, she heard her phone vibrating on her bedside table. It had been months since Kenna had seen or talked to Becca, so it surprised her to see Becca text her out of the blue.

Becca: Hi. I feel so terrible about how we ended things. Do you think we could get together to talk?

Kenna had thought a lot about their falling out as well and wished it had gone differently. She missed having Becca as a friend to confide in and hang out with.

Kenna: I feel bad about it too. I've missed you. We should get together this weekend to chat.

Becca: That sounds great. How about that little cafe by your office? Saturday for lunch?

Kenna: see you there.

When the weekend rolled around, Kenna was more excited than she had expected about seeing her friend again. Things were still rocky with

Emmet and he was absent most of the time, leaving her home alone. She talked to her sister frequently, but she was busy with the kids and planning for the new baby that was coming soon. Her mother was tirelessly working on her campaign and had been traveling around the region for the past few months, doing various speeches and meet and greets.

It had been lonely for Kenna these past few months without Becca to talk to, and she was glad to be speaking to her again. She hoped Becca was doing well and that she had given up on her plans to have a back alley heranon removal.

Winter was upon them now, and snow and ice covered the sidewalks. That day the sun was out, so she decided to walk despite the cold. She dressed warmly in jeans, boots, a wool sweater, and her long down winter jacket, grabbing her hat and mittens on her way out the door. They were meeting for lunch at a small cafe that was near Kenna's office and the walk wasn't too far.

Her boots crunched on the snowy ground as she walked and her breath was visible in the air swirling around her. Wishing she would have worn a scarf, she pulled her coat a little tighter around her neck to stop the chill from getting in. There were small snow flakes lazily falling from the sky, creating a thin layer of fresh white on everything it landed on. She knew that soon the cold weather would prevent her from walking outside, so she was attempting to spend time outdoors before the icy winter trapped her inside.

As she walked into the cafe, she shook the snow off her boots and hat, looking around for Becca. Spotting her in the back corner of the room in a booth, she started toward her. When she arrived at their table, Becca slid out of the leather booth to give Kenna a hug before she sat down.

"It's so great to see you," Becca said as she took her seat.

"It's great to see you too," Kenna replied as she sat across from Becca.

I'm glad we could get together to chat," Becca said honestly.

"Me too, I have missed our talks. I was happy to receive your text," Kenna replied as she removed her coat.

They picked up where they left off as if no time had passed since they last saw each other. Kenna ordered soup and a grilled sandwich while Becca opted for pancakes and bacon, along with a hot chocolate, trying to satisfy her sweet cravings.

They discussed work and family, catching up. Kenna confided in Becca about her frustrations with Emmett and how she feared their marriage would not last. Being that they were no longer client and psychologist they could speak more freely as friends without the underlying professional relationship. Feeling as though she had not been able to vent in months, Kenna laid it all out. She even told Becca about Alec, not that she was attracted to him but just that he invited her to lecture and she really enjoyed it. Finally, Kenna stopped talking and realized that Becca hadn't been able to get more than a few words in for the past hour.

"Anyway, enough about me. What's new with you?" Kenna asked.

Becca took a sip of her hot chocolate and peered at Kenna, a small shadow of a smile on her lips. Her hair was flowing freely around her shoulders and appeared to be thicker and shinier than Kenna remembered. Her pale skin looked more alive and she had pink in her cheeks and her lips. Kenna thought her hazel eyes were brighter even. What's different about her? Kenna thought to herself.

Becca leaned in over the table closer to her and looked around discreetly to make sure no one was within earshot

"I'm pregnant," she whispered with a smile.

Kenna gasped, "So soon? You look positively beautiful."

"We were shocked it happened so fast, and we were expecting to have more time to plan," she replied.

"What are your plans?" Kenna asked worriedly now. She was scared for her friend, but it also overjoyed her that Becca would finally get the child she always wanted.

"We don't have much of a plan yet," Becca admitted. "Once I can no longer hide my growing belly, I will have to quit work and hide out at home. I will give birth at home with the help of a couple of ladies who assured me they have done this numerous times. Shortly after the baby is born, we will have to sell the house and move to a different region with new identities."

"Wow, that's intense," Kenna stated, wide eyed with a solemn face.

The situation didn't even involve her, and it was making her anxious. Knowing that Becca would have to hide her pregnancy from everyone, she felt fortunate that she was the one she trusted to confide in. Deciding then and there that she would be there for her friend through the process, she told Becca that she would help her plan everything and would even be there for the birth if Becca wanted her to be.

"That would be amazing of you. Don't get me wrong, I'm ecstatic about this pregnancy, but the way we went about it does make the process rather lonely and I've missed our talks," Becca said, with tears in her eyes. As she wiped them away with her napkin, she said, "Damn hormones, everything makes me cry these days."

Kenna blinked back her own tears and tucked a strand of loose blonde hair behind her ear. After that, they gushed about baby names and whether they thought the baby would be a boy or a girl. For a moment, Becca forgot she was doing something illegal and was just enjoying her good news with her best friend.

"How far along are you?" Kenna asked, looking down at Becca's belly.

"About twelve weeks is what we figured. It's hard to know because my cycle was messed up with the heranon removal and it's not like I can get an ultrasound to check," Becca replied.

"So we are expecting a June baby?" Kenna asked.

"End of June or possibly July," Becca answered, smiling.

They finished their conversation and stacked their plates and silverware for the waitress before donning their jackets and heading outside. Becca gave Kenna a ride home, so she didn't have to walk in the snow that was coming down thicker than it was before. On their way, they made plans for Kenna to come over for supper and help decorate for Winter Holiday that was fast approaching.

Later that week Kenna arrived at the Wilkins' house for supper and she took off her boots and hung her jacket and scarf on a hook behind the door in the entryway as Lucky circled her feet. Becca had started decorating for Winter Holiday and there were little trees with lights sprinkled throughout the house and garland over the fireplace and up the stair rail. A warm fire was crackling in the fireplace, that gave the living room a cheery glow. The scent of Becca's homemade chicken noodle soup and fresh bread filled the house and was comforting to Kenna.

Kenna helped Becca with the last of the decorations as they sipped warm apple cider and munched on ginger cookies. When Fletcher came home from work, he joined in with them. After supper, they sat down at the dining room table to hatch their plan. Becca had her laptop open to make a spreadsheet for all the steps they needed to consider and expand on.

"I was hoping to finish out the school year," Becca admitted, looking at the other two.

"I don't think you're going to be able to hide your bump that long. You'll probably be showing quite a bit by March, for sure," Kenna reasoned.

"You're probably right. When I get back from winter break, I'll put in my notice to be done before March."

"What about when it's time to deliver?" Fletcher asked.

"I can pick up the two women from the East Side and bring them back here for the home delivery. That way you can stay with Becca," Kenna said to answer Fletcher.

They needed to sell their house, which would be the toughest thing to plan because there was no predicting how long it would take it to sell. Rolling the dice, they decided to list in for sale early in the summer in hopes they would sell it by fall when they needed to leave. Becca had been in contact with the woman from the church basement and she had informed her how her family will get their new documentation with their new identities. As they continued to figure out the logistics of each step, they joked it seemed so farfetched and unbelievable. It would be a miracle if it all worked out.

CHAPTER 16
Fighting Temptations

Kenna was driving on the bridge over the river, heading back to GreyStone. Alec had texted her again a few weeks ago and asked her back as a guest lecture. She had almost declined because she was so busy with work and with helping Becca, but she enjoyed teaching and didn't want the doors of opportunity to close on her. Today she was giving a lecture to an entry level psychology class in the larger auditorium. She had quickly thrown together her lecture materials last night because she had waited until the last minute and she hoped that it was good enough.

She walked into Alec's office and found him at his desk at work. He looked up when she entered the room, and his eyes instantly lit up, crinkling in the corners. She couldn't help but smile back. He was charming and made her feel a spark that had been missing from her life for many months.

Aware that this flirtation they had was

wrong, she tried to keep the conversation professional, but the chemistry between them was palpable. He got up from his chair and moved to the front of his desk, leaning back on it so he was closer to her. She looked up at him from her chair and was distracted by his proximity to her. She could reach out and touch him if she wanted to. Did she want to? She asked herself. Heat began to rise in her abdomen and she had goosebumps up the back of her neck.

"I meant what I said last time we saw each other," Alec said.

"Alec, I'm a married woman. I'm flattered by your interest, but I don't think it's appropriate," she replied, although not very sternly.

"Oh, my thoughts about you are definitely inappropriate, Kenna. And I know you're not happy in your marriage. If you were, you wouldn't talk to me the way you do," he said smugly.

He reached out and put his hand on top of hers on the armrest of her chair. The feel of his skin on hers sent a shock through her whole body and in that moment, she wanted nothing more than to be in his arms. She didn't pull her hand away and when she met his gaze, she knew he wanted her too. Understanding passed between them that they both felt something for each other. Alec glanced at his watch and saw that it was almost time for his next class. He lead Kenna to the large auditorium and helped make sure she was set to go.

Kenna was a wreck inside. She felt guilty for her feelings towards Alec, but she also didn't want to let them go. He made her feel alive and excited, and most of all, wanted. She tried to ignore her internal struggle with her conscious and continue with her lecture.

The grieving process and its steps were one subject she had always been fascinated by. When most people shied away from dealing with death and dying with their clients, Kenna went towards it. She had great sympathy for individuals who were grieving and wanted to help them the best she could. Some days it was hard for her to leave her feelings and work and not take her sadness for her patients home with her. There was a fine line between caring enough and caring too much.

When she finished her lecture, she was satisfied that it had gone well. She was relieved, since she had hastily thrown it together the night before. As the students filed out, she gathered her computer and things in her briefcase. Alec came up on the platform to meet her.

"You're a natural," he praised with his hands in his pockets.

"I'm sure you're just being nice," she replied, although she knew it had indeed gone very well.

"Listen, Kenna, after your last lecture I discussed it with the president of the psychology college. You did a great job then and again today. It's clear you have a knack for teaching. There's a position available for associate professor of psychology and I have recommended you for it," he told her seriously.

"What did he say?" Kenna asked, surprised by his confession.

"He said he thought it was a great idea," Alec beamed.

"I, I don't know what to say. I wasn't expecting anything like this," she said, bewildered.

"You'd be good at it and it's a great opportunity," Alec coaxed.

"I'm just very busy right now and I have a lot going on. I can't juggle anymore, so I'm going to decline. Sorry, I appreciate the opportunity, but I just can't right now." She knew it would be taking on too much.

"Just take some time to think about it, okay? Don't decide right now. I'll keep in touch." Alec brushed her hand with his once more before turning to leave.

Kenna grabbed her briefcase and walked up the aisle of the auditorium to leave. When she reached her car, she was still processing what Alec had told her. Teaching at the college had given her something new to look forward to, a much needed distraction. Associate professor was a great opportunity but also an enormous commitment. She didn't think she could handle it right now with everything else going on.

She was spending more time with Becca, and her practice was booming so much so that she was booking out for weeks and had to do some charting at home in the evenings. Not to mention the stress of her less than ideal marriage that had become mostly one sided. She couldn't remember the last time she and Emmett had a date night, let alone been intimate. It was too much to process right now, and she had to hurry back to her office for her afternoon clients.

Later that day after work, Kenna returned home to her empty house with only Ruby to keep her company. At work that afternoon, she struggled to stay focused on her clients. Her mind kept wandering back to Alec and his offer. She poured herself a large glass of red wine as she cut some cheese and apples to have with crackers for supper. Most days, she didn't even bother asking Emmett if he would be home for supper. He usually grabbed a sandwich from the doctors' lounge and was home late.

She turned on the electric fireplace and snuggled on the couch with Ruby as she ate and drank her wine. As her favorite show played on the television, she knew she should be working on her notes or catching up on housework, but she was unmotivated today.

Before she knew it, darkness fell outside her windows and the bright white moon was in the sky. Ruby stretched and yawned at her feet.

Turning off the TV and fireplace, she poured the remaining contents of the wine bottle into her glass and got up to let Ruby outside before bed. When she stood, she felt woozy and steadied herself with her hand on the sofa. After almost drinking her entire bottle of wine, she was feeling the effects of it and she knew she would pay for it in the morning. She made a mental note to cut back on her wine intake.

Dragging her feet up the stairs, she didn't even bother to wash her face before plopping down in bed. She drained the last of her wine from the glass and set it on the nightstand. As she lay in bed, her mind was pleasantly fuzzy. She felt warm from the wine and her silky sheets felt like they were tickling her legs. Soon thoughts of Alec flooded her brain and she welcomed them. She imagined running her hands through his wavy golden blonde hair as she fell into his deep blue eyes. The feel of his bare chest and abdomen as he held her close. He pulls her in tighter as his gorgeous smile parts and his lips meet hers. She slipped her hand into her underwear and caressed herself while thinking of him and his member. In her drunken state, she was no longer denying it to herself. She wanted him and she was letting herself have him in her thoughts, anyway.

CHAPTER 17
Uncertainty

With the Winter Holiday passed, it seemed everyone was already thinking of spring and wishing the rest of winter away. Winter was her least favorite season, but Kenna was hoping for time to slow down. Soon Becca would have her baby and she would lose her friend forever. She was heading over to Becca's now to help her take down all the winter decor and bring it for donation. Becca was slowly getting rid of most of their belongings. So when the time came, they would take only what would fit in her vehicle.

When she arrived at Becca's, she found her friend sitting on the floor putting little trees and pine cones into boxes next to holiday candles.

"What can I help you with?" Kenna asked after removing her shoes and jacket.

"If you want to start taking the garland off the stair rail, that would be great," Becca replied.

Kenna started at the top of the stairs and was untwisting the garland from the rail. She had made it about halfway down the stairwell when she heard a thump followed be a horrible scream coming from Becca. The shriek coming from her friend sounded feral and Kenna could tell she was hurt and needed help.

Quickly, she ran down the stairs to get to her friend as her heart thudded against her chest wall. In a hurry, she skipped the last step and her sock slipped on the wood floor. She was able to steady herself without falling. As she turned the corner to enter the living room, she saw her friend on the floor sitting on her bottom next to a step stool tipped on its side. She was propping herself up with one arm behind her and one hand was holding her belly. Her face was contorted with pain. She was breathing deeply, her abdomen rising and falling with each breath.

"Oh my god, Becca! Are you okay?" Kenna asked as she reached her side and kneeled down beside her.

"I don't know. When I fell, I landed straight on my ass and I immediately had pain way down low in my belly," she replied with a grimace. "Now it feels more like cramping."

"Can you stand up?" Kenna asked, rising to her feet and extending her arms to help Becca pull herself up.

As she lifted her bottom off the ground, she gasped as she and Kenna looked down and saw bright red blood pooling on the pale wood floor beneath her. She sat back down, afraid to move any more. The color had drained from her face and she looked as white as the snow outside on the ground.

"I feel dizzy, like I might faint," she said.

Kenna grabbed a pillow off the couch and helped her friend lie down on the hard floor. "What can I do?" Kenna felt helpless.

"Call Fletcher," Becca replied with tears in her eyes.

Kenna called Fletcher and asked him to come home right away. She sat on the floor beside Becca while they waited for him. Becca was sobbing now and mascara tinged tears streaked down her face. Kenna didn't know what else to do. She couldn't bring Becca to the hospital, since this was an illegal pregnancy. She was wringing her hands nervously and trying to speak words of encouragement to her friend, but she knew she was in over her head.

Becca's pale face still lacked all color, and she seemed to be getting tired, causing Kenna's anxiety to rise. The blood was pooling around Becca's bottom. Kenna didn't want her to see it and go into hysterics in her current state. If she lost the baby, Kenna was worried she would never recover from it.

"Ah." Becca had stopped crying and placed both hands on her belly. Her eyes had a twinkle of hope. "I feel the baby moving. That's got to be a good sign, right?"

"Yeah, it is a good sign!" Kenna said. "I still

think you need to go to the emergency room."

"You know I can't do that. I would if I could, but what if they made me abort the baby anyway or took her away after she's born? What if they put me in jail? It's too risky and we can't go," Becca argued. Kenna just sighed and watched over her.

When Fletcher arrived, he scooped Becca up and laid her on the sofa. Kenna quickly cleaned up the blood on the floor as she exchanged worried glances with Fletcher. Soon Becca fell asleep with a concerned Fletcher sitting by her side, watching her.

"I'm worried she's lost a lot of blood. She's white as a sheet and felt dizzy," Kenna told him. "Do you know if she's anemic? It's common in pregnancy."

"I don't know. She hasn't been able to have any medical care with this pregnancy because of the way we went about it," He said, his face gaunt and his shoulders slumped forward as he sat in the chair next to her small, fragile frame.

"I'll stay tonight to help watch over her," Kenna volunteered.

"Thank you," he replied without taking his eyes off his wife.

After a while, Kenna brought Fletcher a sandwich and some chicken noodle soup, the steam from the soup swirled in the air as she walked it out to him. "You should eat something," she encouraged, setting the plate and bowl down on the wooden coffee table next to him.

She walked over to inspect Becca. Her body seemed tiny compared to their large leather couch, with a flannel blanket covering her up to her neck. As she checked her pulse, her heart sunk. It was faint, but she could tell it was too high. Kenna understood their fear about going to the emergency room. She knew she would never persuade them to go, but she was becoming alarmed for her friend's life. While Becca slept, Kenna tried reasoning with Fletcher and pleaded with him to take Becca in, no matter the legal consequences to possibly save her life.

"She is the love of my life. Don't you think it agonizes me to see her like this? I want to bring her in and I am worried about her life and the life of our unborn baby. But if I bring her in, she will never forgive me. Not to mention we could both be in legal trouble, and who knows what that entails?" he said as he nervously ran his hands over his head and down the front of his face.

"What about your husband? He's a doctor, right? Can we trust him?" Now Fletcher was pleading with her and needed her help.

She hadn't thought about calling Emmett. Their lives had been so separate lately, she hadn't even considered it. He was a cardiothoracic surgeon, not an obstetrician, but he would probably still know what to do.

Knowing that he wouldn't approve of her

involvement with the Wilkins 'illegal endeavor, she was scared to call him and ask for his help now, but she felt they had no other choice. If Becca died and Kenna didn't do everything in her power to save her, she would never forgive herself. So she picked up her phone and called Emmett. When he answered, his voice was full of worry and concern at why she was calling in the middle of the night. He was still at the hospital because it was his call night and he just got out of a case. She told him about Becca's fall and her symptoms and that they couldn't go to the hospital because it was an illegal pregnancy. After a few minutes, when she had finished laying everything out, she paused for his response.

"Fucking hell Kenna, what have you gotten yourself involved with? Did you ever think of the consequences you could face if they got caught and you were implicated? And now her life is possibly in danger and they're too scared to get medical help. What a fucking mess." He said sternly.

"Emmett, I understand why you're upset and I'm sorry that I kept it from you, but we need your help. Becca's life depends on it," she pleaded.

Emmett let out a heavy sigh on the other end of the line, "I hope I don't regret this. Ask them if they know her blood type," he instructed.

"Do you know Becca's blood type?" she asked

Fletcher. He rose from his chair by her side and went to look through her purse on the bench in the entryway, knowing she frequently donated blood and that she had a card for it.

"AB positive," he replied, pulling the card from her wallet with her blood donation information.

Kenna relayed the information to Emmett along with the Wilkins 'address and apologized again for putting him in this tough position. She was confident that Emmett would be able to help Becca, and she was relieved that he was on the way. Even though she knew he was not done being angry with her about it. He had every right to be angry with her for her choices and for keeping this part of her life from him these past couple of months, and she didn't blame him.

It took Emmett almost half an hour before he arrived in front of the house. Kenna went out to meet him on the front step and apologized to him again, face to face. When he saw the look of concern on her face, he put his feelings aside and got to work. Kneeling beside Becca, he pulled a blood pressure cuff and oximeter from his travel bag. He checked her vitals and found her pulse and breathing rate to be elevated and her blood pressure was low. Becca was so weak and fatigued that she barely stirred while he was checking her over. Placing his stethoscope on her lower abdomen, he listened intently for the baby's heartbeat. He had to reposition several times before finally locating it.

"How far along in she?" Emmett asked as he finished his assessment.

"Almost twenty weeks," Kenna replied.

"With the amount of blood you described after falling, I believe she had a partial placenta abruption, but there's no way to be sure without an ultrasound. It's extremely lucky that both she and the baby appear to be doing okay, but she isn't out of the woods yet. There's a possibility she could still lose the baby," he said to Kenna and Fletcher, and they nodded in understanding.

He pulled two bags of red blood from his bag and everything he needed to start an IV. Once he had it all hooked up, he asked Fletcher for something they could hang the blood bag on so gravity could help get the blood into Becca. Fletcher grabbed the coat rack near the front door and they hung the bag on it. Then they watched and waited. Only time would tell if she would pull through and if the baby was okay. Emmett had to return to the hospital, but he told Kenna what to watch for and instructed how often to check vitals.

She walked him out to the car. "Thank you for helping Becca. I know that what she did seems wrong, but if you knew her and Fletcher, you would know they are good people that were just stuck in an unfortunate situation," she advocated for her friend.

"Keep me updated, and we can talk about the

rest of it later," he replied before getting in the car and driving away.

As the night dragged on, she watched her friend. The exhaustion from the day setting in making her eyelids feel heavy and her muscles ache. Her stomach growled and she realized she hadn't eaten all day. She was too busy making sure everyone else was okay. The second bag of blood was almost empty and she thought Becca's cheeks had slightly more color, which helped ease her angst a bit. Slowly and clumsily, she lifted her aching body out of the overstuffed leather chair, her muscles screaming at her to get some sleep. Stumbling to the kitchen, she tried stretching out her neck that had developed a kink from sleeping in the chair.

After scarfing down a sandwich and drinking a whole glass of water, she wandered back into the living room. She wasn't keen on going back to sleep in the chair. Fletcher was quietly snoring in the chair nearest the couch, and she covered him up with a blanket before sitting back down.

"Hey," Becca said sleepily.

The unexpected sound of her friend waking up startled Kenna. "Hey yourself. You know you gave us quite the scare."

"I am feeling a little better, but I'm thirsty," Becca said.

Kenna jumped up to get her a glass of water and when she returned, she helped Becca sit up against some pillows so she could drink it.

"The baby keeps fluttering every now and then. It gives me hope that she's okay."

"So baby is a she?" Kenna asked with a smile.

"I feel like she is. I just tired of calling the baby it and I got an inkling that she's a girl," Becca said.

"You were asleep but Emmett came over and looked you over and he heard her heartbeat, which he said is good," Kenna said hopefully. Becca's forehead wrinkled and the corners of her mouth turned down in a state of concern.

"It's okay. We can trust Emmett to keep your secret," Kenna reassured her friend.

"I'm sorry if this has put you in an awkward position," Becca apologized.

"Don't worry about me. I'm just glad that you're okay," she said.

"You should go upstairs and get some sleep in the guest room. I'll be okay, and Fletcher will be up for work in a few hours," Becca instructed.

"Alright I will. I'll be back down to check on you in the morning." Kenna yawned as she stood to go upstairs and placed her hand on top of Becca's and gave it a quick squeeze.

When she reached the bedroom at the top of the stairs, she flopped down on the bed on her stomach, fully clothed, and fell asleep almost instantly. With her drool slowly forming a puddle on the pillow.

She slept deeply and didn't stir until the sun started peeking in the windows at dawn, casting a pink glow around the room. Rolling over in bed, she stretched and rubbed her eyes, trying to get the sleep out. Still feeling exhausted from the emotional toll the day before had taken on her, she slowly sat up and sat at the end of the bed. Debating on whether she should call Glenda and have her reschedule all her appointments for the day, she got to her feet and started down the stairs. The wooden stairs creaked with each step and the hand rail slid smoothly beneath her hand.

Becca was sitting up on the couch with her nose buried in a book, and she heard a noise coming from the kitchen, which she assumed was Fletcher making coffee. At least she hoped he was making coffee. Although still pale, Becca looked much brighter. It gave Kenna reassurance that her best friend was going to be all right.

Just as she entered the room, Fletcher walked in from the kitchen with some tea and toast for Becca. The way he doted on her and was always putting her first warmed Kenna's heart. She wished Emmett was more like that.

Although the cold winter weather tried to creep in at the door and windows, the house felt warm and welcoming. There was a fire going in the brick fireplace and the warm scent of a vanilla candle filled the room. Kenna thought her own house felt somewhat cold and sharp in comparison. Not as homey.

"Good morning," she greeted them.

"Oh good, you're up! I need to ask you a favor," Becca said rather rushed.

"What do you need?" Kenna replied.

"Last night I couldn't sleep after I came to because I was worried about the baby. So I've been texting the ladies that helped me with the heranon removal. And although they don't sound excited to help me, they said I could see Dr. J today and she would bring a portable ultrasound machine. They said they usually don't do things like that, but will make an exception for me," Becca said, using her hands as she talked. "Fletcher has some things going on at work today that he cannot miss, so we were wondering if you would drive me to see Dr. J. I don't think I should drive myself after yesterday."

"Yes, I can do that. Just give me five minutes to call my receptionist and have her cancel my appointments," she said.

After tidying herself up a bit in the mirror, Kenna helped Becca to the bathroom. She still felt weak and didn't trust herself walking up the stairs without someone guiding her by the arm. Once they reached the bathroom at the top of the stairs, Kenna waited outside while Becca got ready. Becca was almost scared to go to the bathroom and see how much she was still bleeding, but she had to check.

When she pulled down her underwear, she saw that the pad she had put on last night after the fall was completely soaked with blood and her heart sank. Sitting on the cold toilet, she emptied her bladder and braced herself for what she might see. But when she wiped, there was only a small streak of blood on the toilet paper and none in the toilet bowl. Letting out a sigh of relief, she stood and pulled up her underwear and pants. Suddenly, she felt very lightheaded, and she reached out and grabbed the white pedestal sink in front of her. The cool porcelain against her hands felt soothing and kept her grounded. Once the room stopped spinning, she splashed some cool water on her faced and finished getting ready.

After she was dressed, Kenna led her back down the stairs and they donned their winter coats and mittens before heading out to Becca's car.

The tires spun on the icy road as Kenna tried to pull away from the curb. Once they found traction, the car propelled forward and they were on their way. Becca gave her directions as she drove but she figured they were going to the East Side so she headed in that direction. Once they reached the East Side, Becca pointed to the run-down apartment building and Kenna parked out front so Becca wouldn't have to walk far.

Across the street in a wide alley, there was a group of men gathered around a fire in a trash can, talking and laughing amongst themselves. Kenna realized the East Side differed greatly from the world she was used to. She was acutely aware of her privilege.

Becca got out of the car and disappeared into a tall apartment building that was ridden with safety tape and warning signs. Kenna wanted to join her but Becca asked her to wait in the car. She didn't think Dr. J would take kindly to her bringing new people around. So she sat and waited, looking at her surroundings with great interest.

There were several buildings with the same tape and warning signs that looked like they were about to cave in. She wondered how long they had been like that. The icy streets were filled with potholes, some were so big Kenna was scared they would lose a tire if she hit them. Cars that were parked here and there along the streets were old and rusted. They did not look reliable and some of them looked as if they hadn't run in years.

Graffiti covered most of the dilapidated buildings and some old painted murals that were exquisite. Kenna thought to herself that the artist who created them was very talented. One mural on a brick building depicted an orange sunset over a meadow of flowers. Although beautiful, it looked out of place against the gray snow and garbage lined sidewalks.

After about an hour, Becca emerged from the apartment building, clutching her scarf around her neck, and bolted to the car. When she got inside, she looked at Kenna's questioning face. "The baby is fine!" she almost squealed with happiness.

Kenna let out the breath she was holding with relief. "That's wonderful."

"And that's not all," Becca said with a mischievous grin, "they think it's a girl!"

She took out her phone and showed Kenna a picture. It was an ultrasound image of the baby's profile showing her cute little nose and her hand up by her face as though she were sucking her thumb. "They let me take a picture of the ultrasound screen," Becca stared at her phone screen, her eyes brimming with happy tears.

"I'm so happy for you." Kenna leaned over and gave her a side hug.

"Do they know what caused the bleeding?" she asked.

"Not entirely," Becca answered, "she thinks it was a partial placenta abruption, but she said the ultrasound looked fine now."

"I'm glad everything is going to be okay," Kenna said whole heartedly.

"Me too," Becca replied still staring at the image on her phone like it was the most beautiful thing she had ever seen.

CHAPTER 18
Rough Waters

Once Kenna arrived home after dropping Becca off, it surprised her to see Emmett sitting at the kitchen island waiting for her. His laptop was open and he was catching up on his patient charting. When he saw her walk in, he stopped working and followed her with his stare as she walked into the kitchen to the fridge for some water.

She didn't want to look up as she sipped her water and looked in the fridge for something to have for lunch. Knowing what was coming and how angry he would be, she was dreading the conversation she knew was about to take place. Deciding to get it over with, she shut the fridge and sat beside Emmett on a stool at the large island. Her glass made a loud clinking sound as she set it on the granite countertop and turned to face him. Finally, when she met his gaze, she could see he was furious.

He had disheveled hair as though he had been running his hands through it and dark circles under his eyes that made him look older than he actually was. She knew he was running himself ragged with his surgical residency and she felt bad that she had added an extra layer of stress on him. But part of her was glad he was actually paying attention to her, even if it was for all the wrong reasons.

He dropped his eyes as he ran his hand through his hair in frustration and let out a long, disappointed sigh, "How is she?"

"She is doing much better, and baby is fine," Kenna answered.

"Kenna, what were you thinking getting involved in this?"

"Becca is my best friend, and you would know that if you were ever around. Her and Fletcher are hardworking, responsible, kind people that deserve to be parents. And they've had their application denied four times because of something she did when she was a teenager. It's not right. So they did what they had to do to have a family, and I can't say that I wouldn't do the same in their situation," she crossed her arms defensively.

"It's illegal. Think about the consequences you could face. Not to mention you dragged me into it. What would your mom think of you getting involved in something like this, and during an election year at that?" he fumed. "You're being reckless."

"I'm sorry you feel that way, and I'm aware

of the risks," she answered. "She's my friend, and I'm not abandoning her when she needs me. What if it would have been us that got denied four times? Wouldn't you think about doing the same thing?"

"No, I wouldn't. I wound accept that it was not in the cards for us to be parents," he said.

"Well, I would, and I understand what drove her into doing it," she explained.

"That's crazy," he stated.

"You know what's crazy? Becca and Fletcher getting denied four times when they would make perfect parents," Kenna huffed.

"The restrictions are in place for a reason. We should respect them," Emmett replied. "Did you even consider the impact this could have on your life? You could get in serious illegal trouble by assisting her with this pregnancy. You could even get jail time. If you get caught they could deny our application forever. Then we would never be able to have children," he reasoned with her.

The seriousness of the situation was not lost on Kenna. "I understand there are risks. We will be careful. I promise I won't get caught," she stated, unwavering.

"You're on your own with this, Kenna. I will not be involved, and I hope that you guys don't get caught. For both our sakes," he said realizing that she would not budge.

Emmett grabbed his laptop and went upstairs

to the office to finish his work, leaving Kenna alone in the kitchen to contemplate her choices.

She was torn. The part of her that was a rule follower struggled with the idea of participating in illegal acts. The other part of her, the kind and understanding part, knew that Becca and Fletcher were good people and deserved happiness. It's not like they were hurting anyone and they were certainly capable of caring for their daughter. The system had failed them, and she wondered how many more couples like the Wilkins were out there suffering because of some stupid oversight.

Her stomach growled, reminding her that it was now lunch time and she had skipped breakfast. She warmed up some leftovers and ate sitting at the island. Since she called off work, she knew she would be busy for the rest of the week trying to squeeze patients in that had been canceled today. Already dreading the following day of work, she put her dish in the wash and went upstairs to shower and change.

Soft music played from her speaker in the bathroom as the hot water hit her back, loosening her tight muscles. Soon steam filled the shower and fogged the glass shower door and the mirror in the bathroom. She breathed in deeply, allowing the warm moist air into her nose and lungs. For a long time she just stood in the shower, letting it wash away her stress. The scent of her lavender shampoo filled the air and helped her relax.

After showering, she brushed her teeth, applied moisturizer, and got dressed in black lounging joggers and her favorite sweatshirt from college. She was exhausted, and although she didn't typically nap in the middle of the day, she made an exception and crawled into bed with Ruby following close behind and settling at her feet at the end of the bed.

Soon, sleep crept over her, but her unsettled thoughts plagued her even in sleep. Drifting between sleep and being partially awake, she was in a restless state. She saw Becca and Fletcher with their new baby girl, a picture of pure happiness as the new parents smiled and cooed at the tiny, beautiful infant. She stood watching them from across the room, grinning at the seemingly perfect family. Suddenly there was a dark ominous cloud over them and police rushed into their house at the front door, seizing Becca and Fletcher whilst ripping their new baby from their arms and whisking her away to an unknown location, never to be seen again. Becca cried out in anguish, as though her heart was being physically torn from her body.

She awoke breathing heavily, with small streams of tears leaking out the corner of her eyes. Her palms were sweaty and she kicked off the heavy blanket to cool off. Turning over to look at her phone, she saw she had slept longer than she wanted to, although it felt too short and was disturbing. Yawning and stretching her arms above her head, she sat up and slipped her feet into her fuzzy white slippers. Becca had texted her while she was sleeping to let her know she was doing fine. There had been no more bleeding, and she was planning to return to work the following day. Kenna felt a weight lift off of her as Becca recovered from her injury.

Wondering if Emmett was still in the office, she quietly creeped across the hall and opened the door just a crack to peek in, but the room was empty. She went down the stairs with Ruby at her heals and was surprised to find that she was alone. A small note sat upon the kitchen island and read: Going out, be back late -E.

That's strange, she thought, Emmett never went out. He had been so busy at work she hadn't spent any quality time with him in months and when he actually got a whole day off; they spent it fighting with each other. Then he just left her there to go do whatever it was he was doing. She could understand why he was angry with her. But what he didn't get was that she was angry at him too, and he took no responsibility for the impending collapse of their marriage. Feeling frustrated, she opened a bottle of wine and grabbed her phone to text Becca and check on her.

For the rest of the evening, she sat and fumed that Emmett was still out. Before she knew it, she had finished her bottle of wine and watched several sappy movies. She checked her phone now and then, hoping to see an apology text from Emmett, but it never came.

Finally, she heard her phone vibrating on the coffee table and reached for it hoping he had a change of heart. When she looked at her phone, what she saw made her eyes light up and gave her butterflies in her stomach.

Alec: Hey! What are you up to?

Kenna: Just hanging out at home, you?

Alec: Same. I hadn't heard from you in a while and wanted to check in.

Kenna: are you worried about me?

Alec: not worried, just interested ;-)

Kenna: I've told you, I'm a married woman.

Alec: I know. If you weren't, I'd be over there now.

Kenna: Ha. What makes you think I'd let you in?

Alec: I have a good feeling.

The wine was clouding her judgement, and her frustration with Emmett was not helping. They exchanged numerous texts that bordered on inappropriate and arranged to meet that weekend to discuss future guest lectures. At least that was the excuse she was telling herself when she felt guilty.

The following Saturday, Kenna met Alec at the Daily Cup for coffee and breakfast. She wore a formfitting black turtleneck and her favorite jeans that were always flattering to her figure. He was the picture of effortless style in dark khakis and a navy sweater that accentuated his blue eyes. When Kenna saw him, she smirked flirtatiously before giving him a side hug. The feel of his body against hers left her warm, with tingles running down her back. She took a seat and they ordered hot lattes and muffins, which swiftly arrived at their table with steam wisps over the cups and a sweet aroma of pumpkin trailing behind.

Kenna was pleased to be seeing Alec again, even though she knew she shouldn't be. She knew exactly what he wanted from her and it was getting harder for her to deny that she wanted it too. They talked about work and some ideas she had for future lectures she could give at his classes. When she spoke, he listened intently, his eyes and ears taking in all of her, and he answered her questions and concerns with thoughtful replies.

Kenna was absorbed in the attention she was receiving from him and loving it. She didn't feel guilty anymore. The wedge between her and Emmett had gotten so big that her love for him was fading and making room for her lust for Alec.

"I've really enjoyed working with you," he said with an honest smile.

"Me too," she replied over her latte.

"Maybe we could spend more time together?"

he asked coyly.

"You mean for work?" she asked, but she knew that's not what he meant.

"No, not for work," he said with a sly grin.

She took a sip of her drink; the foam leaving a small trace on her upper lip, making it appear like she had a mustache. "Oh, I see," she replied, not knowing what else to say.

He laughed and leaned forward, using his thumb to gently wipe away the foam while peering intently into her wide eyes. Her foot brushed lightly against his leg and she didn't pull it away.   "   So what do you say?" he asked again.

They were so caught up in their own world that Kenna did not see her mother enter the coffee shop. Victoria sat near the back of the large open room at a small table. She peered at her daughter and the man she was with over a book that she was using to hide behind.

Kenna had been acting strange lately and seemed to be avoiding her, so Victoria had her followed, discreetly, of course. When she saw her and Alec Kingston together at the college, she got this weird feeling, call it mother's intuition, that her daughter was treading in dangerous waters. This meeting today confirmed her fears that Kenna was on the verge of scandal, and during an election year at that. Of her two daughters, Kenna was always the hardest one to parent. She was strong willed with powerful emotions, whereas Kassi was more subdued and disciplined.

After doing some research on this Alec character, Victoria knew he was not the type of individual she wanted her daughter to be friends with. During his teen years, his father had to pull many strings to get him out of trouble numerous times and he had been kicked out of several boarding schools because of bad behavior. Victoria knew she had to squash this relationship like an annoying bug before it got out of hand. She was not about to have her daughter all over the media for adultery during the biggest election of her life.

After happening upon her daughter's relationship with Alec, she had also had Emmett followed and discovered he was damn near living at the hospital. Which Victoria suspected was a large part of the problem. She would need to have a talk with both of them to see if she could help salvage their marriage, at least until the election was over.

Curiously, Victoria had discovered Kenna was also spending quite a bit of time with a new girlfriend. This wasn't alarming other than her daughter had never mentioned this friend to her.

Lately, Victoria had been busy with campaigning. It was hard work and long hours but her dedication was paying off. She was neck and neck with her opponent. All the others had dropped out of the race and only they two remained. Victoria knew she would have to continue to work hard and put in the time to defeat her opponent but it would be possible. She was definitely in the running to become the Region Four Chair.

On the occasion when she had time to call and catch up with Kenna, she found her to be very closed off and their conversations were very one sided and superficial. She usually relied on Kassi to update her on Kenna's life, but it seemed that her pregnancy had created a rift in their normally close sisterly relationship.

Victoria decided she would make time to talk to both Kenna and Emmett separately. And she would do some more digging into this new friendship Kenna had with this unknown redheaded woman. She put on her large dark sunglasses and her long black parka and slinked out of the coffee shop unseen by her daughter.

CHAPTER 19
The Doctor

A couple of weeks had passed since Becca's fall. She had recovered well and was back to her pregnancy bliss, or as blissful as she could be with the constant fear she would be found out. Showing more now, Becca would soon have to leave work and hide out in the safety of her own home until their daughter arrived.

Although Kenna was not the pregnant one, she was feeling stressed and anxious about Becca's situation. Especially the thought of her giving birth at home with no medical help. The more she thought about Becca's fall and the lack of prenatal care and resources she had available to her, the more angry and frustrated she became. Why did it have to be like this? Her friend deserved more than some back alley heranon removal and living on the run from the authorities for the rest of her life.

Kenna had tried to talk to Emmett about her concerns now that he was in on Becca's secret.

He wanted nothing to do with the situation and always encouraged Kenna to stay out of it. This made her even more furious. He was a doctor, for fuck's sake. He should care about patients having access to healthcare when they needed it. After a few attempts, she just stopped talking to him about it all together. Their conversations became less and their attitudes towards each other continued to deteriorate.

Kenna did her own research on illegal heranon removal and discovered that it was happening more than she ever realized. She wished that she would have accompanied Becca when she went back to see Dr. J for the ultrasound. She wanted to give that doctor a piece of her mind.

Not only was she breaking the law over and over by doing the heranon removals, she was also putting women's lives at risk. They received no maternity care and when they need medical care; they are too afraid to seek it for fear of going to jail, or worse. If it wasn't for her friendship with Becca, she might even consider turning this doctor in to the authorities.

The more she thought about it, the more compelled she was to do something about it, but what? Deciding that she should confront the doctor, she devised a plan to get to her. Becca did not give her many details on how she was connected to the doctor, but Kenna knew which building they were in and which day they were there, that is, if it was the same day all the time.

Realizing she didn't have much to go on, she decided to start out with some recon of the area on Monday. That meant she'd have to cancel all of her appointments with clients that day, which she hated doing when her business was doing so well. She didn't want her clients to think she was flaky by continuing to cancel on them. So she hoped that Monday she would get some good information and it would be worth it.

On Monday, she woke and got ready with a purpose. Trying to be unassuming and blend in, she threw on jeans and a sweatshirt, along with a black puffer jacket and black hat. Looking in the mirror, she was satisfied with her bland look. Walking out to the car, she stopped to kick the ice and slush off the fenders before getting inside and blasting the heat. They were past the coldest part of winter and there were some nice days, but it was still freezing. She couldn't fathom why Emmett insisted on running to work every morning.

As she drove to the East Side, she wondered how she should go about this. It would look suspicious if she was hanging out outside all day in this cold, so she decided she would park close and watch from her car. Locating a spot to park directly across from the abandoned apartment building in question, she pulled in and waited. She hoped her newer car didn't look too conspicuous among the run down vehicles all around her.

She leaned her seat back and slouched down so she wouldn't be seen and killed the engine. For hours she watched and nothing happened. A few passersby walked past on the sidewalk, but they didn't seem to see her. She was glad for the cold keeping people indoors. Wondering if she had the wrong day, she sat up and was contemplating leaving when a red car pulled up.

Two young women jumped out and quickly scurried up the steps, looking over their shoulders as they went. Once they were inside, Kenna didn't want to miss her window, so she ran up the steps after them. Opening the door just a crack, she peered after them as they dashed down the long hallway. She slid inside and darted behind the wall of the entryway.

As they started up the stairway at the end of the hall, Kenna ran as quietly as possible as she continued her pursuit. Following them up the stairs while keeping a safe distance, she watched them get off on the third floor. She sprinted up the rest of the stairs just in time to open the door a crack to see which apartment they were going to. The door was not far from her and she could hear one of them women say, "the cradle will fall" before the door opened, allowing them entry.

Anticipating that the women would leave the same way they came, Kenna carefully crept down the long, dingy hallway to the other side.

The hallway was fairly dark, with only a small broken window at the end. Despite this, she could still see the door marked with the number three thirty-three that the two women had entered.

Once she reached the other end of the hall, she ducked into a small alcove where old cleaning supplies were sitting covered in dust and cobwebs. She wondered how long this building had been condemned and when they would actually tear it down. It was common to see entire communities being demolished as the population declined, but Kenna guessed correctly that the government leaders weren't in a hurry to clean up the East Side. They had far more important areas to bring back to nature.

About an hour passed before the women exited the apartment, walking at a slower paced now. The woman with a curvy figured covered by a blue jacket was hunched forward. She leaned on her companion for support down the hall as she had one hand clutching at her lower abdomen. Kenna's heart went out to the woman. She knew that desperation led her here, and she wished she could do more to help. The system was obviously broken and Kenna was realizing just how much.

She waited another ten minutes before approaching the door, clenching and unclenching her hands repeatedly in angst. Suddenly, she felt hot in her sweatshirt and jacket as her anxiety grew. Her heart was pounding and she was holding her breath unintentionally as she reached up and knocked on the door. She heard rustling on the other side before a woman's voice came through.

"Password?" the mysterious voice asked.

"Cradle will fall," Kenna repeated the phrase she had heard the two women use.

The door opened rapidly and a short, thin woman wearing scrubs, a surgical hat, and a mask pulled her inside swiftly. Softly closing the door behind them. There was an older woman changing sheets on the makeshift exam table in the small living room. She presumed the older woman was Dr. J. Kenna stood frozen in her spot, staring like an idiot at the two women. It was surreal to her to be here, a place she knew existed but never expected to see. All the words she wanted to say were lost to her now, but the older woman broke the silence.

"Do you have payment?" she asked.

"I, uh no. I'm not here for your services," Kenna replied.

Dr. J and her assistant cast confused glances at each other before turning back to Kenna. "What are you here for, then? Are you police?" Dr. J asked, although she doubted it by the look of the young woman standing in front of her.

"No, I'm not police. I guess I'm more of a concerned citizen," Kenna fumbled. "I want to talk to you about your practice and how dangerous and wrong it is."

Dr. J raised her brows. "Oh really? Well, then why don't you sit down and enlighten us with all your wisdom?" she said sarcastically.

Awkwardly, Kenna moved around the assistant to sit on the exam table while Dr. J sat back on her stool with her arms crossed across her chest. The doctor intimidated her. She had this presence about her that reminded Kenna of her mother.

"What you're doing is wrong. It's illegal and after these women go through with it, they have to live life on the run, leaving everyone they know and love behind. What kind of life is that? Not to mention how dangerous it is, removing the heranon with no sedation and minimal medical equipment and supplies. These women get no medical care and when they find themselves in trouble, they are scared to go in for fear of being persecuted. They give birth at home in the most barbaric way, again with no real medical care. How can you live with yourself knowing this?" Kenna rattled off while she had her confidence back.

"You're right, about all of it. But you tell me, what other choice do these women have?" Dr. J asked honestly.

"I don't know," Kenna replied.

"I thought you knew everything?" Dr. J replied to Kenna. "Some of these women have applied four or even five times before ending up on my doorstep, and they are desperate for the opportunity to become a mother. They know the consequences and are willing to risk their lives for a child. If I don't help them, who will?" she said.

"Why do you feel so compelled to help?" Kenna asked. "Is it just for the money? Or do you actually have a heart?"

Dr. J let out a sigh, "Because over the last thirty years of my career, I have seen the reproductive restrictions get stricter and more invasive, and I am powerless to stop it. So I help those I can."

"The reproductive restrictions have improved our society greatly. I admit it's not a perfect system, but you can't deny we are making the world a better place," Kenna argued, parroting what she had been taught her whole life. Although she was seriously starting to doubt this herself after seeing the injustice the restrictions imposed on Becca.

"Maybe it appears that way from where you sit," Dr. J replied.

"What do you mean?" she asked intrigued.

"Upper class and even most middle-class women will all eventually get their applications approved, but not here. Why don't you open your pretty little eyes and look around? There are no children on this side of town. The ones that are here hide in the shadows and are only here because of my work. Our government has been denying poor women the basic human right to have children for over twenty years. That's what I mean," Dr. J replied haughtily. "And in doing so, they are eliminating an entire class, slowly but effectively."

Kenna just stared at her. She was not expecting that response and was trying to process all the information that had been given to her. "If that's true, it's not right and someone needs to put a stop to it."

"Who? You?" Dr. J mocked her.

Kenna rose from her seat to leave. When she reached the door, she turned back to the doctor. "If everything is as you say, why do you care so much to do what you do?" Kenna asked curiously.

Dr. J straightened her shoulders back and met Kenna's questioning glare. "I'm from here, not this exact building, but one just like it that was torn down many years ago. My mother raised me and my siblings with nothing in a tiny two-bedroom apartment. We didn't have much, but we had each other. Now women here aren't even getting that chance."

Kenna nodded in understanding before leaving the apartment with the two women still inside. Her mind a flutter of questions. Could Dr. J be correct in thinking the government was trying to eliminate the lower class? It seemed absurd. But the reproductive restrictions had gotten increasingly more difficult and she could see how the poor would be at a disadvantage for their rules. She wanted to know more and was determined to get to the bottom of what the doctor had said.

For the past week after meeting Dr. J, Kenna had been doing research into the reproductive restrictions and all the changes to them over the years. It was a daunting task, as they practically hid the information in the bills and revisions that had to be passed through the government leaders. It seemed to her that over the years, they passed minor changes to the restrictions without drawing much attention. But over time, these slight changes added up to the harsh restrictions in place today. Through her research, she found that most of these changes affected the lower class more severely than the middle or upper class. And ultimately made it impossible for them to get their applications approved.

Growing up, they had it hammered into their heads at school and in the community that the reproductive restrictions were the saving grace of mankind. And they played a vital role in saving humanity and restoring the Earth back to a healthy state. Kenna, like most others she knew, believed that the restrictions were for the best and part of a fair system. Finding out how discriminatory they were now was causing her to doubt everything their government had pushed them to believe.

One day when she was visiting Becca, who was now done working and hiding out at home almost twenty-four seven, she brought up her concerns for the reproductive restrictions after divulging her run in with Dr. J.

"Becca, you've been denied four times. After your denials did you ever do any digging into the reproductive restrictions?" Kenna asked curiously.

"Not really. I mean I looked for ways I could improve my application for the next round but that was it. That is until I turned my focus onto getting pregnant without getting accepted," Becca said as she rubbed her growing belly.

"Well I have been thinking about them a lot lately. Why they were started and the process of how they came to be. Through my research I have found that they have changed a lot over the years and all of these changes affect the lower class more than everyone else," Kenna explained. "I think Dr. J was right about everything."

"It makes sense," Becca agreed.

"But to wipe out a whole class of people? That seems farfetched, doesn't it?"

"I don't know. I mean, if you think about it the lower class needs the most funding and are the ones that use most of the medical resources but don't contribute much monetarily to the system. That's probably why they want to wipe them out," Becca observed solemnly.

"But they are real human beings. People that

just want to live and have children of their own," Kenna said.

"I don't think our government cares about that," Becca added.

"I don't think they do either. What they are doing is terrible if that is truly what is going on."

Having been wronged by the system already, Becca was easy to convince that it was corrupt and had been planned to eliminate the lower class.

They discussed it for hours, Kenna was becoming obsessed with it. After doing arduous research and discussing it with Becca, she decided that something needed to be done to stop it. But what? She wasn't sure what she could do or even where to start. Becca didn't want any part in the action since she was trying to keep a low profile. But she encouraged her friend to keep digging and bring to light the injustices that were being allowed.

Emmett had started talking to her again, but was still his normal, absent self. One night while they were eating Chinese takeout, she brought the subject up to him. She told him about all the information she had found and how wrong she felt it was that the lower class was disadvantaged in the application process. Conveniently, she left out the part where she went to visit the doctor because she knew Emmett would lose his mind if he found out she had gone there. He listened as she rattled off the laws and revisions that had contributed to the unbudging restrictions. After she had finished, she looked at him for his thoughts.

"I think you should stay out of it, Kenna," he said as he took another mouthful of lomein.

"How can you say that?" she fumed. "Someone has to stand up for those who can't stand up for themselves."

"Yeah, someone should, not you. Especially when your mom is the Mayor and is running for region four chair in the next election. Imagine how that would look if you caused a stir right now," he said.

"I'm not sure I have the capability of causing a tiny ripple, let alone a stir," she half joked.

"Just try to forget about it and focus on your practice. In a few short months, we will be able to apply again and we will be busy with that," he said nonchalantly.

Kenna was a little scorned that Emmett didn't support her in something she felt strongly about, but she wasn't surprised. He had been absent before and ever since he found out about Becca, he had been telling her to stay out of it and encouraged her to walk a straighter path. But this was not something she could just forget.

Disappointed in Emmett's lack of support, Kenna found herself reaching out to someone else, Alec. She wanted someone to confide in that would believe her and try to help her in a meaningful way. Although she had only known him a short time, she felt he could be trusted and would have some ideas about how she could make a real difference.

After her talk with Emmett, Kenna thought about her mother and her campaign. Not wanting to derail her mother's career, she decided that anything she did would have to be done as professional as possible. She knew it would take time and would probably never change how things were, but she felt she had to try.

Arriving first at the coffee shop, Kenna sat at their normal table and ordered two black coffees. Alec arrived a short time later and he greeted her with his usual dazzling smile before sitting across from her at the small table. He picked up the coffee and blew on it before taking a gingerly sip, careful not to burn his tongue.

"What's up?" he asked intrigued, he was hoping she wanted to meet to discuss taking their relationship to the next level.

"Theres something I want to discuss with you, and I hope you can help me with it," she said.

Kenna went on to tell Alec about Becca and about her run in with Dr. J, keeping the names and locations out of the conversation to protect her friend's anonymity. Taking a piece of paper out of her bag, she showed him the succession of revisions to the restrictions that had been approved in the past few years. She discussed how these changes have negatively impacted the lower class. When she finished, she waited for his response.

"That's unbelievable. I had no idea," he said.

"Neither did I, and I'm sure not many people are concerning themselves with the reproductive struggles of the lower class," she replied, and he nodded in agreement.

"So, what do you want to do about it?" he asked.

"Well, that's where I need your help. I'm not sure where to start," she answered. "I don't want to do anything to compromise my mom's campaign, though."

"I have some political connections I can reach out to subtly to inquire about this," he said. "Don't worry, I'll be vague about the details."

"That would be great. At least maybe I could get some direction," she replied.

"It's nice seeing you, other than for work," Alec changed the subject.

Kenna wasn't sure how to answer him. "You mean seeing each other as friends?" she asked without looking up at him.

"I don't want to be your friend, Kenna. I want to be more than that," he leaned over the table to be closer to her as he eyed her neck like he wanted to bite it.

Kenna sat back in her chair to put some distance between them so she could think clearly. When he looked at her like that her stomach flipped like she was on top of a rollercoaster and her cheeks immediately blushed. The area between her thighs felt warm as she tried to regain her senses.

"Alec, I know what you want. You've made yourself clear. But, like Iv'e told you time after time, I'm married," she said trying to sound stern but sounding rather husky instead.

"But are you happy?" he questioned her as he sat back in his chair studying her face for the answer.

Kenna was not able to put on a poker face and lie to him. She just turned away from him looking down without answering.

"I could make you happy."

"Please stop," she could feel her defenses against him wavering.

By her request he stopped. He knew that he was breaking down her walls and he could see that she wanted him too. He knew that eventually she would give in to him, and when she did he would be ready for her.

Kenna and Alec parted ways outside the coffee shop and she walked the short distance home in the frigid cold with her scarf covering half of her face and her hood up to shield her from the wind at her back.

Her thoughts we swarming with everything Alec had said to her. She felt guilty for meeting with him outside of work. Knowing how he felt about her, she knew she should stay away from him, but he made her feel so confident, so wanted. She craved his attention and praise like a drug that she couldn't quit. As she trudged through the snow she chastised herself for continuing to put herself in these situations with him.

Maybe if Emmett wasn't so absent and unsupportive of her she wouldn't be looking for attention elsewhere, she thought to herself. Thinking of Emmett and their rift brought up her feelings of loneliness and anger towards him. She wished things were different, that their application hadn't gotten denied. That's what started it all.

CHAPTER 20
Uncovered

The cool air was slowly warming as spring made her entrance. Snow disappeared and the ground was soggy. Victoria stepped out of the black SUV she was in and told her driver to get some lunch before coming back to pick her up. Looking up at the tall building in front of her, she entered the hospital in search of her son-in-law. Giving him a short heads up, she had texted him on the drive over and asked him to have a quick lunch with her at the hospital. He agreed to meet her at the cafeteria, but made it clear he did not have much time, which was fine with her. She was, after all, a very busy woman herself. In fact, she didn't really have time to spend on this lunch encounter today, but she was squeezing it in for fear that her daughter's marriage was falling apart.

When she reached the cafeteria, she scanned the room for Emmett. The large open room was crawling with people, mostly workers in scrubs with the occasional patient visitor sprinkled in. It smelled of greasy french fries.

Seeing that there was no line at the salad bar, she went to fill her plate from there before getting in line to pay. Finally, she located Emmett at a booth near the back, sitting alone in his powder blue surgical scrubs. Greeting him with a warm smile, she took a seat across from him. Briefly, they chatted about his work and her campaign before he turned to her and asked why she wanted to meet today. He could tell she had a purpose for their lunch today and he was not excited to find out what her issue was.

"Even though I have been busy campaigning, it has not escaped my attention that you and Kenna are having a hard time," she said.

"Did she tell you that?" he asked.

"Are you kidding? She doesn't tell me anything," she replied, half joking.

"Things have been somewhat strained at home. They say every marriage has ups and downs and I would say we are in a low spot," he answered disheartened.

"I don't pretend to know what's going on in Kenna's mind, but I know my daughter is unhappy and elusive when we talk. I think she is lonely with you working so much," Victoria said.

"I'm sure that's a big part of it, among other things," he said without divulging the illegal activity Kenna had involved herself with.

"I am concerned about your marriage, and I

think you need to take some time to focus on it, which means stepping back from work a bit. No one went to the lake cabin all last summer. Why don't you plan a getaway and take her there? It has always been one of her favorite places," she suggested.

"I know you're right, and we need to work on some things at home. I'm just tied up at work with this research study and it's hard to get away. In a few weeks, once it's done, I will have time to take a break. I think going to the cabin would do is both some good," he said.

"Just don't wait too long," Victoria warned.

Once they finished with their meal, she bid him goodbye as he went back to the OR and she went to locate her driver. She had a packed afternoon of meetings with her team and an interview with a local news station. The shiny black vehicle pulled up outside the door just as she was exiting. Perfect timing. A chill was filling the gray air and a light drizzle of rain was just beginning.

Victoria returned to her office for her meetings. The large windows looking out onto the dark gray sky showed the occasional white hot flash of lightening and the rain was pouring down in sheets now. A short young man wearing all black entered her office. He was part of her security detail and she had assigned him to trail Kenna. She felt guilty about having her daughter followed. It made her feel slimy to betray her trust like that. But she couldn't rely on Kenna to tell her what was going on and she couldn't afford a scandal during her campaign, so she did what was necessary. The young man continued to stand with his hands behind his back during their conversation.

"So Trent, what have you found out about this new friend of my daughters?" Victoria asked.

"Ma'am, her name is Becca Wilkins and she is an elementary school teacher. There is not anything out of the ordinary with this woman, except it appears she may be pregnant," he replied.

"Why would that be out of the ordinary?" she asked.

"I checked the application approval records from this year and they did not approve the Wilkins, they were denied," he told her.

"Very interesting... Make sure you keep this information between you and me, Trent," she advised him with a stern look.

"I always do ma'am." And he turned on his heel and left her office.

Sitting back in her large leather chair, she thought about the information she had just received. She realized Becca must have had an illegal heranon removal and Kenna was somehow part of it. Surprised that Kenna would involve herself in illegal activity, Victoria questioned what else she was up to. It was time she paid her daughter a visit and had a chat with her about her recent life choices.

The following day, as Kenna walked to her office, she noticed signs of spring approaching. Green grass was starting to poke through the cold wet ground and buds were appearing on the trees that would soon be vibrant leaves. The air smelled of spring rain from this morning, yet the sun was peeking out brightly between wispy clouds. She enjoyed the changing of one season to the next. It was a friendly reminder that change was good, and everyone needed change in order to grow.

Gracefully jumping over a large puddle in her path, she was almost to her office when she felt her phone vibrate in her pocket of her light jacket. Glancing at the sleek glass screen, she saw a text from her mother asking her to get lunch near her office today.

Before Victoria had started on her campaign, it was not unusual for them to meet up for lunch or coffee when she was in the area. But she had been so busy campaigning that Kenna had scarcely seen her mother in months. She admitted to herself that she had also been avoiding her since she had been helping Becca. Although she was an adult and was perfectly capable of making her own decisions, the teenage urge to please her mother but also rebel at the same time overtook her.

Replying via text, she agreed to meet Victoria at a little mom and pop diner near her work.

Kenna took a deep breath as she entered the building and took the stairs to her office. She was already anxious about the lunch and hoped that her mother didn't have any ulterior motives for meeting up with her. She would have to make it quick and be sure not to let anything slip about Becca. Her mother would be furious if she knew what Kenna had been up to with her friend.

Walking into her small but cozy office, she flipped on the lights as she went and the soft glow warmed the space. The light accentuated her colorful watercolor paintings on the wall. She stopped to look at one of her favorite paintings she had ever done. It was a watercolor landscape she had painted from the deck of the family lake house. It overlooked the small lake surrounded by tall hills of pine and birch trees. The greens and whites of the trees reflected off the blue green water of the lake. She smiled as she remembered times spent there. It was there on the deck of the lake house that Emmett had proposed to her on a beautiful fall day, with the brilliant reds and oranges of changing leaves in the background. It was perfect. They were perfect. What happened to them? She wondered again for what seemed like the thousandth time.

Her morning passed by quickly as she saw one client after the next, listening to their triumphs and despair, drinking coffee and taking notes as they talked. Once her last appointment of the morning left, she told Glenda she was going out for lunch and left with her olive green spring jacket hanging over her arm. Victoria had offered to have her driver pick Kenna up, but Kenna liked to walk. It helped clear her head and gave her a boost of energy to get through the second half of her day.

The diner was small and resided in a little old brick building downtown. A faded swinging sign squeaked in the light breeze as she entered the door. Her mother saw her enter and waved at her from a booth by the front window. She was sipping a cup of steaming coffee, leaving the print of her nude lipstick behind on the white cup. She stood as Kenna approached her table and pulled her in to an embrace that lasted longer than Kenna had expected. They took their seats and exchanged pleasantries about the weather and what they would order for lunch. After they had given the aged waitress with a checked apron their order, Victoria clasped her hands together on the table and studied her daughter. She knew she had to choose her words carefully when talking to Kenna as to not drive her away and get shut out.

"I'm sure Emmett told you we had lunch yesterday," she started out.

"He didn't actually, but he was home late and left early so we didn't really have time to talk," Kenna replied, keeping her voice light.

"How has it been going between you two? I know he has been working a lot. It must get lonely being at home without him much of the time," she asked kindly.

"He is very busy, and so am I with my practice really taking off this year," Kenna replied. "We talk when we can, but it's not much."

"That's why I had lunch with him. I think you are both working too much and need to step back to spend more time together. Maybe take a vacation together," Victoria suggested. "With your application period coming up soon, a vacation would do you good before you start trying for a family."

Kenna did not reply right away and instead looked down at her coffee mug she was holding between her hands. "I almost forgot we can apply again soon," she said without looking up at her mother.

"How could you forget? Last year at this time, it was all you could think about?" Victoria asked.

"We've both just been busy, that's all," she replied.

"Busy giving lectures at the college? For that guy, what was your friend's name again?" Victoria asked.

At the mention of Alec, Kenna tensed up, sensing that her mother was trying to pry. "His name is Alec, and yes, I have given a few lectures for his classes. I quite enjoy it and think it's a great opportunity," she answered.

"I'm sure you're enjoying it," Victoria said somewhat sarcastically as her brows raised above the rim of her dark glasses.

"It's not like that, mother," Kenna hissed back quickly.

"Kenna, I am your mother and I could sense that there was something going on with you two when we bumped into each other," She scolded.

Kenna's cheeks flushed pink and she felt exposed. One of her secrets she was hiding from herself, let alone others, was now known by her mother. Now that it was uncovered, it was real and she felt ashamed knowing that she had almost betrayed the person she loved the most in the world. She couldn't bring herself to lie to her mother or meet her prying gaze.

"Whatever was going on, end it. Focus on your marriage with Emmett. I will not have a scandal," Victoria said sharply.

Kenna nodded her head, knowing that her mother was right but resenting her for it at the same time. How she could still find ways to boss her around even as a grown adult annoyed Kenna. "I understand," she said.

Now that Kenna's guard was down, Victoria knew she should ask about Becca to see if Kenna would open up, but she hesitated because she didn't want to push Kenna away.

"What else is new with you? Any new friends?" Victoria asked.

"Nope, nothing new," Kenna replied, her voice still tinged with anger. She thought the question was odd.

"How about your new teacher friend?" Victoria asked casually.

Kenna stiffened at the mention of Becca. She couldn't remember if she had mentioned her to her mother. Maybe Emmett had mentioned her. "Her name is Becca, and we have been hanging out recently," she replied trying to keep her tone neutral. "How is the campaign going?" She tried to change the subject.

"The campaign is going well. We have a comfortable lead from the closest contender based on initial surveys and if things continue on this trajectory, we will win in the final vote. Clayton has been doing a marvelous job. I think he has a bright future in politics," Victoria said.

Kenna smiled. She was happy to hear her brother-in-law was succeeding, but it did not surprise her he had the makings of a politician. She hadn't talked to Kassi much lately, and it pained her to see their relationship strained. Now that the pain from her denial had faded, she knew she should further mend things with her sister. Especially since her new niece or nephew would be arriving soon.

"Does your friend have any children?" Victoria circled the conversation back to Becca, watching Kenna carefully.

"No," Kenna replied. She tensed at the question and wondered what her mother's sudden interest in Becca was all about.

"But she's pregnant now," Victoria said the

statement more like a question, an invitation for Kenna to come clean.

Kenna straightened her shoulders and felt a chill run down her spine as she looked up at her mother. "How do you know she's pregnant?" She gasped and her hand flew to her mouth when she realized how. "Have you been following me?" she asked with a look of shock on her face.

"Kenna, I am just looking out for you," Victoria said matter-of-factly.

"That's bullshit and you know it. I cannot believe you," Kenna said, shaking her head in disbelief.

"What I am concerned about, Kenna, is that your pregnant friend's application was denied, and so we both know what that means regarding her pregnancy. I cannot believe you got yourself involved in something like that. It's not like you," Victoria said, trying to sound concerned but coming off more authoritarian.

Kenna looked at her mother with wide eyes, she was scared that her mother would turn Becca in. "You won't turn her in, will you?" she asked, pleading with her mother now.

"Of course not. I can't have my daughter involved in something like that during an election. I will not turn her in, but you need to stay away from her and the trouble that will undoubtedly follow her," Victoria replied cooly.

Kenna let out a sarcastic laugh. "I should have known this was all about your campaign. Here,

I thought you were actually concerned for your daughter," she said as she got up from the table to leave.

"I am worried about you, Kenna," Victoria said honestly as she looked into her daughter's fiery eyes. Kenna's shoulders dropped as she let out a defeated sigh and turned to leave her mother sitting there alone.

Victoria sat for a while to think about her life and relationships with the ones she loved, something she had not had the luxury to do lately. Sincerely, she hoped Kenna would work things out with Emmett and distance herself from her new friend. She wished that her relationship with Kenna was different and hated that she always came off so cold to her youngest daughter. Maybe when she had more time, she could change all that, but right now she had to get to another meeting.

CHAPTER 21
Family Bond

Kenna was brushing her teeth, the sound of her electric toothbrush filling her head when the feeling of her phone vibrating in her pocket alerted her. She glanced at the screen and saw that Kassi was calling her; she hit ignore and continued getting ready for work. Thinking about Kassi made her regretful. She never intended for the relationship to become so strained because of her jealousy of her sister's pregnancy. They had been so close for all their lives, scarcely ever going more than a few days without talking on the phone.

Her phone lit up again, and this time there was a text.

Kassi:Answer your phone damnit! I need your help.

Kenna quickly called her sister back, eager to know what was so urgent. When Kassi answered, she was talking to her kids and Kenna could tell by the sound of her voice that she was trying to remain calm in front of them. But there was fear in her voice.

"Kassi, what's going on?" Kenna asked anxiously.

"My water broke. I can't believe this is happening. I'm only thirty-five weeks pregnant. Agh," she let out a groan, "I'm having contractions every few minutes and I need you to come take me to the hospital. I don't think I can drive myself."

Kenna was frantically throwing on clothes and running to the door as she listened to her sister groan in pain on the other end. She fumbled for her car keys in her purse to lock the door in her panicked state.

"Where the fuck is Clayton?" she asked as she got into her vehicle and started in.

"He's out-of-town working for mom. The neighbor girl is going to come and watch the kids until Clayton's parents get here in a few hours. Agh, hurry," she pleaded and hung up the phone.

Kenna drove desperately, trying to get to her sister. Ashamed of her pettiness and envy towards her sister, she silently scolded herself for avoiding Kassi during her pregnancy.

When she arrived at Kassi's, she threw the car in park and ran inside with the car running and the car door open. The babysitter was in the family room with the two kids, who waved excitedly at her as she passed. She waved back and it pained her heart that she had not spent much time with them these past several months.

As she entered her sister's room, she heard heavy breathing and saw her sister leaning over the bed with her elbows resting on it. Her normal put together appearance was gone and she stood there with a crooked pony tail and mascara stains around her eyes. Kenna spotted an overnight bag on the floor by the bed and she threw the straps over her shoulder and went to her sister's side.

Kassi grabbed Kenna's hand and squeezed as she felt another contraction coming. "Get me to the hospital. The baby is coming fast. It never went this fast with the others." Kenna could tell from her sister's voice that she was scared and she knew she had to step up and take charge.

"Let's go," Kenna said as she steered her sister out of the room and down the hall towards the front door. The kids looked at their mom with worried expressions as she passed them with Kenna's help. "Everything's okay kids, mommy is going to be okay," Kenna tried to reassure them.

Once in the car Kenna was back to speeding down the road, this time toward the hospital. Kassi gripped the door ledge with one hand and the other hand held her belly. She writhed in her seat and groaned as wave after wave of contractions went through her. They arrived outside the ER door and Kenna ran in for a wheelchair and swiftly took Kassi inside.

Within minutes they were rushed upstairs

and were being assessed by the OBGYN, they strapped monitors around Kassi's belly. The nurses and the doctor were looking at the monitor readings and speaking in hurried, hushed voices. Kassi was in so much pain now she couldn't hold back her screams, and Kenna did her best to remind her to breathe while holding her hand.

"Something's wrong. They look worried and this doesn't feel like it did with my other two," Kassi told Kenna breathlessly between contractions that were now so close together they seemed to never let up.

"Mrs. Brooks, it appears your baby is in distress and we need to act quickly now to deliver the baby safely. Despite being in active labor and in pain, your cervix has not dilated enough for the baby to come through. We need to take you to the operating room to do a cesarean section right away," the doctor explained to Kassi calmly after her last contraction.

Kassi just nodded in understanding to the doctor, with tears filling her eyes. This was not the outcome she had planned for, but she knew she had to do what was needed for her baby. They wheeled her down the hall to the OR, showing Kenna where she could change into scrubs and handing her a white bouffant cap to cover her hair.

After Kassi had her spinal injection, she was lying on the operating room table with blue drapes covering her body. It blocked their view of the surgeon working at her belly. She was no longer in pain. A calmness had washed over both of them as they waited and hoped that everything would be okay.

After what seemed like only a few brief minutes, they heard the triumphant cry of the newborn baby fill the room. They smiled at each other with tears of joy filling their eyes as the doctor held up a tiny, wrinkly baby boy covered in a thin white substance. After cleaning him up and wrapping him in a warm blanket, they placed the baby on Kassi's chest so she could bond with her new baby while they closed her up.

Kenna watched as Kassi kissed the baby boy and he nuzzled his cheek next to hers and sleepily closed his tiny eyes. In that moment, she felt pure joy for her sister and she was no longer jealous of her and her pregnancy. She decided she would do everything she could to rebuild their friendship and be present in her niece's and nephews 'lives.

It was now midday and Kassi was settled in her hospital room with her soon-to-be named baby boy. For being born early, he was doing well and they let him stay in her room. Sunlight filtered in through the window and felt warm on Kenna's skin, and she sat and marveled at her sister. Just hours ago, she was in so much pain and went through major surgery, and now she sat smiling and cooing at her baby as if nothing had happened. Kenna thought she was amazing.

They were both surprised when Clayton breathlessly ran into the room. He immediately went to Kassi's side and hugged her while apologizing over and over for not being there for the birth of their third child. A silent tear trailed down his clean-shaven face as she handed him their baby boy. He smiled and was absorbed by the wonder of new life.

Kenna gave the once-again parents some privacy and quietly slipped out of the room with a little wave to Kassi as she left for home.

Kenna walked down the aisles of the grocery store getting food for the week when she noticed a familiar-looking woman following her. The middle-aged woman was wearing dress slacks and a white button-down shirt. She had short brown hair and kept peering at Kenna over her black rimmed rectangular glasses. Kenna thought it must be her imagination that the woman was following her, so she ignored it and went to the produce section. As she was sorting through avocados, she heard a woman clearing her throat behind her. When she turned to face the woman that had been following her, she still could not remember where she had seen the woman before.

"Hello," the woman said, "my name is Mary, and I rarely do this, but your case really stuck with me."

"I'm not sure what you're talking about?" Kenna asked, confused.

"I am part of the committee that reviewed your application," she paused and looked around to make sure no one was in earshot, "and I wanted to let you know I am sorry we denied your application. It was very strange. It was almost unanimous to approve it and then one member of the committee wanted it denied and he swayed a few of the others and won the vote," she explained.

"Why would he do that if it seemed like a sure thing for the approval initially?" Kenna studied the woman's face for answers.

"I have no idea. Like I said, it was strange. A few of us suspected that there was something more going on. Anyway, I'm sure you'll get approved next round, but I felt like you should know. Have a good day," the woman said as she left Kenna standing in the aisle confused.

Kenna pondered what the woman had told her as she finished her shopping, and it was still on her mind as she drove home. Wondering who the man on the committee was and why he was so hell bent on getting their application denied, she could not come up with any explanations. But she knew one thing, and it was that she could not trust her mother and she had friends in the committee office.

Later that day, she decided to pay her

grandmother Eleanor a visit. She knew that her mother was out of town and she would not run into her there. When she arrived at her house, she found her grandmother appeared older than the last time she had seen her and she was now walking with a cane around the house. Time was catching up with her. Seeing her so frail made Kenna feel guilty for being so absent the past few months.

Eleanor poured them some iced tea and they sat in the sunroom. It was busting at the seam with house plants. They caught up on life and discussed Eleanor's plans for the garden this spring. Kenna was happy to see that her grandmother's mind was not yet failing her and she was as sharp as she had ever been.

"Now that spring is here, I am sure you and Emmett are ready to apply again," Eleanor said in a questioning tone, as if she was inquiring more about the status of her and Emmett's relationship.

"I've just been so busy that it honestly has not crossed my mind," Kenna replied over her iced tea.

"It seemed like this time last year it was the only thought that occupied your mind," Eleanor said questioningly.

"A lot can happen in a year, grandmother," she said bluntly, taking a sip of her tea.

"That is true. People grow and change," Eleanor replied knowingly.

Kenna thought about what her grandmother had pointed out to her. She hadn't thought about getting her application ready again, and this surprised her. She wanted a child, more than anything in this world. Why did she not feel the same about it now? Did Emmett still want to have a family with her? Did she want to have a family with him?

Her thoughts were interrupted when her grandmother asked her to run upstairs for her and get her a sweater from her room. As Kenna climbed the old wooden staircase, she worried at the thought of Eleanor trying to navigate them in her ailing state. When she reached the threshold at the top of the stairs, she saw that the door to her mother's office was open and her desktop was on.

Unable to resist the temptation to look through her mother's things, she quickly went to the office and sat down. She knew she had to make this fast. The computer was locked and she tried several passwords and was getting discouraged when finally she got it unlocked. Her mother had used a password that was on their family computer when Kenna was growing up. Looking nervously at the door every few seconds with her palms sweaty and her heart beating a little too fast, Kenna went straight to her mother's email. Scrolling down to June of last year and stopping at her birthday, Kenna's heart stopped when she found it. An email to someone named Tom. Tears of rage filled Kenna's eyes as she read the words that her mother had typed:

Tom,
Please make sure Kenna's application is denied. Will explain later. Keep this between us.
-Victoria .

She wondered why a mother would do such a thing to her own daughter. How could she sink so low and do something so deceitful?

As calmly as she could, Kenna logged out of the computer and fetched a sweater from her grandmother's room before heading back downstairs. She was so angry and still trying to process everything she had seen that she bid her grandmother farewell and cut their visit short.

When she got to her car, Kenna let out a scream and hit the steering wheel with her palm, wishing it was her mother's face. She allowed her angry tears to fall as she drove home, steaming in frustration.

By the time she got home, she had calmed down and was now advising a plan to confront Victoria. She stayed up until Emmett got home so she could tell him what had happened. At first he was confused and in disbelief, but he also knew what Victoria was capable of.

"But why did she do it?" he asked with his brows knit together questioning.

"That's what I am going to find out," Kenna

said. She had also planned to question her mother on the reproductive restrictions, but she didn't share that with Emmett because she knew he wouldn't approve. If the government was truly trying to get rid of the lower class, Kenna had a feeling her mother would know about it.

The following morning, she texted her mother and apologized for storming out of the coffee shop. She then invited Victoria to dinner one night that week at a new restaurant downtown she had wanted to try. Victoria accepted the apology and invitation, and they made plans for Friday night. Although Emmett was furious at what Victoria had done, he preferred if Kenna confronted her alone. She agreed that the conversation should be between her and her mother.

When Friday night rolled around, Kenna met Victoria at The Table, which was a bistro downtown that had just opened a few weeks prior. After they were seated, their waitress brought a basket of fresh French bread with an herb butter. The rich buttery smell made Kenna's mouth water and she quickly dived in for a bite. As she chewed and listened to her mother talk, she was planning what she would say in her head, and she managed to remain calm even though she was red hot on the inside. Finally, Victoria stopped rambling and inquired about what was on Kenna's mind. This was her shot and she was going to take it. She just didn't know how to go about it.

"How involved are you with the reproductive restrictions?" Kenna asked, trying to sound nonchalant.

"As Mayor I work to uphold the law, you know that. But I haven't had much of a hand in them thus far. Why do you ask?" Victoria was confused.

"Well, after being denied last year, I have done a lot of research into the rules and regulations surrounding the reproductive restrictions. Through the years, it appears they have gotten tighter and tighter and the changes they have made seem to disproportionally affect the lower class. It's like they don't want poor people to reproduce," Kenna explained and waited for a response from her mother.

Victoria aspirated some of her wine at Kenna's discovery and was coughing quietly into her napkin.

When she had finished catching her breath she replied, "Kenna, I'm sure there are reasons for the process in place and I don't think you should be concerning yourself with that right now."

Her daughter had never had the slightest interest in politics and she was wondering why she had started now.

Kenna eyed her mother suspiciously. "So it is true, they are mainly trying to restrict the lower class."

"I'll admit that it seems like the restrictions

in place do affect poor people the most," Victoria said honestly.

"That's so unfair! Can you do something about it? You know, after they elect you region four chair?" she asked.

Victoria thought back to her conversation with the other chairmen. She knew what they expected of her regarding the reproductive restrictions, and she had decided to uphold those expectations. Whether or not it was morally wrong. "When and if I am elected region four chair, I will uphold the current laws. I will not try to change the restrictions," she said, shaking her head.

This made Kenna angry inside. She suspected her mother was going against her beliefs for political gain. She was just another pawn in the game. Her frustration grew and she knew she had to confront her mother about their last application.

"As you are aware, Emmett and I are eligible to apply again in the upcoming months. I keep remembering the last time and the hurt it caused me. Did you ever hear anything about why we were denied from your friends on the committee?" Kenna asked.

Victoria shook her head as she grabbed a slice of the warm bread. "No, I never heard a thing about it. But dear, that was almost a year ago. I think it is time you moved on and focused on your current application. Besides, it's very common and almost the norm to get denied your first time applying, you know that."

Kenna tried to keep her composure as she watched her mother lie through her teeth. "You are probably right, but I have a feeling there was a specific reason they denied our application."

"What reason would that be?" Victoria asked.

"Oh, I don't know. Maybe someone with friends in high places did not want our application to be approved." Kenna said as she stared hard at her mother.

Victoria paused for a second like she was choosing her next words carefully. "And why would they want to do that?" she asked innocently.

Kenna sat back in her chair and crossed her arms over her chest. "You tell me why. I know it was you." Her eyes shot daggers at her mother, and her mouth was set in a hard frown of disappointment.

"Kenna, I am sorry. But you can apply again soon, and it won't be a big deal that you had to wait another year," Victoria said, although she didn't sound sorry.

"This has been one of the worst years of my life! My marriage is rocky, my best friend is having a baby illegally, and my relationship with Kassi was strained because of my jealousy of her pregnancy. All because of you! Why did you do it? Were you just being cruel?" she asked with tears of anger flooding her eyes.

"Of course not, Kenna," Victoria said with a sigh as her shoulders drooped as if the wind had been knocked out of her sails. "We thought it would make our family seem more relatable if you did not get approved the first time around like most people, and if our family is more relatable, it could mean more votes from the middle and lower classes. Votes that could mean the difference for me winning the election," she explained though she knew that this was not the answer her daughter wanted to hear, it was the truth.

"You selfish bitch, you did this for votes? I cannot believe you! What kind of mother does that?" Kenna yelled at her mother as she gathered her things to leave. She'd had enough of her mother's manipulative ways.

"Kenna, please calm down. You're causing a scene," Victoria said calmly.

"Fuck you!" Kenna said through clenched teeth.

She left her mother sitting at that table alone again and went home to Emmett. He was waiting up for her and could see when she walked in that there were streaks of fresh tears down her face and she looked broken. As he hugged her, she sobbed and let herself melt into him, and he just held her and let her get it out.

After a while, Kenna wiped her tears and blew her nose before telling Emmett what her mother had said. Listening intently, he sat on the couch and held her hand as she ranted about her mother's selfishness. He couldn't believe his mother-in-law would do such a thing. Over the years, as she climbed the political ladder, she continued to put her career above her family, but this time she had gone too far.

Later that week, Kenna was surprised when Glenda rang back to let her know that her sister and baby were there to visit her. After telling Glenda to send them back, she got up from her desk to open the door for them. Kassi was wearing jeans and a black flowy blouse that Kenna suspected were her pre pregnancy clothes. She looked great even with the slight dark circles under her eyes from the sleepless nights with a newborn. Her long, dark hair looked thick and shiny as it fell in waves down her back. She carried the baby boy whom they had named Elijah, Eli for short, in his car-seat carrier, happily just riding along.

"What a surprise!" Kenna hugged her sister and then switched her attention to her new nephew. Taking him out of the carrier and holding him as she bounced softly from side to side. He had little hair, but the little that he had was red like his father's and his eyes were light blue, like the sky on a cloudless day.

"We were at the clinic for his six-week appointment and decided to stop in and say hello, also I have to feed him before the drive home," Kassi explained with a tired smile on her face, "and I wanted to invite you to a family dinner this weekend," she said cautiously.

"Will mom be there?" Kenna asked with a look of annoyance.

"Yes," Kassi replied.

"Then I am definitely not coming," Kenna answered as she rubbed Eli's back in a circular motion. He was a calm baby and he snuggled his head into her chest as he breathed softly.

"Kenna, I know what mom did was terrible and I'm sure she regrets it. I'm not saying it was right, but I hope you can forgive her and move past this so we can be together as a family again," Kassi said hopefully.

"Easy for you to say. She didn't have your application denied on purpose for political gain." Kenna was getting irritated. "And besides what she did to me and Emmett, aren't you a bit angry that she is fine with the current laws limiting poor people from having kids?"

"It sounds worse when you say it that way," Kassi said as she plopped down on the sofa exhausted.

"How do you see it?" Kenna questioned her sister.

"I don't know Kenna, I haven't really thought about it. They put the reproductive restrictions in place for a purpose, and I'm sure there are aspects about them that are unfair, but I think we should respect them," Kassi said honestly, "and I think you should let it go and forgive mom. You can focus on your next application and we can all support mom during the final sprint of the election."

"I can't just sit by while this blatant discrimination is going on in our city, and I'm sure throughout the country. I have to do something about it. No one else will."

"What are you going to do?" Kassi asked.

"No idea. I don't even know if I can do anything that would make a difference. Not on my own, anyway," she stated.

"Will you at least wait to start your crusade until after the election is over?" Kassi pleaded.

"Sure. Like I said, I doubt I will be able to make much of a difference, but I have to try," Kenna sighed.

CHAPTER 22
Night of Life

Kenna was driving to the East Side at three o'clock in the morning, and she was wide awake despite the hour. A call from Becca had awoken her, letting her know it was time. She was in labor. As planned, Kenna was going to pick up the two women from the East Side that were going to help with the delivery. On the phone Becca sounded so calm, but Kenna was a bundle of nerves. She flew out of bed, threw on the first clothes she could find, and ran out the door. Now she was focusing on keeping her speed under control so she didn't get picked up on the way to take part in an illegal birth for a child that was conceived illegally.

When she arrived at the old church in the East Side, two dark shapes in the night ran to her car and jumped in the backseat. They greeted Kenna but did not offer their names. As she drove them back to Becca's house, she could hear them talking about the neighborhood.

"These houses are so nice," the first one whispered.

"Yeah, we don't usually get to help with deliveries in nice neighborhoods like this," the other agreed.

Kenna knew that the women usually delivered babies on the East Side, and she knew why. Alec had reached out to her to let her know he was having a hard time drumming up anyone who wanted to support her cause about the reproduction restrictions. It was looking hopeless, and Kenna doubted she could ever make a meaningful change.

Finally, they arrived at the Wilkins' house. It was now mid June and the summer air was warm as they quickly slipped inside the house under the cover of night. The lights were on low and the shades were all closed to hide them from the world outside.

Becca was wearing a comfy night gown and she walked around the living room, pausing to lean over the back of the couch with a contraction. Once it had ended, she thanked Kenna for bringing the women to her and for being there herself. To Kenna's surprise, the women had brought a blow up child's pool with them and they worked on getting it blown up and filled with warm water.

Having just experienced her nephew's rushed, somewhat stressful birth, this was a stark contrast in comparison. Kenna made everyone tea for a boost of caffeine and they drank it as calming music played in the background. The smell of Becca's scented lavender lotion filled the living room as Fletcher rubbed it on her back and massaged it in.

Her contractions became stronger and closer together. She moaned and rocked back and forth to get through them, with Fletcher by her side every second. Kenna brought her whatever she needed and lent her a hand to squeeze when she asked for it. When Becca stood up from the couch to walk some more, she let out a gasp as a gush of water gave way onto the floor. She took it as a good sign that things were progressing well and squeezed Fletcher's hand with a smile. They had waited so long for this and she could hardly believe that it was finally happening. Their baby girl was coming and Becca knew life would never be the same, but she had never been more ready.

The sun started to peek through the edges of the shades with warm, welcoming light, with hints of orange. Kenna could tell Becca was feeling a great deal of pain and yet she continued to emit a calmness through the room. Soon she could no longer stifle her cries as the pause between her contractions was less than a minute.

The two women took her by the arms with Fletcher's help and got her into the small pool. Fletcher sat in the pool behind her, and she leaned back against him. The women each kneeled down next to the pool, one on each side, with their sleeves rolled up past their elbows. Kenna kneeled next to the taller woman with black hair whom they had been calling Grace, although that wasn't her real name, and reminded Becca to breathe.

Soon Becca's contractions were so close together there was no break between. She did her best to breathe between her guttural moans and occasional swear words.

"I feel like I have to push!" she yelled while she grasped Kenna's hand, still leaning back on Fletcher in the pool.

"That's normal. You can go ahead and push with the next contraction," Grace instructed.

When the next contraction came, Becca gritted her teeth and began to bear down as Grace counted to ten. Then she stopped and started to pant until the next contraction came on less than a minute later and she pushed again.

"You're crowning. I can see a little bit of baby's head," Grace said.

Kenna wondered what Grace did in the real world. She had a hunch she was a nurse. Becca looked tired but determined and as she felt the next contraction come on, she pushed with everything she had. Kenna watched as the baby's head slowly inched forward until it was all the way out.

"That was great! That was the hardest part. Come on, you can do this!" Grace cheered her on.

"It hurts so bad!" Becca cried

"Only a few more pushes left!" Grace encouraged her.

Kenna could tell when the contractions were coming just by looking at Becca's face and body language, and she reached for her hand and held on as she pushed. This time she didn't hold back and she yelled a deep, throaty sound. Grace reached down and helped to free the baby's shoulders and after that, the rest followed swiftly behind.

"You did it!" Kenna cheered, smiling at her friend.

Grace picked up the baby and clamped the cord before laying her on Becca's exposed chest and placing a towel on top. "She's a girl and she's beautiful. Congratulations."

After a few minutes, they helped Becca out of the pool and into some dry clothes before she sat in the recliner to nurse her baby for the first time. They let Fletcher and Becca get to know their daughter while they cleaned up.

"She sure is something, huh?" Becca asked Kenna as she stared at her brand new sleeping baby.

"She sure is," Kenna agreed with a warm smile. She thought the baby was the prettiest baby she had ever seen. "Did you think of a name?" Kenna asked.

"Emma Louise, and I'll call her Emmy Lou," Becca said, beaming. She didn't know it was possible to feel this much love for someone she had just met, and the joy she was experiencing was overflowing. Even though everything that surrounded Emma's conception and birth was illegal and had to be done in secret, Becca knew she would do it all again to get here. She would go to the ends of the earth for her little girl.

After they cleaned everything up and they ensured Becca was doing well after birth, Kenna left to drive the two women back to the East Side. What a surreal night they just had together, an illegal home birth that couldn't have gone any better. Two new parents that deserved to be parents more than anyone else Kenna had ever met. The two women looked as tired as Kenna felt. They had just been through so much together that Kenna had worked up the courage to ask them some questions.

"How many babies do you deliver?" she asked.

"I lost count a while ago on the total, but we deliver a few a month consistently. Sometimes more," Grace said.

"Really? I didn't realize it was that common," Kenna stated.

"Yeah, it has been for years. We usually deliver babies on the East Side. Those are the women that need our services," she answered.

"I have been looking into that. The reproductive restrictions really make it difficult for low-income households to have children," Kenna replied.

"Difficult? They have made it impossible for the lower class to reproduce. It's a terrible system that is prejudiced against the poor and it is unbelievable that it's our reality," Grace rattled off. Kenna could tell she felt strongly about it.

"Why do you do it?" Kenna asked curiously.

"All of us that help have ties to the East Side in one way or another, and it makes me angry that the people there are having their right to have children taken away from them by the government. So I do what I can to help," she said. "Even though it doesn't seem like much."

Kenna felt the same way as Grace and desperately wanted to do something about it. Hearing another person talk about it with the same passion she felt gave Kenna hope that there were others out there that would want to help.

Kenna spent most of her free time over the next couple weeks helping Becca and Fletcher pack and get rid of a majority of their belongings. Their house had sold and they had to be out in two weeks. She was getting depressed thinking of her life without Becca and her family. They had been through so much together this past year, but she knew they had to go if they wanted to give their daughter a life where she could be free. Although she knew it wasn't possible, she hoped they could see each other again someday.

Today, she was driving Becca back to see Dr. J while Fletcher stayed home with Emma. It was time to have her heranon replaced, so she didn't conceive again and blow her cover. When they reached the East Side and parked in front of the old apartment building, they quickly looked around to make sure no one was watching. It surprised Kenna to see two small children watching them from a window in an apartment building across the street. As soon as she met their eyes, they ducked out of sight. Wondering how many children were hiding in the shadows on the East Side, she turned to walk into the building with Becca.

They crawled over the yellow tape and went in the broken door down the long hallway to the stairs. They walked in silence until they found themselves in front of room three thirty-three and knocked to enter. Once they were inside, Dr. J greeted them in her usual fashion and they all stepped aside to give Becca some privacy while she changed.

"Dr. J have you ever tried to make a change in the reproductive restrictions? Like through the correct political channels?" Kenna asked.

"Many have tried and failed. They get shut down before their cause reaches any one of importance. I, myself, have not tried to do it. I help the best way I know how," she said as she turned back to Becca and the task at hand.

Heranon placement is usually done with some anesthesia on board, but there was none of that here, and Becca was not looking forward to this painful procedure. Normally, after a woman has a child, they wait six weeks to place the implant to allow the uterus time to heal and shrink back down to normal size. Becca didn't have six weeks. So she lay on her back on the table and spread her legs apart, dreading what was coming next.

As Dr. J inserted the cool metal speculum, Becca's body tensed involuntarily. She was still sore from giving birth, and the speculum felt like sandpaper against her private parts. As she had just went through labor, her cervix was not yet completely closed and the dilation went by quickly and was less painful than the last time. Becca held on to the edges of the table and squeezed her eyes shut with every step and counted the minutes until it was over. Dr. J then grabbed a very long tool with a small blade on the end and another equally long tool with a grabber on the end that was holding the heranon. Looking through her surgical glasses with magnifiers on them, she inserted both long tools into Becca. She spent several minutes embedding the heranon into the uppermost part of her uterus.

Becca let out a small yelp when Dr. J made the cut, but otherwise she breathed through the procedure as gracefully as she possibly could with her legs open. At last it was over and she slowly sat up with some help from Kenna and sat on the edge of the bed, catching her wind before wiping up and getting dressed.

"You are leaving town, correct?" Dr. J asked Becca.

"Yes," Becca replied.

"My assistant will give you the information you need for the documentation you requested," Dr. J instructed.

The assistant wrote down an address and a passcode for them. They were meeting with some guy they called Zeek after leaving here. Becca thanked Dr. J and her assistant for everything they had done for her and they left the dingy apartment. The address was also on the East Side. When they arrived, they found themselves in front of a dive bar that looked like it attracted a rough crowd.

Unsure what to expect, they nervously went inside. The place was empty except for a few regulars sitting at the bar. They turned to stare when the ladies entered through the door. Becca cautiously approached the bar. The bartender was a heavyset man with a balding head and long beard. She leaned over the bar to ensure she would not be overheard and whispered the passcode "hidden in shadows". He nodded and motioned for them to follow him to the back of the bar. He led them to a dark narrow staircase that went to an even darker basement and left them there.

Becca went down the narrow staircase first, with Kenna close behind. When they reached the bottom, they were surprised to see a large man standing outside a metal door with a handgun in a holster on his hip. Kenna swallowed nervously as they approached him. He insisted on patting them down before letting them gain entry to the doorway. Kenna started to refuse but knew that Becca needed her with her and so she complied as this strange man patted up and down her legs, arms and torso. She was thankful that he wasn't very handsy and it was over with quickly.

Once they entered the room, there was a middle-aged man smoking a cigarette at a desk in the middle of the room. A small lamp on the desk cast a weak glow on his face and the smoke circling around his head.

Kenna didn't think anyone smoked cigarettes anymore and was wondering where he even got them. The door slammed shut behind them and another armed man stood on this side of the door.

The man behind the desk motioned for them to sit in the two chairs across the desk from him.

"You must be Becca?" he asked, looking at Kenna. She shook her head no and motioned toward Becca, who raised her hand, indicating she was the one he was referring to.

"Right. Okay then, we should have everything you need. Do you have the cash?" he asked Becca this time.

"Yes, it's all here." She handed over a small bag filled with stacks of twenty-dollar bills.

They waited as he counted the money, talking aloud to himself. Kenna gripped the armrests of the chair she was sitting in and tried to tell herself to relax. Going through this whole process with Becca, she had found herself in more sketchy situations than she had seen in her entire life and the stress was getting to her.

"Two thousand," he said when he had finished counting. I'm going to need another five hundred bucks from you today to give you all the documents.

"We agreed on two thousand," Becca stated bravely.

His face turned into an angry scowl. "I know what we agreed on, but I'm telling you I need another five hundred right now."

Becca started rummaging through her purse looking for cash, but she only had two hundred dollars on her. She was about to cry at the thought of not getting everything they needed to leave town with her little family and start over. The stress and constant watching and waiting to get caught was taking its toll on her, and Fletcher too.

Kenna fished her wallet out of her purse and gave her three hundred dollars. Becca looked at her with tear-filled eyes and mouthed a thank you before accepting the money.

"Here you go, now give my the paperwork," she said triumphantly keeping her chin up.

He handed her a thick manila envelope, and

she opened it to inspect the contents before they left him. It was all there: new birth certificates, social security cards, license and passports for her, Fletcher, and Emma. Becca was now Elizabeth and Fletcher was now Mitchell. Emma still got to be Emma, since no one knew about her yet.

"How do we know these will work?" Kenna asked.

"Lady, I am the best in the business for fake documents, probably the best in the country," he bragged.

"Are there many people who do what you do? In the other regions too?" Kenna asked curiously.

"Yeah, this happens all over the country. Lots of people running from lots of different things," he put out his cigarette in an empty drink glass on the table.

After replacing the precious documents back in their folder, Becca nodded to the man and stood for her and Kenna to leave. They got out of there as fast as they could. When they emerged on the sidewalk in front of the bar, they both let out a sigh of relief, as if they had been holding their breath during the whole encounter.

Becca clutched the envelope to her chest. It meant everything for her to live without fear with her family. They had cleaned out the rest of their bank accounts and retirement funds, and they were set to leave in the morning.

Kenna returned the following day to give a

final farewell to her friend as she left to travel across the country with her family in tow. She knew they couldn't tell her where they were going. They needed to disappear to everyone, including her, and she could accept that. She had to accept it. There was no other choice.

There she stood in their front yard, watching as they buckled Emma in her car seat. Fletcher gave her a small wave before getting into the driver's seat. Becca turned to her friend, neither one wanting to say goodbye but both knowing they had to. Kenna opened her arms and embraced Becca for the last time. Silent tears streamed down both of their faces as they held on to each other, reliving everything they had been through together in such a short period. When she finally pulled away, Becca wiped the tears from her face with the back of her hand.

Meeting Kenna's tearful gaze with her own, she said, "Thank you for everything. You've been the best friend I've ever had."

"You too," Kenna felt like Becca was dying, not just leaving forever. In a sense, Becca was dying, so Elizabeth could be born and go on with her new life. "I will miss you, a lot."

And with a last wave out the window, Becca and her family drove away. Kenna hoped that in some twist of fate, their paths would cross again. Maybe when things settled down, Becca would reach out. She tried convincing herself this wasn't the end of their friendship, but deep down, she knew she would never see her again.

As she walked home, she felt sorry for herself and this new void she felt inside, a hole that she felt needed repairing. Over the past year, she had spent so much time focused on Becca and her life, living through her, that she had forgotten to live her own life. Now it was time to get back to living.

CHAPTER 23
Making and Breaking Connections

Kenna had a new focus after Becca left and it was to fix everything in her life that she had been neglecting. Her marriage with Emmett and preparing for their next application the following month was her first priority. Although she still felt passionate about the wrongness of the reproductive restrictions, her lack of plan and connections left her feeling hopeless.

To her surprise, Dr. McColfax had emailed her and asked her to return to the university to be a guest lecturer for one of her classes. Kenna was delighted at the invitation and the opportunity to work with one of her favorite professors from when she was in school.

Going back to the GreyStone reminded her of Alec. She hadn't heard from him in quite a while and her mind was much clearer on the subject of him now. Debating if she should even let him know she was coming, she wanted to see if he had any connections to help her with her crusade against the restrictions. She also wanted to tell him she was not interested in him in any way other than working together professionally when it was appropriate. In the end, she decided she would just casually pop into his office for a quick conversation as to not make a big deal about it.

Dr. McColfax taught higher-level classes consisting mostly of graduate students and she asked her to be a guest lecture on a subject she didn't expect, starting your own practice and the business side of starting out. Her prepared lecture materials were merely copies of her monthly budgets and income. Along with information on how to get the proper licensing to own a small business. Surprisingly, she rather enjoyed putting it all together and was looking forward to teaching again.

She didn't know what her future held but she knew that over the past year she had enjoyed guest lecturing and was interested in being more involved at the college in some capacity, she just wasn't sure what that would look like and didn't want to abandon her young but very successful practice.

The following week she went to the college and gave her lecture. Afterwards, she was sitting in Dr. McColfax's office discussing future opportunities for her at the college. Kenna knew that Dr. McColfax was always getting involved in politics and had friends in the circuit, so she decided to casually bring up her thoughts on the restrictions to see if she had any information.

"Dr. McColfax," Kenna started.

"Please call me Judy," she replied.

Judy, I recall your keen interest in politics. Lately, I've been researching reproductive restrictions. I was wondering what your thoughts are on them?" Kenna asked.

Dr. McColfax looked at Kenna over her glasses. "What are your thoughts on them?"

Through research, I discovered that the government has covertly included clauses and regulations on reproductive limitations in the guidelines over time. They seem to have targeted the lower class," Kenna paused for a reaction, but didn't get one, "they've made it impossible for poor people to reproduce, and I don't think it's right," she finished.

The professor turned in her chair with the tip of her glasses in her mouth. "I see. You're sure of this?" she asked.

"I can give you my notes and the documents I found. The congressional records are public. It just took a lot of digging to find the minor changes every year. They were all small and seemed reasonable, but as they added up over the years, it's become clear to me they are prejudiced against the lower class."

"Send me what you have so I can review it. I

have a friend at the capitol that I think would be interested in this," Judy said.

"I will send it to you later today, and I appreciate your help with this. I didn't really know where to start," Kenna said graciously.

"What about your mother? Didn't she want to help your cause?" Judy asked curiously. She had always been a fan of the mayor and her support of women's rights.

"She made it clear that she will not help with this. She feels the restrictions are just," Kenna replied cooly.

"Interesting," was all the professor would say in return.

The two women said their goodbyes and Kenna reached across the mahogany desk to shake Judy's hand before she left. For the first time since uncovering the deep buried secrets of the reproductive restrictions, Kenna felt like she could do something to make a difference. She just needed the right people on her side.

As she exited the office, she turned to look at Alec's door. It was shut, but she could hear him inside. For a moment, she debated if she should even stop and say hi to him, but she knew she should tell him once and for all that she was not interested in his advances. So she opened the door.

What she saw next was unexpected. Alec was on the other side of his desk and his face was buried in the neck of a half-naked young woman sitting on his desk as he pumped his dick into her over and over.

"Oh my gosh, I'm sorry for interrupting," she mumbled as she closed the door, looking away from them. Not knowing what to do, she left.

"Kenna? You're not interrupting, Asha was just leaving," Alec yelled after her, trying to recover.

He swiftly pulled out of the girl and pulled up his pants, running after Kenna as he tried to fasten his belt.

"That wasn't what it looked like," Alec yelled pathetically.

"What it looked like was that you were fucking one of your students," Kenna said, unamused with raised brows.

Alec didn't respond right away. He was searching his brain for a reasonable excuse but was coming up empty.

"I swear it's over between me and her. It was just a mistake, a moment of weakness on my part," he explained.

"I don't care who you screw, Alec, but having sex with a student in your office is insanely unprofessional," she said sternly.

"I know." His face was full of guilt as he brought his hand up and rubbed the back of his neck in frustration.

"It doesn't change the way I feel about you," he said meekly.

Kenna rolled her eyes and crossed her arms

over her chest. "The only reason I even stopped at your office today was to let you know I am not interested in you what-so-ever and you need to stop your advances if we want to work together professionally in the future. Although I'm not sure I want to work with someone who routinely screws his students in his office," she added hotly.

He had failed to come up with an excuse and he didn't want to lose Kenna, so he acted without giving it a second thought. Alec grabbed Kenna by both shoulders and pulled her in and planted a hard, eager kiss on her lips.

Kenna got her arms between her and Alec and pushed off as hard as she could to separate them. She stared him down with fire in her eyes, and when he started to advance toward her again she pulled her arm back and let her fist fly into his face. Once he was doubled over in pain clutching his damaged nose, Kenna took the opportunity to slip away. She was breathing heavy and her head throbbed with rage as she cursed his name under her breath.

Alec, still cradling his nose, knew his chances with Kenna were over, and it was useless trying to convince her otherwise. So he went back into the building in search of Asha to make up with her. If he couldn't have Kenna, he at least wanted to get laid.

A few days had passed since Kenna had

walked in on Alec and she was relieved that she hadn't heard from him. She knew she should tell Emmett about him if she hoped to fix their marriage, even though the kiss was uninvited. Not looking forward to the conversation, she decided she would get it over with that night. It was time for Emmet and her to apply again, and she didn't want him going into an application without knowing that she had an inappropriate link to another man. It just didn't seem right to do that to him.

When he came home that night, she waited up for him in the kitchen. Needing some extra courage to go through with it, she opened a bottle of red and was on her second glass when he arrived.

"What are you still doing up?" he asked as he grabbed a wineglass out of the cupboard and poured himself a modest glass.

"I have something I need to tell you," she knew there was no turning back now. She needed to just get it out. Her stomach was in knots and she felt like she was going over the hill of a rollercoaster as she tried to find the words to tell him.

"Emmett, our marriage has been rocky at best this year and as we drifted apart, I became interested in another man." There it is, out in the open. She wished she could pull it back to the depths of her and keep it there instead.

"What happened?" Emmett wouldn't look at

her. He had his eyes fixed on his glass as he stood at the island with his jaw clenched and his mouth in a hard, straight line.

"He tried to kiss me and I punched him in the face," she answered, ashamed.

Quickly, he brought his eyes up to meet hers, they were wide with fury. "I'm going to kill this asshole."

"No, Emmett, I'm just as much at fault as he is. You can blame me. Besides the one unwanted kiss, I promise nothing physically happened between us."

He let out a small sigh of relief. "So what was it, then?" he asked sadly.

"It was nothing, just a flirtation. And it's over," she replied honestly.

"How could you do that to me? To us?" He wouldn't look her in the eyes.

"I don't know. I didn't mean for it to happen," she said just above a whisper. "I've been so alone while you've been devoted to your residency."

"That is so fucking selfish. Poor Kenna didn't get enough attention while I am working so hard to build a better life for us, for our family." He had never used this tone of voice with Kenna before. It shook her core to see him so angry with her.

"You have every right to be upset. I'm sorry a thousand times over, and if you can find it in your heart to forgive me I promise to spend the rest of my life making it up to you," she pleaded with an even sincere tone.

Silence fell between them for an uncomfortably long minute. He finally met her sad hazel eyes with a look of disappointment. "I'm sleeping in the guest bedroom tonight," he said callously as he turned his back to her and went upstairs.

Once he left her there, she cried. She cried from embarrassment for herself and for her guilt. Sitting there alone, she wished he would have yelled at her, she knew she deserved it. As she wiped her eyes and nose, she wondered how their marriage had gotten to this point, but she knew how. She had blamed it all on Emmett, on his absence and lack of participation. But the truth was, she was equally to blame. When things got tough, she went looking for affection elsewhere instead of sticking it out.

Wondering if he would forgive her, she sat alone in the dark feeling defeated. She hoped he would forgive her and that their marriage was salvageable. The farthest thing from her mind was the application process and if they would still go through with it.

The next morning Kenna was surprised to see Emmett sitting at the island drinking coffee and eating a piece of toast waiting for her. He had slept in the guest bedroom last night and hadn't said another word to her about their conversation last night. She descended the stairs and approached him cautiously.

"I had all night to think about our

conversation last night, and I've decided to forgive you and move past it. This year has been tough for us and I'm man enough to acknowledge that I have been putting my work above our marriage and have not been putting in any effort. I respect you were honest with me, and I trust it won't happen again," he said somberly. After he had been up most of the night thinking about their fight and his anger was dissipating. He knew they were both to blame for the shoddy shape of their marriage and he was willing to take some responsibility and move forward. He hoped that she would be willing to put in the effort if he was and they could still forge a future together.

"It won't ever happen again," Kenna said, shaking her head as tears threatened to spill out of her eyes.

"So, what do you say? Do you want to work on us with me?" he said as he reached his hand out to her.

"I want nothing more," she said as the tears finally spilled over and trailed down her cheeks. Taking his hand, she went to him and he held her and rubbed her back as she tried to regain her composure.

"Alright then, what do you say to an entire weekend away with me at your family's cabin?" he asked with a smile. He knew it was her favorite place in the world. A long weekend together with no interruptions from the outside world is exactly what they needed. What their marriage desperately needed.

She pulled her face out from his shoulder and looked at him, surprised. "Really? You mean it?"

"Absolutely," he replied.

She turned to run back upstairs and he called after her, "Where are you going?"

"To pack!" she yelled back excitedly, and he chuckled at her enthusiasm.

When the weekend finally rolled around, Kenna was buzzing with anticipation. It had been over a year since she had been to the cabin and she couldn't wait to get there. For as long as she could remember, her family spent a couple weeks in the summer at the lake, and it was easily her favorite place. The lots were heavily wooded, with tall pines giving the cabins privacy from each other. There was no cell phone reception for miles. That was what she loved about it, the ability to disconnect from the world and just enjoy nature and the peacefulness of your own thoughts.

Emmett was driving and Kenna looked out the window as they headed out of the city. After driving through a small suburb, they reached wide open green space with only the rolling hills, trees, and the road in front of them. It was early on a Friday morning, so there were few cars out where they were.

Kenna was amazed at the progress they had made returning old developed areas back to nature. Even during her short lifespan, the drive between the city and the lake had changed so much. When she looked out at the green hills and meadows, she could see no trace of the densely populated cities that were there many years ago. No trace of the various roads and water systems that had been ripped out as they repaired the damage done by humans and gave the land back to mother earth.

They listened to relaxing music as they drove. Neither one feeling the need to speak as they held hands over the center council and enjoyed the quietness that nature provided. Every once in a while, they exchanged shy smiles and squeezed each other's hands. It reminded Kenna of their first weekend they ever spent away together. She had taken him to the cabin and they spent the weekend swimming in the lake during the day and tangled in each other's arms all night. She blushed at the thought and turned to look out the window.

The drive took just over an hour and they arrived at the cabin before lunch time. The cabin was two stories, and the basement had a walk out on the lakeside. It was sided with cedar shakes that had faded with time. The lakeside was comprised almost entirely of windows with a large deck coming off the top level. There was a short stairway down to the lake and hundreds of feet of private lake shore with a beautiful sandy beach. Not too far out from their beach, there was an island of boulders with pine and birch trees on it. She and Kassi used to swim out to it when there were younger and pretend it was their own private island.

It was midsummer now and the days were hot, perfect for being out on the water. Although it was prime time to be at the lake, there were not many boats out, which wasn't that unusual. Most of the cabins out there were just weekend cabins and many of them only had occupants for a few weekends out of the summer. Kenna had packed a swimsuit for swimming in the lake but with no one around, she bet they could get away with hot tubbing naked. At least she hoped they would hot tub naked.

After Emmett had finished bringing in all their bags and groceries, he joined her on the deck with mojitos in hand. They sat in Adirondack chairs watching the calm lake and the occasional fish jump while they sipped their drinks. Every once in a while, they would hear a loon calling or a chipmunk rustling in the trees. There were only sounds of nature to bother them here.

They packed a picnic and took the canoe out on the lake for lunch. Emmett packed more drinks. Lake George was large, and there were many secluded bays to tuck into for a picnic. They paddled along the shore and then further into open water. Kenna leaned her head back and let the warmth from the midday sun warm her face and neck as they easily cut through the calm, clear water. She had been to the lake countless times, but its beauty was never lost on her. The water was bluer than most lakes. It was almost turquoise on a cloudless day. The sandy and rocky lake bottom was easily visualized even at greater depths, and Kenna loved spending time in the water there.

"We should plan another trip up here this summer. Soak up the warm weather while we can," she said.

"Yeah, that sounds great," Emmett replied.

They stopped paddling in the middle of a bay with no houses on the shore. Tall pine tree-covered hills surrounded them. It was serene. The air was fresh here, and she breathed deeply, taking it all in.

As they munched on cheese and crackers with fruit, Emmett poured them both another drink. They normally didn't drink this much alcohol this early in the day, but they were on vacation. So Kenna shrugged and took the crisp, refreshing drink from him and had a sip.

"I'm really glad we could finally get away together," she told him.

"It was way overdue," he replied.

"I'm not going to lie. This year has not been my favorite year of our marriage," she said honestly.

He chuckled. "Yeah, it hasn't been the best," he looked at her and shaded his eyes from the sun with his hand. "I'm sorry for that. I've been pretty selfish and throwing everything I have into this residency."

"I've been selfish too. When our application got denied, I made everything about me and instead of being supportive of you. I was childish and blamed you for not being around," Kenna admitted.

"I took you for granted. I got tunnel vision with this residency and put everything else in life on the back burner, including you. Expecting you to just wait around for me when I wasn't putting any effort in to our relationship. I'm sorry for that," he apologized sincerely.

"I'm sorry too," she said without bringing up her emotional affair again, he knew what she was sorry for.

"Residency is almost over and after boards I will have some time off before starting work, time to focus on what's important, us," he said, rubbing her upper arm with his hand. She had gone so long without his touch, she craved it and now that she was finally getting it she didn't want him to stop.

"I'd like that," she said, and she meant it.

Out of nowhere, a dark gray cloud closed in on them and suddenly they felt the cool sprinkles of rain on their skin. They quickly packed up their food and started paddling for home. As the rain started to come down harder, they laughed as it soaked through their clothes and splashed in the bottom of the canoe. After they reached the shore, they hopped out and pulled the canoe on the beach before running inside.

Once they were inside the warmth of the cabin, they looked at each other giggling at their drenched appearance. Emmett moved closer to Kenna and took her face in his hands and kissed her softly. He pulled his lips away from hers to meet her eyes and she saw a hunger in his eyes, one that matched the hunger her body felt for his. Kenna clung to him. It was crazy how he could still make her feel weak in the knees. They started removing their wet clothes without breaking their kiss. Their clothes made sopping sounds as they hit the floor. Soon they were standing in the entryway in nothing but their underwear. Their hands roaming each other's bodies like they were discovering fresh territory all over again.

She pressed her body against his as she put her arms around the back of his neck. Rain was tapping hard against the windows. He bent down and scooped her up in one fluid movement, her legs wrapped around his waist as he carried her down the back hallway to the bedroom. As he softly laid her down on the bed, the low sound of rolling thunder sounded outside and soon more flashes of lightning followed. Without fumbling, he reached behind her and undid her bra while kissing the side of her neck.

He was on top of her now with one of his hands holding both of hers above her head as he made a trail of deep kisses from her neck to her breasts. Stopping at her nipples, he cupped her breast in his hand as he circled her nipple with his tongue before sucking on it gently. He moved down slowly, tickling her with his tongue as he went. When he reached her navel, he started pulling off her panties with his free hand and she slowly raised her hips so he could remove them.

He caressed her with his tongue and fingers until she was moaning from the pleasure. When he knew she was close to climax, he moved back on top of her, entering her with his hard erection. She gasped euphorically as he thrust into her over and over again while his tongue explored the inside of her mouth. Pulling him into her with her hands on his ass, she was grinding against him voraciously, trying desperately to satisfy her craving. He knew she was on the verge of finishing, and the sound of her blissful moans drove him to a divine orgasm.

He collapsed next to her in bed and they held each other as they slowed their breathing, recovering. She rested her head on his shoulder and traced her finger along his chest and abdomen, watching his chest rise and fall with each breath. They laid that way for a while, listening to the thunder and the sound of the rain falling through the trees.

They made love again before getting out of

bed in search of food and water. She was wearing one of his shirts and he was in only his briefs as they stood in the kitchen flirting with each other as they ate their pizza.

"That shirt looks good on you," he said as he stared at her hard nipples through the white shirt.

"You don't look bad yourself," she eyed his bulge in his briefs. She loved having his undivided attention at last. The way he was looking at her this weekend, with the same hunger she felt for him, resonated in her core and pulled her to him like a magnet.

He finished with his pizza and walked over to her wrapping his arms around her waist. Her nipples brushed against his skin through her shirt and got even harder. His hands trailed down the small of her back and cupped her naked ass. She could feel herself getting wet again from his touch.

"If we don't put some clothes on, we probably won't leave the bed for the rest of the weekend," he said huskily in her ear.

"What's wrong with that?" She answered playfully as she nibbled on his ear.

He pressed himself into her and she could feel his hard cock between her thighs with only the fabric from his briefs separating him from her wet velvety sex. His hands traveled up her shirt and he circled her nipples with his fingers before giving them both a playful tug. She groaned into the side of his neck and felt his member twitch against her.

With one movement he lifted her onto the counter as her lips found his, her tongue entered his mouth caressing his. He tugged down his briefs and they fell to his ankles, the head of his dick already settled at her opening. When he couldn't take it any more he entered her fast and she inhaled sharply without separating her mouth from his. As his shaft slid into her her soft walls closed down around him.

Once he was fully inside of her he stayed there and returned her eager kisses before slowly pulling out and driving into her again. He felt her inner walls shudder against his shaft reciprocating to him.

"Fuck, baby." He pulled out slightly and drove into her again. "You feel so good."

"I'm close," she whispered into his ear before laying a playful bite on his neck. It was almost enough to drive him over the edge.

"Come with me," he breathed as he thrust into her again.

Her head tilted back as the orgasm took her and she moaned his name. She clamped down around his shaft and his grip tightened on her ass as he pushed into her, fully sheathed in her.

He shuddered as he came in her depths, burying his face in her hair. She could feel his cock pulsing inside of her as his orgasm spilled into her.

They collapsed into each other breathing heavily, he was still buried inside of her. She wrapped her arms around his neck and pulled him in tight, breathing him in.

"I've missed this."

"Me too," he said.

"We should probably get dressed now," she whispered as she traced small circles on his upper back.

"Good idea," he said slowly pulling out of her before helping her off of the counter.

After their lunch quickie, they ventured out to the hot tub to watch the rain from the comfort of the covered deck. Both in the nude, the hot water caressed them tantalizingly. They talked easily and laughed as they enjoyed each other's company. Being at the cabin together was erasing their problems of the past year and restoring them back to who they once were together.

After their skin had wrinkled, they got out of the hot tub and raced to the shower together. In the shower Emmett took Kenna in his arms and planted a sweet kiss on her forehead as he held her tight. They stood that way for a while letting the water run over them. He picked up the bar of evergreen soap and rubbed it on her back and over her shoulders, using his other hand to help wash her. She pulled away from him so that he could run his soapy hands over her chest and her breasts. Once he was finished she took the soap from him and rubbed his back and chest, her hands traveling along his body washing it away.

After they had finished with their long hot shower, she was surprised to see the rain has stopped and the sun was casting a serene golden glow through the clouds. Emmett started making a fire in the pit down by the lake, and Kenna joined him there with snacks and wine. There they sat for hours. Soon the stars were above them. It had been so long since Kenna had seen the stars. She hadn't left the city in over a year. They were so bright here, it was hard for her to tear her eyes away from them.

"Our application window is open again," Emmett said, breaking the silence. "When do you want to start working on it?"

"Are you sure you want to have a baby with me, after the year we've had?" she asked somewhat sarcastically.

"I want to if you want to," he answered honestly.

She turned to smile at him. "I'll start the process as soon as we get back then."

"Good," he nodded and turned his attention back to the lake.

The loons were putting on a show for them tonight, and they could hear calls from all around the lake. It was one of her favorite sounds and she hadn't realized how much she'd missed it.

"How are things going with your mother?" he

asked.

"Wouldn't know. I haven't talked to her," she replied, still looking at the sky.

"I don't blame you. What she did was inexcusable," he said, "but I think we should forgive her someday."

"It's not just about what she did to us," Kenna replied. "She knows the government is using the reproductive restrictions to eliminate the lower class, and she's fine with it. She made it clear she wouldn't do anything to go against the restrictions."

"How is that going?" he asked. He had encouraged her not to get involved before, but now that Becca was gone, he realized she was passionate about it and would not give up on it. If it was that important to her, he wanted to be supportive.

"I discussed it with one of my old professors and she was going to reach out to her political contacts, but I haven't heard back from her yet," she sighed. "Anyway, I promised Kassi I wouldn't continue with it until after the election was over."

"That's a good plan. Get through our application process and the election, and then worry about your crusade against injustice," he said, half teasing, and it made her smile.

They retired to bed and after one last lovemaking session, they fell asleep and didn't stir until morning. She awoke before him, surprisingly, and decided to go for a walk along the lake as the sun rose. Following the shore along their bay, she walked through the sand and ended up on the other side of the bay, facing their cabin. Taking in the view of it, she stared as the orange and pink sunrise reflected off the cabin windows and off the water before her. She reached into her pocket for her phone to take a picture. This is how she wanted to remember this place. Maybe someday she would even paint it.

When she got back to the cabin, the smell of freshly brewed coffee greeted her at the door. Emmett was up reading at the table with a steaming mug in front of him. They spent the rest of their weekend relaxing by the lake and enjoying each other's undivided attention.

The following morning Kenna was melancholic as she packed their bags to leave. The weekend had been amazing and she felt that she and Emmett had rekindled what they had been struggling to find this past year. She desperately hoped that they wouldn't forget what was important when they returned to their busy lives in the city.

Emmett, sensing her sadness, entered the room and wrapped his arms around her. "Don't worry, we will make a point to come back here more often," he reassured her.

They drove back to the city with a newfound appreciation for their marriage and each other, and they were both determined not to let it go.

CHAPTER 24
Taking Chances

Kenna and Emmett had settled back into their routine at home but made time to spend together. He was busy studying for boards and she was being supportive in any way that she could. While he was busy with that, she started getting their application together, which was easier than last time since they had already been through it once.

Thinking back to last time and the grief it caused made her nervous to put herself out there again. But knowing that they should have been approved last year, she realized that there was no reason for them to be denied this year. She hoped things would go as they should this time, without meddling from her mother.

The election for Region Four chair was just weeks away now and the rest of her family was consumed with it. Victoria had reached out to her a few times to apologize, but Kenna never replied to her. When she remembered how low her mother had gone, she still got so angry she thought her head would explode. The anger came from the heartache she had caused by her own mother using Kenna's life as a pawn in her game.

This time it was Kassi who reached out to Kenna, asking her and Emmett to join them as a family for an appearance with a local television show. She knew Victoria had put Kassi up to asking her. How would it look having Victoria's family there to support her upcoming election but one daughter missing? Not good for appearances. Kenna pondered on what was more concerning for her mother, their troubled relationship or Kenna's refusal to engage in the political game and display support for her. She guessed it was the latter.

"Emmett and I will not take part in the television appearance or any other public display of support for that woman," Kenna said, referring to their mother.

"I really wish you would reconsider. Please? Do it for the family, not just for mom," Kassi pleaded with her.

"I'm not budging on this Kassi, you're wasting your time," Kenna meant what she said.

Later that day, Kenna was surprised to hear a knock at the front door. Ruby went running toward the door, barking to alert her. She saw the black SUV parked in the street through the window and rolled her eyes. Of course, it was her mother. As she opened the door, she didn't try to hide her aggravation from Victoria.

"What do you want?" Kenna asked.

"Kenna, you're being very rude. Aren't you going to invite me in?" Victoria asked, dejected.

Without answering, Kenna opened the door and stepped aside to let her mother through. "If you have come to ask me to do the tv show, I already told Kassi I wouldn't do it."

"Kenna, I know you're angry at me and understand that. But this is crunch time with the election and I need the whole family to stand behind me on this. This is very important and is a once in a lifetime opportunity," she pleaded with her daughter.

"Even if I could just move past what you did to me and Emmett personally, which I am not ready to do, how can I show support for someone who agrees with the government overstep using reproductive restrictions to eliminate the lower class?" she said, becoming agitated.

Victoria's face was twisted in anger as she snapped back, "That is enough talk about the restrictions! I have tried asking nicely, but since you're acting like a spoiled brat, I'm forced to try another approach. If you don't show support for me in these last few weeks before the election, I will make sure your application is denied again this round."

Kenna looked at her mother with disbelief. "You wouldn't dare."

"Try me," Victoria was unwavering.

"Fine, I'll do your stupid fucking tv appearance, but after this election is over we are done." She opened the door and gestured for her mother to get out.

Victoria nodded to her daughter and took her leave. Once safely inside the black SUV, she sighed and shook her head. The conversation had not gone how she had planned it in her head. She was digging herself a hole where it came to Kenna, and she feared their relationship would never be the same. As a mother, it hurt her to see her daughter so against her. Sitting up tall, she straightened her shoulders and put her sad thoughts out of her mind. She turned her focus on winning the election. It was so close she could almost taste it. Hungry for power, she was willing to risk everything to get to the top.

The following week Kenna obediently met the rest of her family at the studio for the tv appearance. She wished Emmett was there, but he couldn't get out of his on call shift. Everyone was dressed to impress and they appeared to be a well put together, supportive family. Kenna wondered what people would think of their mayor if they knew who she really was. At least, what she had become.

They were live on the air, so they had been coached on what to say beforehand. There they all sat on a long blue couch and there was an audience, although it was hard to see them with the spotlights shining at them. The show host, a young woman with big teeth and a snug red suit dress, was asking Victoria interview questions and the rest of the family just had to sit and look nice. The producers reminded her to smile frequently throughout the interview. What a joke.

After they had finished asking Victoria questions, they asked Clayton a few and then moved on to Kassi. They were moving down the line toward her. She froze, not sure what she would say when they got to her. And then she had an idea. She could go rogue and say something about the reproductive restrictions being unjust.

This wasn't really the right time and place for it, and she thought about her mother's threats to get her next application denied. Doing this would put her future family on the line, not to mention further complicate her relationship with her mother. Her mother had the power to make sure she never got her application approved. Kenna doubted she would actually go through with getting her denied again, but lately she wasn't so sure she knew her mother, or how far she would go. The show was live and most people in their region were probably watching. If she wanted exposure for her cause, this would definitely accomplish that. Finally, the host was in front of her, asking her what she thought about the upcoming election.

"I admit I don't usually follow politics, however recently I've become concerned with the reproductive restrictions and how unfair they are towards the lower class. They make it impossible for low-income couples to have children," Kenna said to the host. Holy shit, she thought to herself, I actually did it. I'll probably regret this.

When she turned back toward the rest of her family, she saw her mother's eyes throwing daggers at her. Kassi was just looking at her with her mouth wide open in disbelief. The show host was not sure how to handle it, so she just nodded as Kenna spoke and then gave the cue to the producers to cut to a commercial break. Kenna waited for the wrath that she knew awaited her.

Victoria stormed toward her with her heels slapping the stage angrily. "What in the hell was that? What do you think you're doing?" She glared at Kenna with her hands on her hips.

"I'm bringing awareness to the wrongness of the reproductive restrictions," Kenna replied matter-of-factly. She turned to go, leaving the rest of her family there to continue the charade without her. Smiling to herself as she walked away, she was satisfied with the trouble she had stirred up. She wondered if Emmett had seen it, she hoped he would continue to support her with this. Seeing as everyone else in her family wanted her to drop it.

Victoria clenched her fists at her sides and stomped her foot in frustration. She knew Kenna had just made the election harder for her to win. Even if she won, she would have to deal with her daughter's fight for a change in the restrictions afterward. She rubbed her temples with her fingertips and returned to her seat to finish the show.

They continued with the rest of the interview without mentioning Kenna or her outburst, doing their best to redirect the conversation back to Victoria and her plans for the region if she were elected Region Four Chair. She did not address the reproductive restrictions again.

It did not come as a surprise to Kenna that after her spectacle on air, she was not asked to participate in any more pre-election public appearances. Which was fine by her. After the show, Emmett had come home from work late in the night and woke her up. She wasn't sure if he would be pissed or encouraging.

He flipped on their bedroom light and sat on the bed next to her, still in his scrubs. She sat herself up in bed to talk to him and was surprised to see him grinning at her.

"Did you see the show?" she asked as a yawn escaped her.

"I did. I think everyone did," he replied.

She shot the rest of the way up in bed and was now wide awake. "Really? Were people talking?"

she asked excitedly.

"Yeah, people are talking and I'm sure if it's floating around the hospital, it's going around the rest of the city too," he said. "You really went for it, huh?" he joked.

"I did. I didn't plan for it and in the moment I wasn't really sure it was a good idea, but something inside of me just propelled me forward," she explained.

"Do you think your mother is going to cause more trouble for our application?" he questioned gently.

"I don't know, but I hope not. I still have a sliver of hope that she wouldn't stoop that low," she replied.

"What are you going to do next?" he asked her.

"I don't know, but I know I've got to follow this up with something. There's no turning back now that it's out. I'm just one woman and I'm not sure how much of an impact I can make myself," she admitted.

He kissed her forehead. "All you can do is try," he said before getting up to shower and change for bed.

As he showered, she laid in bed, her mind racing with thoughts of what happened earlier. She imagined people throughout the entire city, and probably the entire region, talking about her and what she said on tv. The thought gave her anxiety, but also excitement. Without planning it, she had reached a vast audience and shed some light on how discriminatory the restrictions are. There was no way she was getting any sleep tonight.

As though it had read her mind, her phone vibrated on the nightstand next to her head and she reached up to grab it. There was a text from Judy.

Judy: You were right about the reproductive restrictions. I have reached out to my friends at the capital and they want to meet. By the way I saw you on tv, it was amazing.

Kenna read the text a few times before it really set in. People who actually had the ability to change laws wanted to meet with her. She couldn't believe it was actually happening. After replying to Judy, letting her know she would be thrilled to meet with her and her contacts, she went to tell Emmett about it.

He was just getting out of the shower and had a towel around his waist. His dark hair was curly when it was wet and he smelled fresh, like his rain scented body wash. Kenna paused at the door, eyeing up his naked body. His wet abs shined in the light. She felt warm between her legs and tingly on the back of her neck. It almost distracted her enough for her to forget why she came in the bathroom in the first place.

"Judy just got back to me. She said her friends at the capital want to meet with me to discuss with restrictions," she said with her eyes wide with excitement.

"That's great baby," he replied, and he meant it.

"This could be the chance I've been waiting for. The chance to make a real change. With help from the right people we can make an impact that matters."

"It's great seeing you take charge on something you are passionate about. Like you found a purpose and it lit your fire. It's very sexy."

He took her in an embrace, his hand sliding up her shirt onto her back, causing goose bumps to spread up and down her spine. As he pulled her in closer, his towel fell off, revealing his nakedness pressed up against her. She took off her shirt as she lead him to the bed. She got on top of him and they made love, but she was in charge this time. And he loved it.

CHAPTER 25
Cast Your Votes

Victoria was in her office trying to do damage control after what Kenna had done on tv. The final election was just days away and she couldn't believe her daughter would pull such a stunt, and on regional television no less. She took off her glasses and rubbed her temples before getting out some ibuprofen and throwing it back with a swig of water. This storm Kenna had created was causing her stress on top of the monstrous election stress and she was having headaches daily.

In a few minutes, the chairmen from Regions One, Two and Three would arrive at her office for an emergency meeting. They had undoubtedly heard of Kenna's spiel and wanted to chew Victoria's ass for letting it happen. She was dreading listening to what they would say.

If the stress she was feeling now was any indication of how her next four years in office would go, she wasn't sure if it was worth all the effort she was spending getting there. She almost wished she had just retired. It's not like she needed the money. She wanted the power, and today she was questioning if it was actually worth the fight and the sacrifices she had made. But there was really no turning back now.

"Ugh," she muttered to herself as she clutched her chest. It was happening again. She had been getting these chest pains for the past couple weeks, particularly when she was stressed, which seemed to be all the time lately. It had been happening so frequently she knew it was not just going to go away on its own and she finally broke down and made an appointment. Since she was the mayor, her primary care doctor arranged it for her to see cardiology right away tomorrow, thank goodness. She was hoping they could fix this. It was the last thing she needed right now just days from the election.

There was a knock at her door and then the chairmen from the other regions appeared in her doorway. She invited them in and Amos closed the door behind them. They sat in the chairs across from her at her desk, and they all had displeased looks on their faces.

"To what do I owe this surprise visit?" Victoria asked, feigning confusion.

"We saw your daughter on TV. Her outburst has caused quite the stir," Felicity said coldly.

"There has been talk about the reproductive restrictions being prejudiced against the lower class across all of our regions," Amos chimed in.

"I apologize for what my daughter did. I can assure you that I do not share her views on the restrictions and will continue to follow your plan," Victoria said.

"That's great and all, but now that the word is out, it's going to take a lot of damage control to keep this snowball from growing out of control," Jeffrey spoke up.

"I understand that this unforeseen turn of events has inconvenienced you all. And I swear I will work hard toward restoring the citizen's faith in the reproductive restrictions," Victoria pledged.

The three other chairmen exchanged doubtful glances. Victoria was nervous. She knew she needed their support. Not to mention these were the people she would work with for the next four years, and she didn't want to make it difficult before she even got started.

"Squash this now before it becomes a much larger issue," Felicity demanded through clenched teeth.

Victoria nodded in understanding. The three chairmen rose from their seats and exited her office, closing the door behind them. Sighing, she dropped her head into her hands as she rested her elbows on her desk. She hoped things would not get any worse. She didn't think she could handle anything else being thrown at her right now.

"Damn it," she swore to herself. The chest pain was back and she grabbed her chest as she focused on her breathing and remaining calm. It felt like everything she had worked so hard for was close enough she could reach out and grab it, yet it was slipping so far away at the same time.

The next day, she arrived at the cardiology office hoping to fix one of her problems so she could tackle the next one. When she arrived, she was immediately escorted back for her appointment without having to wait in the waiting room. The cardiologist recommended a stress test and they got moving to work her in right away that day.

Emmett was in clinic seeing patients and saw Victoria as she walked down the hall for her stress test. He didn't approach her, but he was curious why she was there.

They hooked her up to a bunch of monitors and had her walk on the treadmill. She started out slow and was doing fine, but when they increased her speed and she immediately had chest pain and had to stop the exam. Her EKG was abnormal, they told her.

They quickly brought her back to the exam room with the cardiologist. Emmett knew he shouldn't, but when he saw no one was watching, he stood outside the exam room door. It was cracked open, and he could hear their entire conversation.

"Mayor Carson, it appears you have pretty

severe coronary artery disease and we would recommend you have a heart cath today. We would likely have to place several stents," the cardiologist told her.

"That can't be right. I'm healthy and have had no heart issues," she stated, confused by what the doctor was telling her.

"Did anyone in your family have heart disease?" he asked.

"My father died of a heart attack in his early forties," she answered, still confused about what was happening to her.

"Likely it's hereditary, then. Your cholesterol is high even though you're at a good weight and have no other co-morbidities," he assured her. "I'm surprised the high cholesterol wasn't caught sooner."

"Well, I hate hospitals so I don't go in unless something is wrong and honestly, I have not needed to go in for anything in years," she replied, "and I can't have surgery today. The election is in three days. I don't even have time to be sitting here talking to you now."

"I don't think you understand. You're at risk of having a massive heart attack. One that could definitely be fatal. I highly recommend we take care of this today, sooner rather than later," he advised.

"After the election in four or five days, I'll do it. But not before," she said, unwavering.

He sighed, "If that's what you want, it's your

choice as long as you understand the risks. I will prescribe some nitroglycerin and a baby aspirin, along with a cholesterol medication. You need to make sure you don't do intense physical activity and try to keep stress levels low."

She laughed at that. Her life consisted only of stress right now.

"If you feel chest pain, chew a baby aspirin and take a nitroglycerin tab. Then you should go to the ER. There's a good chance we will be doing your cath and stents emergently in the next few days instead of just electing to do it today," he scolded.

"I understand, doctor. I've got a very important next three days and after that I'll do it," she promised.

Emmett was caught off guard when the door opened, and Victoria walked out, almost bumping into him.

"Emmett, what are you doing here?" It surprised her to see him standing outside her door.

"I work here," he said, trying to think of how he could defend his eavesdropping.

"Right. Did you hear my conversation with the doctor?" she asked as her eyes narrowed to slits.

He was trying to decide if he should lie and say no to cover his ass, but he also wanted to try to talk Victoria into doing the surgery sooner, since her life was at risk. He sighed and dropped his hands to his sides.

"Yes, I heard. And I really think you should do the surgery. Please Victoria, you could die," he tried to convince her.

"Mind your own business, Emmett, and if you tell a soul about what you heard, I'll make sure you can no longer practice medicine," she retorted. She turned to walk away from him down the hall and he stood there, wishing he would have lied to her.

He knew he couldn't tell Kenna without breaching privacy laws and putting his license at risk. Frustrated, he ran his hands through his hair as he went to the next exam room. There was nothing else he could do or say about the situation without breaking rules. After calming down and straightening out his white coat, he went to see his next patient.

When Victoria reached her vehicle, she instructed her driver to take her directly to their campaign office. She planned to practically live there for the next three days until the election was over. The numbers were close between her and her opponent, but she was leading slightly. They were in the home stretch and she had no intention of letting this little health issue hold her back. Her mind was already back on track to winning and she pushed her heart concerns back to the far corners of her mind.

Three days later, Kenna and Emmett were at

home watching the election results on tv instead of being at the election headquarters with the rest of her family and campaign crew. Emmett made some fresh buttery popcorn and took a seat next to Kenna on the couch. He still hadn't said or done anything about Victoria's heart condition, and he knew he wouldn't. There was too much at risk. He just hoped that she would have surgery for stents shortly after the election and then he could stop worrying about it. If Kenna found out that Emmett knew about it and didn't tell her, she would be upset. Even though she was fully aware of how the privacy laws work as a provider herself.

Kenna shoved a handful of popcorn in her mouth as her mother appeared on the screen. The buttery salty taste made her crave a glass of wine and she went to grab a bottle of red and two glasses for them. The counting of votes would take hours, but she knew they would watch the whole thing. She wasn't quite sure if she was hoping her mom would win or lose. She was torn. Victoria was still her mother, after all, and she had seen her work hard her whole life to get to this point. She deserved it and Kenna knew that, but knowing how her mother felt about the reproductive restrictions made part of her wish Victoria would lose. If her mother was determined to uphold the current restrictions it would be harder to make changes.

The leaderboard showed a real-time count

as the region's major cities submitted their final results. It was a close election and as the numbers rose Victoria and her opponent were neck and neck, one pulling ahead for a few minutes before the other rose to the top again. Two announcers were talking about how this was the closest election for region chair in history thus far. Kenna and Emmett kept shoving popcorn in their mouths until their bowl was empty, even they were feeling the stress from close election.

This continued on for three more hours and it was now late into the night. Emmett had fallen asleep and was snoring softly on the couch beside Kenna. She could not tear her eyes from the screen, not even for a minute. The camera occasionally focused on her mom and the rest of the family, waiting for the results. Clayton was pacing. He had loosened his tie and was wearing a baseball cap with their campaign logo. Kassi sat stoically in a chair next to mom. She looked perfect, as always, in a beige skirt suit and her long brown hair flowing freely around her shoulders. Victoria looked poised as she sat next to Kassi, but she was not engaging in any conversation. Kenna wondered what was going through her mind.

"This is it," Victoria thought to herself. "Victory is almost mine." It had been a long night for everyone, but the adrenaline of the election was keeping them awake. Thankful to have Kassi and Clayton by her side, she still wished Kenna was with them. She didn't have time to focus on it now, but she knew eventually when things slowed down a bit, she wanted to repair the damage she had done with Kenna.

Earlier in the night, when she had fallen behind her opponent for about a half an hour, her stress rose and she couldn't do anything to control it. The chest pain returned. She had to walk away from the noisy, stressed environment and find a quiet room to take her nitroglycerin and chew her baby aspirin. After taking some time to relax and do some breathing techniques she remembered from the last time she took a yoga class, the chest pain stopped. Thank goodness. She just needed to get through tonight. She just needed it to be over. After her chest pain went away, she returned to the others in time to see her numbers pulling ahead once again.

There was only one major city left for the count, Thayes, and the numbers were pouring in by district. Victoria kept her eyes on the leaderboard. She was in the lead but only by a little over one hundred votes and could lose the lead any minute. Come on, come on. She repeated in her head. The surrounding noise was deafening, and the air was thick with tension as everyone had their eyes on the board awaiting the last count from the last district of Thayes.

Kenna didn't realize she had scooted herself to the edge of the couch and was perched there staring at the tv awaiting the final count. Her mother was still ahead, but not by much. She held her breath. Any second now, the results would be in. "And our new Region Four Chair is... Victoria Carson!" The announcer shouted out excitedly. The camera focused on Victoria and her family. Victoria was holding Kassi in an embrace, happy tears streaming down Kassi's face with a big smile. Clayton was pumping his fist in the air and high-fiving some of the campaign staff around them. Her mother was the picture of grace with a humble smile and after she let go of Kassi, she turned to the crowd with an elegant wave and a small bow.

As she watched them all together, a few quiet tears crept from her eyes and slowly trailed down her face. She wished she was there with them, but she hated her mom at the same time. She didn't know how that was possible. After waking Emmett, she let him know her mother had won and he was glad for her, but like Kenna, he was still angry at her and didn't jump for joy.

They went to bed with Ruby trialing behind them. Tomorrow was a big day. It was their application review, and they were eager to get it over with. Kenna had made sure their application was perfect, down to the smallest detail.

Emmett was done with his residency now and had accepted a position as a cardiothoracic surgeon at the hospital downtown. This more than doubled their previous salary. There was no reason they should get denied again. And although the sting of their previous rejection was still felt, they were both confident this would be their year. Unless Victoria messed it up for them again, but Kenna didn't think she would do that. Although she had done it once before...

Their review was early in the morning, so they each set an alarm on their phone and went to sleep shortly after crawling into bed. Tomorrow could be the best or the worst day ever. Again.

CHAPTER 26
Here We Are Again

Today was the day, again. Kenna and Emmett woke up early to the sound of both of their alarms going off on their phones at the same time. Normally, she would hit snooze at least once, but today she sat up right away with her alarm. The combination of the election results last night mixed with her anxiety about today made for a lousy night of sleep.

She and Emmett brushed their teeth together in the bathroom. The only sound was the humming of their electric toothbrushes. While getting ready, he kept giving her small, reassuring smiles and brief comforting touches on her back as he moved between the bathroom and his closet. He could tell she was tense and wanted to help her relax. He also knew there was no way they would get denied again unless Victoria did the unthinkable. Again.

"How does this look?" he asked as he stepped out of his closet wearing dark khaki slacks and a light blue button-up shirt.

She looked him up and down before replying, "Looks good."

After selecting a black knee length pencil skirt with black tights and pumps paired with a white flowy button up blouse, she examined herself in the full-length mirror. She kept her makeup light and natural, then tied her hair back in a low pony with her blonde waves trialing down her back. Her hair had gotten so long over the winter, and she was surprised that it was more than halfway down her back.

After letting Ruby out, they opted to grab coffee on the way and left the house, locking the door as they went. Their car was conveniently parked right outside their front door.

When they reached the car, Emmett turned to Kenna with a playful smile. "Feels kinda weird doing this again, right?"

"Oh yeah, I'm getting some serious déjà vu," she replied with a small laugh and a wave of her hands.

He loved how she used her hands when she talked and that her smile had been so bright since their weekend getaway to the cabin. Wanting Kenna to be happy had been his key priority since passing his boards, and he knew having a baby would be everything to her. To them. He hoped that his mother-in-law didn't meddle in their business again.

As he drove through their neighborhood and

then downtown, he turned on the radio to fill the silence. He looked down at Kenna's lap as she fidgeted with her fingers. Reaching over the center console, he took her hand in his and gave a comforting squeeze. She looked up, giving him a small smile and a knowing look.

They got coffee at a drive through. She was thankful he didn't go to the same one they had gone to before their last application review. This day was weird enough without going to the same coffee place. She drank her iced coffee, that was just a little too sweet, as she looked out the window trying to distract herself.

"It's going to be fine," Emmett reassured her. "They have absolutely no reason to deny our application again."

"They really didn't have a good reason last time, but they still rejected us," she pointed out.

"It won't happen again. Plus, with your mom winning the election last night, she would have nothing to gain by blocking our application again. She's not the type of person to do it just out of spite."

Emmett was right about that, Kenna knew. Her mother may use them as pawns for her personal gain, but she didn't believe she would do anything intentionally hurtful for no reason. But then again, she was finding that maybe she really didn't know her mother very well after all.

They arrived at the Sector Building, Emmett parked in a different parking ramp than last time and she was grateful again for the change. When she got out of the car, she looked at the large office building and let out a deep sigh, one she had been holding in for most of the car ride. Then, hand in hand, they started towards the entrance.

They made their way to the familiar waiting room and took a seat facing the tv. A morning show was playing and they were discussing the close election from the night prior. The last thing Kenna wanted to think about during this meeting was her mother. When she thought of her, she instantly thought about the betrayal she had done to her and Emmett. But there she was. Her mother's face was everywhere now and would be for a while. Kenna was just going to have to get used to it.

Kenna tore her attention away from the tv and looked at a magazine on the table next to her. It was more than a year old. That didn't matter since she wasn't really interested in reading it, just using it as a distraction. She peeked over her read and observed the others in the waiting room. Their appointment was early and there was only one other couple there before them. Just to the right of her they sat, two men with their hands intertwined between them and their faces directed at the television.

She wondered if they would find a surrogate. They were scarce now that the government had regulated what they could charge for their services. The pay wasn't worth the effort they had to put in now and only the wealthy could afford to pay them more under the table to persuade them to carry a child.

They looked like a pleasant couple, and she hoped they found a surrogate. After another few minutes, the couple was called back through the heavy metal door. Kenna rubbed her hands together in her lap. She knew they were next. Her thoughts were bouncing between dreading the review and wanting to hurry and get it over with.

She looked over at Emmett. He was looking at something on his phone, but he stopped and looked at her with his full attention. He put his phone away and slid his hand closest to her around her back, resting it there while he used his other free hand to reach for hers. His touch felt good on her skin. As he slowly brushed his hand along her back in small circles, she could feel some of her anxiety melting away. She loved that he could help her keep calm and clear her mind just by being present.

Emmett did not look anxious at all. Not that he ever did. He was always a stoic and calming presence. It was part of what made him an excellent surgeon. He could remain calm and level-headed, even in the most stressful cases. She wondered if he was as nervous on the inside as she was on the outside, but she doubted it.

The elevator off to their side opened and another eager couple stepped off and made their way to the check-in desk. The woman's heels clicked on the hard floors as she walked. Being here again and seeing the other couples waiting reminded Kenna of Becca. A little over a year ago was the first time she had seen her. Little did she know then that their friendship would flourish because they bonded over that fateful day.

She missed Becca. Over the past year, she had become a big part of her life and she hadn't prepared herself well enough for her departure. She often wondered where they went and how they were doing, if they were getting settled in their new life yet. Did they go to Region One, which was not as densely populated, and where it was constantly rainy and drizzling on the coast? Or did they go to Region Two, where it was always warm and only ever snowed up in the mountains? Maybe they went south to Region Three, which had a mix of mountains, coastline, and prairie. She could play this guessing game all day, imaging who they would become now. Still, she held onto the hope that she would see her friend again someday.

Kenna's attention was brought back to reality when Emmett stood, pulling her up with him as he went. The woman must have called their names, but she didn't hear it. They made their way to the big door and followed the woman down the hall. She felt like she was being carried down the hall by an external source and not by her own two feet.

Once they were seated in the familiar review room with the review committee staring down at them, her heart raced. It took everything Kenna had not to run away from the fear of being rejected once more. She scanned the faces of the committee members and wondered if the man who helped her mother last time and denied them was still here. She hoped not. There was one familiar face. The woman who had approached her at the grocery store was staring back at Kenna with kind eyes. Kenna hoped the woman would stick up for her today if needed.

Finally they started the review, peppering Emmett and herself with question after question. She answered them honestly and professionally, hoping that they liked what she was saying. Emmett, of course, was a rockstar when it came to answering their questions. Again, she was happy and thankful to have him there by her side.

The committee could find no faults in Emmett and Kenna through their questioning, and she knew they should be approved. She still had doubts in the back of her mind because of what had happened last time. If the same thing happened again, she vowed to wring her mother's neck with her own two hands.

"I think that is enough questions," the woman Kenna met at the grocery store stood from her seat and addressed them. "Emmett and Kenna Foster, congratulations. We are approving your application. Unanimously, we agree that you would make excellent parents and wish you the best on this new adventure," she winked at Kenna.

Kenna let out all the air she was holding in her lungs and threw her arms around Emmett's neck. Happy tears were squeezing out of her eyes as she hugged him. He kissed her on her forehead and lifted her off of the ground with his embrace. After a long minute, he pulled away and took her face in both of his hands, tilting her face up and planting a soft kiss on her lips.

"See I told you, nothing to worry about," he said jokingly.

She laughed and kissed him again before turning to the committee to thank them. They both left the center of the room and walked toward the exit. This time when they passed the woman at her desk outside the door, Kenna smiled at her and walked down the hall with her head held high and a new determination.

Leaving the building this time around was so different from the last time. She was practically skipping she was so filled with enthusiasm. Last time it felt as though her life was ending, and today it felt like her life was just beginning. Unable to contain her smile, her cheeks were starting to hurt. She could tell Emmett was happy, too. He wasn't as obvious to read as she was, but he had a certain bounce in his step that hadn't been there before. Out of the corner of his eye, he kept stealing glances at her. He hadn't seen her this happy in over a year and was relieved to see it.

When they reached their car, Kenna gave an excited shriek. "I'm going to make the appointment for my heranon removal first thing Monday," she told Emmett.

"That sounds great. Let me know when it is so I can take you," he still had a few weeks before his credentialing was put through and he could start at the hospital.

Kenna called Kassi to let her know the good news. She was thrilled for them. They made plans to go out to brunch to celebrate. After choosing a restaurant downtown, Emmett and Kenna headed there to get a table while Kassi and Clayton made their way to downtown. Once they arrived at The Stone, an up-and-coming brick oven pizza joint, Kenna turned to Emmett before they got out of the car.

"I am so happy and I don't want anything to ruin our day, but I can't help being a little sad that we aren't celebrating with my whole family. Like we were supposed to last year," she admitted.

"I know, love," he said gently, putting a loose strand of hair behind her ear. "It's okay to feel sad about that. Sadness and happiness are not all-or-nothing emotions, they can live amongst each other."

"You're right," she replied and wiped her eyes.

"You always know what to say."

"I don't know about that, but I'm glad you think so," he said as he placed his hand on her thigh.

She checked her makeup in the mirror and did a quick touch up under her eyes before they went into the restaurant. The place was warm, even with the air conditioner on. With a large brick oven and cooks putting pizzas inside using huge pizza peels, the open kitchen was a sight to see. An aroma of just baked crust and melty cheese filled the air. It smelled amazing and Kenna's stomach was letting her know it was not happy she skipped breakfast.

They chose a table close to the windows and ordered a pitcher of mimosas for the table. They were celebrating, after all. As they waited for their brunch dates, they chatted excitedly about their plans for a baby. Where the nursery would be, and names they liked for a girl or for a boy were just a couple of the topics they discussed while eating the complimentary breadsticks as they gabbed happily.

Finally, Clayton and Kassi arrived. Emmett and Kenna rose to greet them. Kassi hugged Kenna and squeezed her tight. They congratulated the couple on their success with their application review, and once they were seated they all rose their mimosas in the air and gave a victorious "cheers."

As their scrumptious pizzas, Hawaiian and

supreme, were brought to their table, they were catching up on each other's lives. Clayton would work for Victoria at the capital now that she was Region Four Chair, a gigantic step for his career. Kenna was happy for him. He worked hard for his family and it was paying off. She just hoped politics wouldn't change him like it obviously did her mother.

Kassi gave Kenna the name of her doctor she recommended for having her heranon removed and later replaced. She had been through it three times, after all. She told Kenna to name drop their mom and she could probably get in the same day. Normally, Kenna didn't enjoy doing things like that, but this time she might make an exception because she was so eager to get started. She had been waiting a year for this and she didn't want to wait any longer before becoming a mother.

After they had finished eating and were just waiting for the check, Clayton and Kassi gave each other a knowing look that did not escape Kenna's attention. She waited, confused about what was coming next.

"Kenna, now that you've been approved and will hopefully fall pregnant soon, I think you should try to forgive mom. I know what she did was wrong and I'm not sticking up for her that way, but it's hard having a divided family for everyone. As you go through pregnancy and the birth of your first child, you will appreciate having family there for you. I think that if you continue this feud with mom through all of that, you will regret it later on," Kassi said.

"I appreciate your concern and I'm sure I will eventually forgive mom. Family is important to me and I want my future children to have family around. But right now when I think about her, I still mostly hate her and it's going to take some time for that feeling to go away," Kenna replied icily.

Kassi just nodded in understanding. She hoped they could all be a family again someday. After they paid their bills, they all walked out together and Kassi hugged Kenna and congratulated her one last time before leaving.

"Please think about what I said," Kassi whispered to Kenna as she pulled away from their embrace.

"I will try," Kenna replied halfheartedly.

Emmett and Kenna had a short drive home and when they arrived, they relaxed on the back patio for a while. The anxiety from the morning and the excitement afterwards had worn them both out. They assumed their normal position with him sitting on the patio couch and her laying down with her feet on his lap. He rubbed her feet gently as they relaxed.

"You know, Kassi has a point. What your mom did was terrible, but here we are now and they have approved our application. You're going to want your whole family around once we have a baby," he said calmly.

"Oh no, not you too. Why does everyone think I should jump at the chance to forgive that woman?" Kenna said, feigning annoyance.

"I will support you in whatever you decide. But I don't want the years to pass, leaving you to regret never fixing the relationship with your mother," he explained.

"Sometimes I hate it when you're right," she uttered, teasing him mildly.

But she knew he was right and she wanted to forgive her mother. She just didn't know how yet. When they had left the application review and she called Kassi to tell her the news, she also wanted to call her mother to let her know she'd be a grandmother again. But then she remembered they weren't speaking. Or at least she wasn't speaking to Victoria.

Kassi was right, all she had to do was name drop their mother and the clinic worked her in that same day on Monday. Emmett drove her to the appointment and they were just waiting for their turn to go back. Kenna couldn't believe it was actually happening. Everything was falling into place quickly and she was excited, but there were some feelings of guilt along with the excitement. She wanted to fight the unjust laws surrounding the reproductive restrictions and yet she still applied and got accepted. It was not lost on her that there were many woman less fortunate than herself that would never have what she was about to have. This made her feel guilty for being so excited about the possibility of having a baby soon. Maybe even as soon as nine months from now.

These thoughts were pushed out of her mind when the nurse called her and Emmett back to the procedure area. He walked slightly behind her with his hand at her waist, giving her support with his presence. The doctor talked to them both briefly and soon she was lying on the procedure table and was given sedation.

When she woke, she didn't remember a thing from the procedure and Emmett took her home to rest. She was a fatigued and a little sore from the ordeal, but she was filled with joy and hope for what their future held.

CHAPTER 27
Beginning the Fight

Kenna had taken a couple days at home to recover from her heranon removal. In that time, she had been in contact with Judy, planning when they could meet with potential supporters. She knew she needed help to take this on and it was a relief to her to finally be getting help from people that could make a real difference. As hopeful as this made her, she also knew that she would be going against her own mother as she started her role as Region Four Chair. She didn't know how she could forgive her and, at the same time, wage war against the restrictions that her mother stood to uphold as part of her political agenda.

It was all so complicated. To think that just a little over a year ago, her life was vastly uncomplicated. So much had changed and she knew it would continue to do so. All she could do was fight for what she believed was right while living her own life and trying to grow as a person.

Her phone buzzed in her pocket and she retrieved it to see that Judy had finally gotten back to her with a date and a time for their meeting. She looked at the date, confused, and then looked at her phone calendar. The meeting was tomorrow. Kenna had thought she would have more time to plan and go through her material before having this meeting. After replying to Judy that she would be there, she ran upstairs to organize her research so she could present her case to these politicians.

The following evening, she met Judy and three others at a quiet, dimly lit supper club close to GreyStone campus. She did not recognize the three politicians, but that was not surprising to her as she never really paid them attention before last year. They had each worked in politics for years in Region Four and they all knew her mother.

"Have you tried getting your mom on board? Her political stances are compatible with being against these reproductive laws and their unfairness to the lower class," a woman named Alice, who held the title of City Seat here in Thayes, asked.

"I discussed it with my mother and she made it very clear that as Region Four Chair she would uphold the current reproductive restrictions and would not go against them in any way," Kenna replied.

They all exchanged glances around the table. Victoria's stance on this was out of place with her prior political beliefs.

They discussed the evolution of the restrictions and when each minor change was snuck into the guidelines. Eventually leading to where the laws were today. They delved into the population numbers in Thayes and how the East Side was experiencing a disproportionate decline in numbers relative to the rest of the city.

"I am surprised no one has caught this before, and that no one has tried to stop it," a man named Xavier said. He was the Region Legislator and apparently had major pull at the capitol.

"No one has cared that the lower class is getting eliminated, or no one has noticed. The people that would have the power to say or do anything about it all get their applications approved. So why would they question the system?" Judy pointed out.

Kenna knew how true that was. She would have never questioned the system until she heard Becca's story and witnessed what was going on at the East Side with her own eyes.

"So, what's the next step?" Kenna asked, eyeing the others.

"I'll file a motion to review the reproductive restrictions and make changes. This will take a little while to put together. We have to be very specific about the change request and cannot leave anything out. Then I will have to get other politician signatures to put the motion through, after that there would be a hearing to discuss it. This will take time, but if we stick with it, I think we can make some actual changes," Xavier said.

"I agree and I can help with the motion," another politician by the name of Veronica chimed in. She was the Region Recorder and had just gained her seat after being a lawyer for many years.

"Is there anything we can do in the meantime?" Kenna asked.

"You can generate public support for these changes," Xavier answered back while Veronica and Alice nodded in agreement.

Kenna didn't have the slightest idea how to do that, but when she looked at Judy, she could see the wheels turning inside her head.

"We will take care of that," Judy said with a confident smile.

The other three left after their conversation, leaving Kenna and Judy at the table to plan their next move.

"What's your plan?" Kenna asked excitedly.

"Well, I know it's coming up soon, but I think we should organize a march at the Region Address," Judy answered.

Kenna sat back in her seat to consider this. The Region Address was surely the biggest public political event in the region, so it would be an excellent opportunity. But that would mean they had less than a week to put it together. She felt a twinge of guilt about planning a public demonstration that would ultimately oppose her mother during her first major speech as Region Four Chair.

"We won't have enough time," Kenna reasoned.

"It will be tight. But I think we can do it if we work hard at gathering supporters over the next five days. This event will definitely get us the most coverage," Judy stated.

Kenna knew Judy was right. There was a large media presence at the speech, as well as an enormous crowd. If they could generate the numbers, they would get noticed. She had doubts they could drum up enough support in such a short period.

"How do we do it?" Kenna asked.

"I'm going to reach out tonight to all the political and feminist groups I am a part of and try to drum up numbers that way. As well as having them share it on all their social media pages. I'll put flyers together tonight and we can distribute them tomorrow door to door to businesses," Judy was formulating her plan as she talked.

"Got it. I'll help with flyers tonight and see who else I can reach," Kenna said.

Kenna was not part of many groups and she doubted any of her friends and acquaintances would be interested in the March. She was at a loss on where to find more supporters.

They left the restaurant, and Kenna went to get her vehicle to drive to Judy's house. Once she reached her car, she texted Emmett to fill him in on the plan.

Emmett: That's great, good luck.

Kenna: Thanks for your support. Don't wait up.

When she looked up from her phone, her eyes wandered toward the East Side and remained there. For a moment, she just sat and stared. Then it hit her. The East Side is where she would find her supporters. But how would she reach them?

She tried to come up with a game plan as she drove to Judy's. They spent half the night designing flyers and printing them off for distribution. And by the end, she was exhausted and just crashed on Judy's couch for the night.

The following day, they hit the streets with their flyers and went into all the businesses downtown. Hanging them up in the windows and handing them to people they saw. Most of the people that were interested in what they had to say were young women. Kenna hoped that their interest would lead to their support at the March. She guessed that less than half of these people would actually show up when it mattered.

When they had finished, she decided she would try her luck on the East Side. She went door to door to all the open businesses and even tried a couple of apartment complexes, but felt like she was getting nowhere. After a couple of hours, she sat down on a park bench, feeling defeated.

Then something caught her eye. It was Grace, one of the women who helped with Emma's birth. Kenna watched her go into the old church, immediately she stood up and walked briskly across the playground to follow her. As she entered the church, she heard a door towards the altar slam shut and went to it. When she opened the door, she saw a narrow dark stairwell and followed it down to the church basement.

Grace was standing in the middle of the room talking to another woman. They both looked up, surprised when they saw her. Grace stared at her, confused for a few seconds, trying to remember where she knew Kenna from.

"I'm Kenna Foster, you helped my friend Becca," Kenna explained.

"And why are you here?" Grace asked with a worried expression.

"I'm organizing a march in protest against the reproductive restrictions and I need supporters," she said awkwardly as she thrust a flyer into their hands. "It's taking place in a few days during the Region Address."

Grace was silent for almost an entire minute. "That's amazing," she said without taking her eyes off the flyer in her hand.

"We need numbers in order to make a real

impact. Do you think anyone from here would be interested?" Kenna asked hopefully.

"I will try reaching out to some contacts and see what I can come up with," Grace replied. "Can you come back here tomorrow night?"

"Yes, I can do that," Kenna replied enthusiastically. For the first time today, she was hopeful.

Emmett went to the hospital for an onboarding meeting before he started his official job. While he was there, he wanted to snoop to see if Victoria had returned for a heart procedure as recommended. He knew he couldn't go into her chart because that would be against the rules. But he did have access to the OR list for surgeries every day, which was something he had to look at daily for work and wasn't breaking any rules. So he checked the list for her name on all dates from the election night to now. Nothing. Damn it Victoria, he swore to himself silently.

Why couldn't she just follow her doctor's orders? He didn't know what to do. If she understood the risk she was taking by putting this off, maybe she would understand. Or maybe she thought she was above death and it would never get her. He shook his head as he contemplated his next steps.

He hoped he wouldn't regret it, but he decided to pay his mother-in-law a visit. He grabbed his jacket and sent her a text asking if she was at her new office at the capitol before heading that way. She returned his text immediately and confirmed she was at her office that day.

The capitol was close to the hospital downtown so he left his car parked and walked instead of trying to find parking at the capitol. After he made his way through security and the check-in desk, he took the elevator up to the top floor, which was now Victoria's new office as Region Four Chair.

When he arrived at the top floor, they directed him to sit in a small waiting area until Victoria was available. The entire top floor was devoted to Victoria's office along with her closest staff, and it was fancy. Emmett was almost surprised at how fancy it was. A mix between modern and classic, there was beautiful light hardwood flooring in a herring bone pattern throughout with large modern rugs in the offices and waiting area. The walls were a dark emerald green with hints of gold patterned wallpaper. The ceilings were taller than one would expect in an office and the doors had to be ten feet tall as well. A large gold chandelier hung from the ceiling over the reception desk and a coffee bar in a dark walnut built in shelving area sported a high end espresso maker. Emmett correctly guessed that each piece of artwork on the wall was worth more than a year's salary for him.

Victoria's assistant, a young woman with dark hair pulled back in a tight bun with sleek dark glasses and tailored trousers, ushered him back to Victoria's office. When they opened the strangely tall doors and stepped inside, he could see Victoria's new office was larger than the entire first floor of his house and appeared to be more of an apartment. The grand ceilings and flooring continued throughout.

"Wow, your new digs are pretty nice," he said to Victoria as she walked up to greet him.

"I know, it's gorgeous. Which is great because I'll be spending so much of my time here I'll practically have to move in," she replied.

After letting her assistant know she could leave them, she walked Emmett back to a gigantic room that housed her desk and workspace. Instead of sitting at her desk, she motioned for him to sit on the couch in a separate area that was more comfortable. She sat opposite of him in a high back armchair. On the coffee table between them sat a tea set and pastries on a silver tray. So fancy, Emmet thought to himself as he grabbed one croissant and poured them both some tea.

"So, Emmett, what brings you here?" she asked calmly. Now that the election was over, she was more relaxed and less on edge. Her chest pain had completely come to a halt in the past few days since the election. As Region Four Chair, she was busy but it wasn't anything she couldn't handle.

Emmett set down his cup and looked at her

seriously. "Victoria, I came to plead with you again to stop putting off heart surgery. You need stents and every day you put it off you're putting your life at —."

"I hear your and Kenna's application was accepted. Congratulations, I am ecstatic for you both," she interrupted him before he could finish his sentence.

"Thank you. We are excited. But we also want our future child's grandmother to be a part of their life, and you can't do that if you're dead," he replied sternly yet sarcastically.

She smiled at his small jest. "All right, Emmett, I will call and schedule the procedure. I just didn't have time to do it before and the Region Address is coming up in less than a week, but after that I will do it."

He had forgotten about the Region Address. The annual speech at the capitol by the Region Chair was the biggest one, discussing plans for the future and the current situation in the region. There would be a crowd of tens of thousands of people there to hear his mother-in-law speak. It was impressive.

"Please schedule it. Don't wait. And take it easy before then," he pleaded.

"Don't worry about me. I'll be fine. Just worry about giving me another grandchild," she teased.

Emmett smiled and shook his head as they finished their tea. Again, he hoped Kenna would forgive Victoria soon, before she let it go too far.

He planned to try to convince her again tonight, and probably every night, until she finally listened to him.

He took his leave, and Victoria got back to work on her speech. She had several meetings today to get it perfected before the big day.

Emmett was at home when Kenna walked in just before supper, beaming from ear to ear. She dropped her things on the entryway table and plopped down next to him on the couch.

"You wouldn't believe the day I've had," she said, still grinning.

"Try me," he said as he closed his laptop and put it off to the side. He had been making a real effort to be present since their weekend away.

She spent the next half an hour filling him in on her meeting from last night and working with Judy to get the flyers made and distributed. Last, she told him about her surprise encounter on the East Side and how she was going back the following evening.

"Is it safe for you going there alone? I think I should come with you," he said protectively.

"Most people who are interested in our cause are women, and I think it would intimidate to them if you came. I'll be fine and I'll call you immediately if anything happens," she reassured him, although, she was not concerned for her safety. She trusted the women she spoke to and did not fear harm from them or any other woman on the East Side.

When they went to bed that night, they laid in the dark holding each other.

"Are you ready to forgive your mother?" Emmett asked her again.

"I suppose I should soon," she sighed heavily. At this point, she was getting less angry when she thought about her and more sad at the thought of not having her in their lives.

"So?"

"I promise I will talk to mom tomorrow." She knew it was time.

He didn't tell her he had gone to see her today. She would wonder why, and he knew he couldn't tell her the real reason, so he didn't mention it.

The next day, while Kenna and Emmett were eating breakfast, she texted Victoria and asked if she could come talk to her today. Her mother replied swiftly that she would be thrilled to see her. Kenna set down her phone and finished her oatmeal and fruit. She felt lighter now that she had decided to forgive Victoria, like she was no longer weighed down by the burden of hating her. Emmett had noticed Kenna humming this morning and her attitude was bright. It pleased him to see her perking up.

After getting ready for the day, they left the house together, sharing a quick kiss on the stoop before departing to their destinations. Emmett was going to the hospital and she was headed to the capitol to pay her mother a visit. He asked her if she wanted to ride with him, but she declined and chose to walk outside and take in the warm morning sun.

As she walked, she thought of what she wanted to say to her mother when she arrived. Resolved to forgive her mother, she also wanted to try once again to change her mother's mind about the reproductive restrictions. Now that she was Region Four Chair, she had the power to overturn the restrictions and Kenna still held a small hope that she could reason with her mother. Rather than allowing the discussion to turn hostile, she made a conscious decision to communicate her feelings in a composed and imploring fashion that wouldn't provoke her mother's defensiveness.

The sidewalk downtown was filled with people trying to get somewhere, and Kenna blended into the crowd as she walked. Most people who lived and worked downtown didn't even own a car. Good parking was scarce. The sound of their shoes striking the pavement and the buzz of conversation all around her distracted her thoughts away from her mother. She continued to the capitol building, taking in the blue skies and warm breeze as she went.

After a few more blocks, she found herself at the capitol steps. Pausing to look up at the building, she was taken by its stateliness. There were wide concrete steps leading to a courtyard with a huge, elaborate fountain. A few people were sitting on the fountain ledge and some benches nearby, drinking coffee and eating breakfast. The building was old and grand, with large columns and ornate windows that contrasted with the modern skyscrapers of downtown.

Kenna imagined her mother standing on the terrace in just a few short days, giving the Region Address to the entire region. Still in disbelief that her mother now held so much power, she admitted to herself that she was enormously proud of everything her mother had accomplished.

Slowly, she climbed the steps to the capitol and crossed the terrace to enter the arched front door. Immediately, she felt the cool rush of air conditioning as she entered the main lobby. After going through security, she made her way to the elevator. Her shoes clacked against the marble floor and the sound echoed down the hallway.

The golden elevator doors opened and she stepped inside, along with several other people, and pressed the button to the top floor to her mother's new office. Two women directly in front of her were whispering to each other privately. Kenna thought she heard one of them say restrictions and something about a protest. Kenna's ears perked and she leaned forward to hear what the women were saying, but the elevator door opened and the two women stepped off, leaving Kenna curious about their conversation.

When she reached the top floor, she was alone in the elevator. The door opened revealing the reception desk, and Kenna stepped off, admiring the large golden chandelier as she passed under it. The young woman at the desk directed her to a small waiting area off to the side. Kenna sat in a rich velvet chair that was surprisingly comfortable as she admired the decor all around her. After only a few minutes, Victoria's assistant arrived to walk Kenna back to her mother's office. She glanced in the other offices as they walked past on their way and saw Clayton sitting behind a desk, but he did not notice her.

When she entered Victoria's office, she was distracted by the size of the space. It seemed more like living quarters than an office. Her mother came to greet them and thanked her assistant before dismissing her. Kenna noticed that her mother looked very well and her mood was bright. She looked like her old self. During the election, she thought her mother looked worn down and her mood was always stressed. She was glad to see that Victoria had recovered from the election.

They went to the small comfortable seating area and Victoria sat next to Kenna on the sofa. The proximity felt awkward to Kenna since she and her mother had not been on the best terms lately. She cleared her throat and positioned herself so she was facing her mother.

"I'm glad you came to visit me, and I hear congratulations are in order to you and Emmett!" Victoria said with sincerity.

"Yes, thanks. We hope to grow our family as soon as possible," Kenna replied, trying not to let the awkwardness she was feeling show in her voice. "I'm happy to see you too, mom, and I'm ready to put our mistakes behind us and move forward," Kenna replied.

"I think that's a great idea, and I can't wait to become a grandmother again."

"I want you to be part of our lives and our children's lives, even if we don't agree on everything," Kenna said cautiously.

"You mean the reproductive restrictions?" Victoria asked knowingly.

"Yes, I do. Unless you have changed your mind about them?" Kenna asked hopefully. "I still maintain my stance against the restrictions and hope to somehow help change the laws so poor people can have children if they desire. I just don't think it's right how they are being discriminated against because of their financial status."

Victoria sighed and shook her head as she answered, "Honey, I am not a monster, and I understand what you are feeling. But things have to be this way. Look at how far we have come and all the good that has happened as a result of the reproductive restrictions. The country is no longer overpopulated, and we can give back to the environment and keep it sustainable. All the children born are wanted, planned, and there are no longer children in foster care. Because there are fewer people in need of government assistance, we can better help our poor and they can live healthier, easier lives even if that means they won't have children. Sometimes sacrifices must be made for the greater good."

"By refusing the applications of the poor, the system is basically eliminating the lower class. It's snuffing out a whole class of people. Real people, who live and breathe just like you and I do. People who should have a chance at parenthood," Kenna stated calmly. She didn't want to cause a fight, but wanted to let her mother know where she stood.

"Maybe someday you'll understand why I must uphold the current laws. It is for the greater good," Victoria tried to reason with her.

"I don't think I will ever understand how you can stand behind these laws that are clearly discriminatory and wrong," Kenna replied, "but I don't want us to be estranged because of this, so if you have not changed your stance on the matter, we will just have to agree to disagree."

Victoria nodded her head in understanding. Part of her wished Kenna would just drop her obsession with the restrictions so they could all move on. The other part of her knew Kenna was right, but she had agreed to uphold these restrictions when she became Region Four Chair and she could not go against her word now. Even if she knew it was wrong. She had made the deal and now she had to live with it.

"Well, I am sure you have more pressing issues to attend to, so I will leave you to work," Kenna said as she rose from her seat.

"We should plan to get together soon. Are you going to attend the Region Address?" Victoria asked hopefully. It was her biggest public speech she had ever given and she hoped her family would be there for support.

Kenna felt a catch in her throat at the mention of the Region Address. Knowing she couldn't tell her mother about the protest, she still felt guilty for keeping it from her. She feared the protest would hurt her mother and cause stress during her first important public appearance. But she also believed in their cause and was not willing to give it up to protect her mother's feelings or political office.

"Yeah, I'll be there," Kenna said with a reassuring half smile.

She embraced her mother and held her close before leaving her office. Although she could not convince Victoria to change her mind, she was happy that they were on speaking terms and hoped that the protest wouldn't take that away.

CHAPTER 28
Have a Little Faith

Not knowing what to expect at her meeting in the church basement, Kenna hoped she could convince a few hand fulls of supporters to come to the capitol for the march. It was only two days away and she had no idea how many people would show up. She was afraid no one would come and they'd be standing there in front of the capitol looking like idiots.

On her drive over to the East Side, she couldn't shake the negative thoughts that plagued her. She was almost certain this meeting was a waste of time and wouldn't produce the numbers that she so desperately needed. Tomorrow, she was going to see Judy and the others to get a rough number for the march the following day. She hoped Judy could use her connections to drum up support and that she was more successful than Kenna.

After parking a few blocks away, Kenna walked toward the old church. It was getting late and dusk was upon her. The warm summer night was strangely comforting to her as she snuck into the church inconspicuously. The dimly lit church was empty and eerily quiet. She thought about just leaving rather than go through the disappointment of being the only one who showed up for this gathering.

She descended the dark staircase behind the altar, being here alone in the dark was creepy and she realized her heart was pounding and she was holding her breath. Letting out an enormous sigh, she told herself to keep moving forward.

When she opened the door at the bottom of the stairs, she was met with light and this helped ease her anxiety. Suddenly, she inhaled sharply in shock. There were faces staring back at her. A lot of faces. The large dingy church basement was packed wall to wall with mostly women of all ages. Kenna looked around, trying to gauge just how many there were, but she lost count. She knew it was in the hundreds, which was more than she ever would have dreamed of.

There was an awkward moment of silence while Kenna caught her bearings. Then Grace approached her and lead her to a makeshift platform at the front of the room. She wasn't sure what to say, she hadn't exactly prepared a speech. But they were all waiting silently and intently, focused on what she had to say.

"Thank you all for coming here tonight. My name is Kenna Foster and I, along with several others, am trying to fight against the reproductive restrictions." She looked around the room, making eye contact with several women as she talked. They nodded their head in understanding as she continued.

"Our government has unjustly engineered the reproductive restrictions to stop poor people from having children. Ultimately, they are trying to wipe out the lower class." Looking around in anticipation, she expected them to be shocked, but none of them were.

"We need to stand together against the restrictions and make the rest of the region, and the entire country, aware of what has been going on." A few shouts of agreement echoed through the crowded room.

"Come, march with me in protest of the restrictions at the capitol during the Region Address. We have two days, tell everyone you know to come march with us. We will make an impact, and they will hear our voices," she held up her hand triumphantly.

Someone toward the back of the room started clapping, then another, and another. Soon the room was loud with thunderous clapping and cheers from the crowd. Kenna couldn't believe it. For the first time, she felt like she was truly making a difference. The smile on her face was genuine as she stepped down from the platform and approached Grace at the front of the crowd. Grace had tears in her eyes as she clapped and cheered with the rest of the women.

"Thank you." Grace leaned in to tell Kenna above the noise.

After the cheering subsided, people started filing out in small groups and Kenna stayed to talk with the women and answer their questions. After the last group left almost two hours later, Kenna was still high from the rush of it all. Grace had stayed behind as well, and she was beaming at Kenna.

"That was amazing." Grace clasped her hands in excitement.

"It was more than I ever expected," Kenna replied.

"This could be the change we need. If we can change the restrictions, we won't have to run this illegal operation anymore. The children of the East Side would no longer have to live in the shadows and families wouldn't have to flee on the run just to stay together." Grace looked at Kenna with hope in her eyes.

"We will make a change. I promise you that. It may not be easy and it's going to take some time, but I won't stop until I make this right."

The two women left the basement together, turning out the lights as they went. Outside of the church, Grace gave Kenna her number and her real name, which was Sienna. She wanted to help in any way she could, and Kenna promised to keep her in the loop.

She drove home to tell Emmett what had

happened and she couldn't wait to tell Judy in the morning. This was it. They were really going to make it happen. The adrenaline was finally wearing off and Kenna was exhausted. So exhausted that she didn't notice the black SUV that followed her from the church to her house.

The following morning, she woke with a new confidence and excitement for the future. As she got ready and had breakfast, she hummed to herself and seemed to float around the kitchen. Emmett smiled as he watched her. He was proud of the woman she was becoming and was happy to see her newfound confidence. There was nothing more attractive than a confident woman with a purpose.

When she left the house, she noticed an envelope sitting on their front step. Curious, she bent down to grab it. Her mouth formed a straight line in confusion as she opened it and revealed a note written in messy red writing, *END THIS NOW OR WE WILL.*

Glancing around her and down the sidewalk looking for whoever left the letter, she didn't see anyone around. She felt a mixture of anger and fear from the threat, but she would not stop now. Not wanting Emmett to see the note and worry, she folded it and put it in her purse before heading to Judy's. If he knew she was being threatened, he would try to persuade her not to participate in the march, and there's no way she was missing it.

She wondered who left the note and how much they knew. Kenna had tried to keep the church basement meeting a secret, but with that many people in attendance, it wouldn't be a surprise if the word had gotten out. It had to be someone working for the government. They would be the ones with the most to lose. The thought of the government coming after her frightened Kenna, but not enough to derail her plans.

When she arrived at Judy's, she saw the others were already there. Immediately, she showed them the note and shared her concerns with them. The note did not phase the others. Apparently, this sort of thing happened all the time in politics and they quickly waved it off. This eased some of Kenna's fears. If they weren't worried she wouldn't be either.

"There's nothing they can do to stop the march," Judy said to Kenna, peering over her glasses. "Don't let them scare you."

Kenna nodded in understanding. "I met with a group of supporters last night on the East Side," she said excitedly.

"How many do you think were there?" Judy asked without looking up from what she was doing.

"Over three hundred," Kenna said with a sly smile.

Judy abruptly looked up from the paper she

was holding and peered at Kenna with a look of surprise. A slow smile pulled at the corner of her mouth. "Well done."

They discussed their numbers. Judy had also managed to get over one hundred supporters that agreed to show up to the march.

"That's enough to be seen and heard," Kenna said, sitting back with her arms crossed over her chest.

"It sure is." Judy slapped the table in triumph.

For the next few hours, they went over details for the march. Where they would start and what route to take, they would end the march at the capitol steps right in front of Victoria giving her speech.

Kenna still felt guilty that she would publicly be going against her mother during one of the most important speeches of her career. She wished she could have persuaded Victoria to support them, but she knew now that would never happen and she accepted it.

When the plans were all decided, Kenna and Judy sent out text chains to supporters, letting them know when and where to meet. Then they got to work painting banners for tomorrow, in bold black and white, easy for the media to see and send their message across the country.

When Kenna got home later that day, she jumped in the shower to wash the paint off of her arms and out of her hair. After she got out of the shower, she saw Emmett sitting on their bed, with the note written in red sitting beside him and a look of great concern on his face.

"Kenna, why didn't you show me this?" He held up the note.

"I didn't want you to worry. Did you go through my purse?" Her shoulders tensed in accusation.

"No, it fell out of your purse and I found it on the floor thinking it was mail we had missed," he said honestly. "Are you in danger? If you are, you better tell me."

"No, I talked to the others and they assured me this sort of thing happens when you make waves with the government." She sat next to him on the bed.

He sighed and pinched the bridge of his nose. "You need to promise me that if you're in any trouble, you will tell me and that you'll back off."

"I promise." She laid her hand on his.

"Alright," he sighed, but he did not look very convinced.

Emmett left to run a few errands and Kenna noticed a black SUV sitting in front of their house. She went to the front door and opened it to investigate. The back window of the vehicle rolled down and she was bewildered to see Clayton looking at her.

"Kenna, get in. We need to talk," he demanded.

She got into the back of the SUV with him. "What the hell is going on Clayton?"

"I know about the march you've planned for tomorrow, and I came to tell you to shut it down." He shifted in his seat so he was looking at her.

"Even if I wanted to shut it down, which I don't, I couldn't. It's too big now." She crossed her arms over her chest defensively. "Does mom know?"

"I haven't told her yet because I didn't want her to stress with her speech coming up, but I will have to tell her." Clayton shook his head in annoyance.

"You do what you have to do and I'll do the same," Kenna replied cooly.

"I warned you not to do this." Clayton looked at Kenna with pleading in his eyes.

She stared at him for a moment, confused by what he meant, and then she understood. "You're the one who left me the note? That's fucked up Clayton," Kenna said, pointing a finger at him.

"You know what's fucked up? Going against your mother the way you are. That's fucked up," he said, irritated, as he ran his hand through his hair.

"I have to stand up for what I believe is right." She opened the door and left him sitting in the backseat alone.

CHAPTER 29
Play the Game

Victoria was getting ready for her speech. She had just sat down for hair and makeup, which was sure to take two hours. Clayton came into her office carrying coffee and a forlorn look. He did not want to break the news about the protest to Victoria. Especially since her own daughter was the one who'd organized it.

"Chairwoman Carson," he greeted her formally.

"Clayton, I've known you your whole life. Just call me Victoria," she took the coffee from him.

"Victoria, I have some information I need to share with you." He put his hands in his pocket nervously.

"Well, I can tell by your face that it's bad news. Come on, tell me what's going on." She sipped her coffee.

"We have heard that there is a protest march planned today, against the reproductive restrictions." He rocked back on his heels.

"Please don't tell me Kenna is involved in this," she sighed as she set her coffee down.

Clayton was silent, but his lack of response only confirmed what she already knew. Of all the days to plan a march, why did Kenna have to choose today? She was about to give the biggest speech in her career. One that would be broadcasted at a national level, and she didn't have the time or the energy to worry about Kenna's little side project.

"I tried to dissuade her." Clayton looked up nervously.

"We all did," Victoria said, taking off her glasses to rub her eyes.

"What can we do?" Clayton asked.

"Nothing. We do nothing. Today will go on as planned, and we will ignore Kenna's display of idiocy. Hopefully, it will be such a small group it will go unnoticed by all. Then we will try to put out any fires that arise after the day is over," she answered tiredly.

Clayton left her to get ready and went to make sure everything was in order for the speech. Already regretting his choice to agree to several media interviews this week on behalf of Victoria, he knew this week was going to be a shit show.

Victoria hoped this would fizzle out and Kenna would move on to something else, like planning her family. She hoped that the other region chairs would not get word of it. Not wanting to answer to them. The stress of it all had caused a slight pain in her chest. She chewed a baby aspirin and tried to ignore it. She just had to get through today.

Kenna had gotten up early, before sunrise, to get to Judy's. They were going to the starting point of the march together early, before anyone else arrived. Everyone was meeting in a parking ramp that was a few blocks away from the capital. That way, there would be room for everyone. Kenna drove and after they parked, they set up a large folding table with banners and signs for people to carry.

They still had over an hour before the meet time and over two hours until the start of the Region Address. So they were a little shocked when people began to show up. Lots of people. And they just kept coming in like a constant stream over the next hour and a half. Initially Kenna was trying to keep a head count to have an idea of how many there were, but it was impossible to keep track with the amount of people that kept coming.

Finally, it was time to start the march. Kenna and Judy were at the front leading everyone, and Kenna looked back at the sea of people that were following behind her. Thousands of women and some men from all walks of life stood looking back at her. The magnitude of what they were about to do finally hit her. She turned around and took a deep breath before taking the first step forward on their path.

It was a sight to see. Everyone marching toward the capitol. All wearing white shirts and holding signs protesting the reproductive restrictions. As they neared the capitol, they caught the attention of the media. Kenna ran ahead of the group and stopped to talk to one reporter.

"What are you guys marching for?" the reporter asked.

"We are marching in protest of the reproductive restrictions. They are deliberately targeted towards the lower class to stop them from reproducing. And we won't stand for it anymore."

"Can you tell us what you mean by that?" The reporter pushed the microphone in her face.

"The income requirements, housing requirements, and past criminal record guidelines all target the lower class unfairly. Because of these harsh restrictions the lower class is getting wiped out. We are marching for reproductive freedom!" She threw her fist in the air as she looked directly into the camera in front of her. Adrenaline pulsed through her and was giving her a high she had never known before. She never knew she could feel this way, she had tasted the excitement and she liked it.

Kenna ran back to the front of crowd and continued on. When they were almost to the capitol steps, they chanted, NO RESTRICTIONS, over and over. Victoria was in the middle of her speech, but the sound of their chants soon overpowered her voice. She tried to keep everyone's attention by speaking louder, but everyone was curious about the large group marching through the crowd chanting and soon it was clear Victoria was no longer the main attraction.

Victoria stopped speaking and looked at Kenna. They met each other's eyes and just stood there staring at each other while Kenna continued to chant with her group. Victoria studied her daughter, who was leading a group of thousands, and she forgot all the words she had planned on saying. She knew that this would cause a stir. One that was far bigger than she was prepared to deal with, and she dreaded the aftermath of it. But part of her was proud of what her daughter had accomplished, even if it meant more work and stress for her in the end.

Kenna stared back at her mother and wished that they were on the same side, not pinned against each other.

Suddenly Victoria's face become contorted with pain and she grabbed her chest. Kenna watched in horror as her mother fell to her knees and then forward onto the ground.

"No!" Kenna screamed as she ran toward her mother. There were so many people in front of her she was trying to get through the crowd, clawing desperately with her hands, trying to move people out of the way.

When she finally made it through, she ran up the capitol steps two at a time and outran the security guards coming after her. After she reached her mother, a group of Victoria's staff surrounded her. Kenna dropped to the ground by her mother and Victoria reached for her and took her hand. Kenna leaned in to hear her mother.

"Fight your fight." Victoria breathed quietly. Then she gasped and Kenna felt her grip go limp.

There was no life left in Victoria's eyes. She was gone. Kenna sobbed as she clung to her mother's lifeless body.

CHAPTER 30
The Aftermath

Emmett was standing further back in the crowd and when he saw Victoria fall, he whispered "fuck" to himself before fighting his way to the front of the crowd. When he reached the capitol steps, a line of security guards stopped him and would not let him through. In the distance, he could hear a siren and he soon saw the ambulance arriving. The crowd parted as it arrived to let the vehicle through, so he ran to it. They loaded Victoria in the back of the ambulance and Kenna jumped in with them before it took off with sirens howling.

As he watched the ambulance drive away, he saw Kassi watching helplessly from where the ambulance left. When he got to her, she looked at him with her tear-streaked face and leaned into his shoulder, sobbing.

"Come on Kassi, we have to get to the

hospital," he urged her as he patted her back.

"Let's go." She pulled away from him, wiping her eyes.

Running through the crowd on the path the ambulance had left, they didn't even bother stopping for Emmett's car in the mess of traffic leaving the capitol. They ran all the way to the hospital and didn't stop to catch their breath until they had entered the ER entrance.

Clayton was in the hallway and when Kassi saw him she ran to him, looking at him for answers. He just shook his head and looked down, telling her what she needed to know. She slumped down into a chair next to him with her face in her hands, her shoulders deflated as grief raked her body.

Emmett looked around the waiting room and down the halls, searching for Kenna. He found her in a small room off the hallway, the one where they bring you to tell you bad news. She was sitting in a chair, staring at the wall with tears streaming down her face. She was pale and he was worried she may pass out.

"Kenna I am so sorry." He kneeled in front of her chair.

She didn't look at him. Instead, she kept staring at nothing. "They said it was a heart attack and she had seen cardiology and was planning to have surgery tomorrow." A sob caught in her throat. "Did you know?"

Emmett sighed and tilted his head down.

"Kenna I couldn't tell you, it's against privacy laws and she told me not to. I begged her to get the surgery as soon as possible, but you know how stubborn she can be."

"You should have tried harder." Getting up from her chair, she left the room. She wanted to blame someone and Emmett was an easy target. A sob choked out of her throat and she braced her hand against the wall in the hallway as her other hand went to her mouth to cover her sobs. There was an empty hole in her heart that caused a deep aching in her chest. Her mother was gone and she had spent the better part of the past year avoiding her. She hated herself, blamed herself. The march had caused her mother stress during the most important speech of her career, a march Kenna had organized and lead. It was her fault that her mother was dead and Victoria's statement of encouragement before her death did little to calm Kenna now.

Emmett leaped to his feet to follow her. When he reached her he grabbed her by the arm, spinning her around towards him. Wrapping his arms around her as she fought against him, he held her firmly until she stopped fighting. She buried her face in his chest, her cries muffled against him. Soon her tears left gray blotches on his white shirt, but he just held her and let her cry.

After a couple of hours, they went home. Kenna was dreading the following day when they had to discuss funeral arrangements and, at some point, needed to do a press release. Clayton would take care of that. Neither Kenna nor Kassi wanted to be in the public eye while they tried to grieve.

❦

It had been an entire month now since Becca, now Elizabeth, and her family had made it to Region Two. The drive had taken two days and they had to stop frequently to feed Emma and change diapers. She was so relieved to have made it. After settling in Caldonia, a larger city in Region Two that was located on a large bay on the ocean, they quickly got to work on setting up their new life. They chose a larger city so they could blend in easier and disappear. In smaller towns, people ask questions.

After spending a week in a cheap hotel, they found a quaint little townhouse to rent. It was on a hill and she could see the bay and the large ships going by from the upstairs windows. Fletcher, now Mitchell, found a job at an auto shop. He had to start out at entry level, but Becca knew he would advance quickly. She was going to stay home with Emma until she was old enough to go to school, as long as they could afford it. The sale of their house had given them a nice safety net to fall back on.

One night after putting Emma to sleep, she was laying in bed next to Fletcher, who was fast asleep. He was snoring softly. She watched him sleep and her heart swelled, she was glad that he was hers. He was working so hard to make a good life for their little family. Even though they didn't have much, they had each other, and that was more than Becca could have asked for.

She was watching the news to fall asleep and wasn't even paying very close attention until an announcement came through, mentioning Region Four. A clip appeared on the screen of a march of thousands of people at the capitol. Becca shot straight up in bed when she saw Kenna leading the group and their banners about the restrictions. Her mouth was hanging open in disbelief as she watched.

Suddenly, the camera focused on Victoria on the capitol terrace as she fell to the ground. Becca gasped and her hand flew to her mouth. The news announcer then stated that the Region Four Chair had died and they were waiting for more information regarding the cause of death, but no foul play was suspected.

Becca's eyes began to tear up as she thought of her friend and the hardship she was going through. She wished so badly that she could see her, or at least reach out to offer her condolences. But she knew she couldn't. This was the life she chose and she was resolved to it.

When they got home from the hospital, Kenna went straight to their bed and curled up in the fetal position. She didn't know how she had any tears left to cry and wondered if she would run dry. What she felt beyond her sadness was an overwhelming feeling of guilt. Guilt for being estranged from her mother for the past several months. More guilt for organizing a march that caused her mother to have a heart attack. And most of all, guilt for blaming Emmett when she knew she was the one to blame. She wondered if Kassi would blame her, too. She should.

Most of all, she was mad at her mother for being so stubborn she thought she was above death. Putting off her lifesaving surgery after she was told several times that she needed it right away. But that wasn't surprising to Kenna. Her mother hated hospitals and avoided them if she could. Kenna also wasn't surprised her mother kept her diagnosis hidden, considering her mother's private nature and tendency to keep things to herself.

As Kenna cried and wondered how life would go on without her mother in it, she drifted into a deep sleep. The emotional toll of the day had worn her out and she crashed for almost twelve hours before waking groggily with sore, puffy eyes.

When she got downstairs, she found Emmett watching the news and drinking coffee. He immediately got up from his seat and asked her what she needed and what he could do.

"Just hold me for a minute." She went to him with her arms open.

"I'm so sorry Kenna," he breathed into her hair.

"I'm sorry too. I lashed out at you yesterday and you didn't deserve it." She tilted her chin up to look him in the eyes as she apologized.

"It's not your fault either, you know," he stated while rubbing the small of her back.

"It feels like it is."

"Kenna, your mother knew she was at risk and she stubbornly refused a surgery that could save her life. She was a ticking time bomb and she knew it."

"The stress of the march could have put her over the edge though," she reasoned.

"The stress from the speech itself probably put her over the edge, and that's on her," he said putting his hands on her shoulders and pulling her back from him so he could look her in the eye. He wanted her to know, no needed her to know that it wasn't her fault. It wasn't anyones fault except maybe Victoria's.

The day was a blur as they made calls and decisions about her funeral and assets. Kenna and Emmett went to stay at Victoria's house with Eleanor, so she wasn't alone. Her memory continued to digress and Kenna feared with her mother gone it was time to put her in a nursing home. The thought of it broke her heart. They decided that Kassi and Clayton would permanently move into their mother's house and would care for Eleanor for the rest of her days. Kenna and Emmett would get the lake place and would see to it's upkeep.

Kenna sat back and let Clayton and Kassi make most of the decisions regarding her funeral and on a public press release. She wondered who would take her mother's place as Region Four Chair. It was such a pity that her mother worked so hard for years to get to where she wanted to be and then she died before she had a chance to enjoy it.

Kenna vowed to herself that she would enjoy life to the fullest. Spend more time at the lake, have the family she always wanted, and remember that marriage takes work and is not always easy.

A few weeks went by and Kenna had returned to work. She was trying to get back to living her life, but it was so hard sometimes. She wondered when it would get easier. Emmett was taking her up to the lake cabin this weekend. He thought some fresh air and time away from the public eye would be good. Several journalists and media channels had contacted her asking for an interview, but so far, she had turned them all down. She didn't feel up to it, not yet anyway.

When she was done with work, they left for the lake. She was glad to be getting out of the city and wished that they were staying longer than just for the weekend. They arrived and unpacked. It was still early in the evening, so they sat on the patio overlooking the lake. At dusk, the loons started calling to each other and the sound reminded her of her mother.

"Mom loved the call of the loons." She smiled at Emmett with tears in her eyes.

He squeezed her hand and nodded in agreement. They sat in silence, watching the stars and listening to the loons until they went to bed.

The following morning, it startled Kenna to see Judy was calling her. She didn't have good service in the cabin, so she ran outside with her phone and up the hill a ways, trying to get a better signal.

"Hello? Judy, can you hear me?" she asked as she walked up the hill.

"Yes, I can hear you. Kenna we did it!" she exclaimed excitedly.

"Did what?" Kenna asked bewildered.

"The motion that we filed to change the reproductive restrictions was accepted! In a few months, it will go to the floor for discussion and we can make changes" Judy explained.

"That's amazing! I can't believe we actually did it," Kenna replied, out of breath from trudging up the hill.

"It will still be a long road. Some politicians don't like change and others will be bought out for their vote to keep the restrictions the same. We will have to lobby and stay in the public eye so that no one forgets about us," Judy paused on the other end.

"Judy, are you still there?" Kenna checked her phone for service.

"Yes, I'm here. Kenna, I know that your mother's death has been very difficult for you and the last thing you probably want to do is talk to the media. But we kind of need you to do it. Your face is the one everyone remembers from the march and people of the Region, and probably the rest of the country are interested in hearing what you have to say."

Kenna rubbed her forehead and paced back and forth. "I know you're right, but I just don't think I have it in me right now. I need some time."

"You don't have the luxury of time. You have already made big waves that can lead to big changes, and I know you have what it takes to see this through," Judy said encouragingly. "Plus, you gave all the supporters your word that you would fight for them. Please don't let them down."

Kenna remained silent while she contemplated her options. "All right, I'll do it. First thing when I get back to the city, I will set up some interviews."

Once their weekend at the lake was over and they returned home, Kenna kept to her word and set up interviews with everyone that was willing to talk to her.

"Kenna, please tell us what started your

interest in the reproductive restrictions," a young, fashionable male reporter asked her during her first tv interview after the march.

"Well, as you know, my and my husband's application was denied last year. That's what kind of sparked my interest. Then through a friend, I saw a side of the reproductive restrictions that I never knew existed. A side where most people get their applications denied, that's what is happening in the East Side and in other poverty stricken areas in the other cities and regions."

"What did you do next, after you found out that lower income people weren't getting their applications approved?" he continued.

"I started researching the restrictions and the laws that surround them. I dug into all of the accessible documents I could get my hands on that would give me an insight into the restrictions. Through this research I found that the restrictions have been getting increasingly more strict, and they affect the lower class the most."

"What changes do you want to see?"

"For starters we want to change the three things that really put the lower class at a disadvantage. We want to lower the income requirement along with loosening the housing and past criminal history requirements." she stated confidently.

"What do you say to people who think

what you're doing is wrong, and will hurt our society?"

"I think that this topic is one that can evoke many different opinions, and that individuals in the middle and upper classes may not be very concerned with the reproductive status of the lower class. But the elimination of an entire social class is not right, no matter how you look at it. If the government has the power to do it there's no telling what other freedoms they could and will take away from us, from all of us."

"So you're not concerned that children will suffer with unfit parents due to your proposed changes?"

"I wouldn't say that I'm not concerned, we are aware that there will be social issues with these changes. But if we are successful, people will be more free to make their own choices regarding reproduction. And that's what it should be, a choice."

"How do you think your mother would feel about this if she were still with us?" he asked the question everyone wanted to know.

"I think she would be proud of me," Kenna subtly wiped away the water that started to leak from both eyes. "She would encourage me to fight for what I believe in, whether she believed in the restrictions or not."

"Thank you for sharing with us today," he praised as he rose from his seat and extended his hand to her.

Over the next several weeks, she did dozens of interviews and public appearances, successfully explaining why the reproductive restrictions were wrong and what changes she hoped to see. The entire country was now invested in getting the laws overturned, or at least changed drastically.

Kenna had previously thought that the past year was the worst year of her life. But now, looking back, she realized how much she had grown and accomplished. She felt satisfied that she did everything she could to fight for what she believed was right. She made a tremendous splash, one that sent ripples across the entire nation. And she was just one woman.

EPILOGUE
5 Years Later

Kenna parked her van along the curb in front of their brownstone. Before getting out of the vehicle she paused to look at their home and into the windows that were flooded with a soft golden light. It was late spring and everything was green. The grass along the sidewalk was thick and luscious and the leaves had finally all opened on the trees. For her, spring meant change, new beginnings and new chances. She had learned through the past few years to welcome the change and enjoy the ride.

She ascended the steps into their home anxious to get to her people and spend some time with them before bedtime. When she closed the front door and wandered into the kitchen the scene before her warmed her heart. At their kitchen table sat their oldest daughter Tori, short for Victoria, she had her tongue poking out the side of her mouth with a look of intense concentration on her face. At only four years old she was quite the motivated young lady and she had already decided she was going to be a doctor like her daddy. Kenna wouldn't be surprised if she actually followed through with it.

Tori was working a thick marker over a large white poster board, she loved helping with her mother's campaign. She was running for City Seat, an entry level political position. One that could help her get her foot in the door at the capital, she would use it as the stepping stone she needed to advance further. She wasn't sure how far she wanted to go, but she knew she wanted a seat at the table, the table where important decisions were being made.

"Hey honey," Emmett called when he saw her approaching them. He was spoon feeding little Ellie, short for Eleanor, in her high chair. The infant was covered in some orange puree that looked consistent with sweet potatoes. She saw her opportunity and smeared the goop all over her dark hair while her father was distracted.

"Looks like someone needs a bath tonight," Emmett sighed shaking his head at his youngest daughter with a chuckle.

Kenna tried to stifle her laugh but was unable to do so and Ellie started laughing too before proceeding to rub the substance all over her shirt. Emmett raised his eyebrows at Kenna but was still smiling.

"What? She's adorable when she's making a mess." Kenna pointed to the always happy, rolly baby.

"Mom, do you like my sign?" Tori asked Kenna hopefully.

"Oh baby girl, I love it. I think it's your best one yet." She planted a kiss on top of Tori's blond head.

"How are you feeling? About today?" Emmett asked as he attempted to wipe down the baby.

"Okay. A little sad, but ready for the change." Today had been her last day at her psychology practice. She had continued lecturing at the college and eventually accepted the job for associate professor which then opened the door to a full time professor position that she took. She knew she would miss her clients and the satisfaction of helping people through their problems, but she wouldn't miss the tough cases. The cases that really got to her, the ones that she couldn't leave in her office and ended up bringing home with her. After several years, those cases start to wear you down and she knew she needed a change.

"I'm proud of you, for everything you've done," Emmett stated as he looked at his wife lovingly.

"I'm proud of you too, mommy," Tori cooed from her perch. Kenna's eyes glossed over with happiness at the sound.

"Thank you," she replied to both of them. "We

better get these girls in the tub, tomorrow is a big day," Kenna said with a clap of her hands. Tori groaned at her impending bedtime and Ellie started to yawn still sitting in her high chair.

Tomorrow was voting day and she was full of angst. After getting both girls tucked away in their beds they turned in. Kenna had a restless night, plagued with thoughts of failure. An even scarier thought, what if she won? She would officially be a politician and she didn't have the slightest idea how to be one of those. Her mind kept racing with these thoughts and she tossed and turned until she finally sat up with her alarm.

"How did you sleep?" Emmett asked groggily as he rolled over in bed beside her.

"Like garbage," she replied rubbing the sleep from her eyes.

Emmett gave her a knowing look, she was always the worrier. "Everything will be okay. If you don't win, we still have our life here together with our girls. And if you do win we will support you." He propped himself up on his elbow and used his other hand to rub her upper arm. She took comfort in his touch and laid back down beside him so he could hold her for five more minutes before they got up for the day.

Getting both girls up and ready for the day was like herding cats, but eventually they all made it out the door on time. Emmett drove Kenna's van to the campaign office as the girls sang happily in the back seat. When Kenna started to fidget with her wedding ring Emmett reached out and squeezed her hand before tracing soft circles over it with his thumb. She took a deep breath and tried to mentally prepare for the day before they arrived.

When they arrived at the campaign office they were greeted by Judy and Kassi, they were already drinking coffee inside. Judy had managed Kenna's campaign and had done a smashing job.

"Kenna, do you want coffee or something to eat?" Asha walked up to her and asked. She was in grad school now and had been Judy's TA last year. They brought her on to help with the campaign and Kenna was pleasantly surprised by her work. She had finally moved in with Alec, but he was waiting to propose until she finished grad school.

"Yeah that would be great, thanks," Kenna replied.

It was going to be a long day of waiting. After the polls closed around the city they would have to wait for the results from all the city districts to be counted. They sat and waited, then waited some more.

It was after dark when Emmett and Kenna finally made it back home. Kassi had taken the girls home with her so they wouldn't be up too late. They peeled their clothes off and fell into bed next to each other.

"How does it feel?" Emmett asked.

"Weird. I can't believe I'm a politician now. If you would have told me five years ago that one day I'd be City Seat, I wouldn't have believed you."

"Where do you want to go from here?" He was studying her face.

"I don't really know. I supposed I'll keep going as far as I can."

"How far do you want to go? Region Chair?"

Kenna thought about it for a second and thought of her mother becoming Region Chair just to die shortly after, before she really got a chance to make it worth while.

"Maybe," Kenna answered with a shrug of her shoulders.

Emmett looked at her worriedly, he glanced down before returning his eyes to hers.

"I just don't want it to change you. You know?"

Oh Kenna knew alright. She knew that her mother had changed throughout her career and it wasn't for the better. Changes that she probably regretted at the end, but Kenna reminded herself that she wasn't her mother and she was not destined to follow the same path.

"I won't let it change me," Kenna said as she stroked the side of his face with her fingers.

"Good." Emmett pulled her in and pressed his body against hers. He kissed her gently, as he held her tight. She felt herself relaxing in his warm embrace, and she knew she was right where she was supposed to be in life. Everyday she was thankful to have him and their girls and she knew that with her family by her side she could take on anything she set her mind to. Finally she drifted off to sleep content.